P9-DFR-265

Next of Kin

Books by Gladys Hasty Carroll

Novels

As the Earth Turns
A Few Foolish Ones
Neighbor to the Sky
West of the Hill
While the Angels Sing
Christmas Without Johnny
One White Star
Sing Out the Glory
Come With Me Home
The Road Grows Strange
The Light Here Kindled
Man on the Mountain
Next of Kin

Collected Short Stories

Head of the Line
Christmas Through the Years

Nonfiction

Dunnybrook
Only Fifty Years Ago
To Remember Forever
Years Away From Home

Gladys Hasty Carroll

Next of Kin

Little, Brown and Company • *Boston* • *Toronto*

ABIGAIL E. WEEKS MEMORIAL LIBRARY
UNION COLLEGE
BARBOURVILLE, KENTUCKY

813
C319ne

COPYRIGHT © 1974 BY GLADYS HASTY CARROLL

ALL RIGHTS RESERVED. NO PART OF THIS BOOK MAY BE REPRODUCED IN ANY FORM
OR BY ANY ELECTRONIC OR MECHANICAL MEANS INCLUDING INFORMATION STORAGE
AND RETRIEVAL SYSTEMS WITHOUT PERMISSION IN WRITING FROM THE PUBLISHER,
EXCEPT BY A REVIEWER WHO MAY QUOTE BRIEF PASSAGES IN A REVIEW.

SECOND PRINTING

T11/74

Library of Congress Cataloging in Publication Data

Carroll, Gladys Hasty, 1904–
 Next of kin.

 I. Title.
PZ3.C2354Nh [PS3505.A77533]   813'.5'2   74-12269
 ISBN 0-316-13005-2

Designed by D. Christine Benders

Published simultaneously in Canada
by Little, Brown & Company (Canada) Limited

PRINTED IN THE UNITED STATES OF AMERICA

To
Caroline and James Watson

Next of Kin

*[Being Entries Handwritten in an Old Ledger
with Mottled Covers under the Heading
"The Sturtevants and the Crowleys,
by William Crowley"]*

Tuesday, May 9, 1972

If Bart were alive tonight, he would say, "Well — tomorrow is First Pasturing Day." Every May ninth, after putting the Crowley Family Bible back on the shelf and winding the kitchen clock, he used to close the clock door with a soft snap, turn toward Kate and me, slip a thumb under one of his galluses, and say, "Well — tomorrow is First Pasturing Day." He did that as long as he lived, though for years before he died we didn't have any cows. Bart was always one to look ahead. He liked to have everything in good order in its proper place and according to his Bible, his clock, and his calendar. . . . Fog and rain all day, so I didn't get the bicycle out of the shed. Spent the morning scrubbing the kitchen floor with the last of the seasand, then spread newspapers and blacked the stove and set Kate's curtains to soak. They are getting so thin I don't dare put them to the washboard again. Studied all afternoon a bundle of the notes I took from Melura Sturtevant's diary. Very hard for me to make out now. Wish they were in ink, but I had no ink up there. Had to work by lamplight today, the sky was so dark. Eyelids pretty swollen tonight.

Wednesday, May 10

Hippies back at Sturtevants'. May be some of the ones who have been there before, may not. A motorcycle roared by me as I was pushing my bicycle up Tanner Tom's Hill coming home from the village with my groceries, and by the time I got to where I could see it through the trees the front door up there was open, so they must have had a key. I would have heard the noise of breaking in, if there had been any, after their motor was shut off. Tonight there is a faint light in the kitchen wing.

No use in my paying any attention to it and I keep telling myself so. Still I seem to see Bart looking over the parapets at me with the same awful urgency that was there after he couldn't speak and lay on his bed trying to tell me what his tongue wouldn't move to say.

I talk to him.

I say, "I know, Bart. You want me to go up there and find out what is going on. You think if you were still here and able to climb the hill you would, no matter what. You felt that place was your responsibility however many years had gone by since Sturtevants came there or contacted you, and you and Kate brought me up to feel the same way. It had been more and more a Crowley job since Alexander Sturtevant and Dobbin Crowley got here in the 1660's, and that place meant about as much to Crowleys as the Crowley place. I have to say it doesn't to me because this has been my home for close onto seventy years now and deep inside of me there is a knowledge you could never have of what it is to be homeless. Still I love the Sturtevant place because you and Kate loved it, and I want and have tried to do for it whatever you wanted done.

"But it is no longer possible, Bart, for one man with no authority to protect an isolated, deserted set of buildings and stretch of field and woods. Not even you in your heyday could have done it, if your times had been like these."

I tell him:

"You must realize I have tried. It has been harder for me than it would have been for you because as you very well know I am naturally a mild man and want no trouble with anybody. Nevertheless, three times summer before last I went up there and told groups of young people hanging about that this was private property, and I must ask them to move on. The first two were agreeable enough; said they were hitchhiking to Canada and only stopped for a little sleep in the shade (though of course our lane is no direct route to Canada or anywhere else, and a more unlikely place to get a hitch could hardly be found), or that they were only picking up a few Summer Sweetings to eat with bread and cheese they had bought in the village. They said there should be a sign to warn people off and I agreed with that, so before the next group got there I had painted and put up three neat, plain signs: PRIVATE DRIVEWAY and DO NOT ENTER and NO TRESPASSING PLEASE.

"But the signs didn't stop the third group and they gave me more difficulty. I had been uncertain as to which of the travelers before them were male and which female yet had no doubt both companies included some of each sex. However I was quite quickly convinced that the third group was made up entirely of young men. They were insulting and somewhat threatening, but I stood my ground and before nightfall they did leave though not until I had had to stand by helplessly while they painted what looked to me like a hex symbol on the stable door and over my three warning signs. They used an oily dark fluid they had brought along in a can and I was never able to cover it with any paint I had. As soon as my paint dried that symbol would come through. I took down the signs, but that mark is still on the stable door. . . . And they did not go very far (perhaps because by then it was late in the season and the nights growing cold) — only to the old Hasey place about a mile north on Route Four. That too has been unoccupied for several years and I don't know who owns it. Anyway, those young men settled into it, nobody put them out, and they stayed there until nearly a year ago when it burned down. They told the firemen they had been away when the fire started — out berrying, they said, but the firemen saw no berries they had picked — and came back when they heard the siren. Don Stedman driving along another road two miles or so off saw the smoke and called in the alarm. Nothing is left at Hasey's now but the chimney, and Old Dan's stone walls and the rotting pasture bars defaced by the hex symbols.

"You know what the coming of spring used to mean to us, Bart. Now I have learned to dread it. In winter everything around me is much the same as I have always known it, except that you and Kate are never visible to me. In the quiet I still hear your voices, your footsteps, the small sounds she makes as she dips water, beats cake batter, slices apples, cuts patches to mend a mitten or a pair of pants; and you putting new taps on our shoes, shelling corn to pop, whittling, tightening a loose doorknob, making of the cat, and snoring in the next room after you have gone to bed. Snow is the heavy theater curtain separating the past from the present and future, the stage from the house (whether the house be empty, sparsely occupied, or crowded; blank, attentive, or restless; quiet or noisy; cheering or abusive). As soon as that curtain is drawn, the stage — the past — comes alive and real and I am part of it, lost in it, safe and restored and myself in it.

"I see your eyes twinkle, Bart. You say, 'What are you running on like that to me for, Billy? I never was to a theater in my life.' Kate remonstrates with you. 'Land sakes alive,' she says. 'Leave the boy alone, Bart, do. He has to tell *somebody* what's going through his head.' But you tell her, 'He'd better save it for his book.'

"Kate is right. I do need somebody to talk to. Somebody who listens. Somebody who knows how it used to be here and wants to know how it is now. This book is for those who never knew, don't know they want to know, and never will know unless I tell them.

"Fall is next best to winter. Each day is quieter than the day before. In the color of the leaves, the heap of pumpkins by the back door, the cawing of crows, the scampering of mice between the partitions, the smell of frost and of smoke from the burning cornstalks, the rifle shots of hunters there is the promise of winter coming close, a stirring in the raised curtain and a sifting down of iridescent particles of dust from its folds. Then the snow comes again . . .

"But by April, as the days lengthen and I begin to take time from my books, papers, and old pictures to figure up what I have for seed and what I must buy to plant and where I shall get Eli Martin to plow with his tractor (he got a new,

much heavier tractor last year) I do begin to grow uneasy, to
keep an eye out on all sides lest I am being watched or even
about to be pounced upon by strangers. And I, of course,
become the Sturtevants and the Crowleys — your Sturtevants, Bart, and your Crowleys, those I knew and many
more you told me so much about and I have studied so much
that I feel as if I knew them.

"A year ago I got so edgy I went hunting for that last
letter you had from Horace, Jr. Finally found it up attic —
that one you got in 1957 where he said he was leaving the
next day for Europe, to be gone about six months, and would
send your five hundred dollars for the year as soon as he got
back; but you never heard from him again.

"Then I wrote to him.

"I told him you died six years ago and left the Crowley
place to me. That I was living here alone now, and had tried
to do for his place what little I could, but unless it got major
repairs soon it wouldn't stand much longer. Also that we
were beginning to have quite a lot of trouble around here
with groups of young people who seemed to feel free to move
into unoccupied houses for periods of days, weeks, or longer;
and some of them did serious damage before they left. I told
him about the signs I had put up, but said I couldn't do much
for his place unless he gave me the authority to and wrote
out a paper I could show the police if they had to be called."

I tell Bart:

"I knew he was unlikely to be at the same place now, but I
put my return address plain on that envelope, and I printed
PLEASE FORWARD in the lower lefthand corner; and no
answer to it ever came nor was my letter ever returned to
me. So however hard it may be for you to understand and
believe (and nothing is supposed to be hard where I know

you and Kate are) you have to accept the fact that Crowleys have done all they can ever do for Sturtevants. I have accepted it. Now you and I both have to stop worrying about it. I realize that is easier for me than it would have been — or maybe is now — for you, because my personal obligation is only to you and Kate. When I study and make a record of what I learn about the Sturtevants I do it because you and the earlier Crowleys cared as much about them as about yourselves, and often, it seems, more; and because of the feeling I have that we are doing it together, talking it all over and trying to figure it out together as we did here for so many years. But the Crowley place is *my* place, the Crowley house is now my only companion, my family, and I could concentrate on it every waking hour the rest of my life. My one real worry is about what will become of it after I go."

I ask him:

"Did you ever look *that* far ahead, Bart? If you did, I wish you had told me your thoughts about it. It is a puzzle I can't solve. Eli has promised to feed Cat if ever I can't. But there is no reason why the place should be left to him, and I know Kate could never bear the thought of his wife Flo turning this kitchen upside down."

Friday, May 12

Yesterday was another rainy day but Cat and I were snug enough. Kate's curtains had dried in Wednesday's sunshine and I sprinkled them and rolled them up that night so they were ready to iron and hang in the morning. After that I worked on the papers, and Cat lay on the rug in front of the stove and slept. It was warm enough so I left the back door open a little while. I like to hear the sound of the rain on the shed roof. But a motor kept starting up, sputtering, back-firing, and stopping on the hill and that bothered me, so I closed up. It was near one o'clock when I stopped to rub my eyes and stretch. Cat rolled over, blinked at me, stretched, too, and went to the door and mewed. So I let her out and went to bed.

This morning it was later than usual when I rustled up the fire. Slices of breakfast oatmeal were just beginning to sizzle in Kate's spider when somebody turned the bell on the front door. It made me jump. I don't know as I'd ever heard that bell before since I used to ring it myself when I was six or seven to see if it would bring Kate to exclaim and invite me in as if I were a friend she had been longing to see for years.

I pushed back the spider and went in through to wrench open the door which had been closed all winter. There on the step stood as bedraggled a pair as you ever saw. Both bare-foot, in blue jeans patched in red and black, grimy T-shirts, and plaid jackets, with water running in streams from hair hanging to their shoulders.

I knew well enough where they had come from. I didn't say anything. I just stood and looked at them, watching them drip.

One of them, the bearded one, said, "Hi. Any chance we could buy some vegetables of you? Some eggs? Milk?"

The other one just smiled, saying nothing. Cat came curiously around the corner of the house, half-hidden in the budding lilacs.

I said, "Nope. Nothing left in the cellar this time of year

fit to sell. Don't keep a cow. Hens, neither. Any milk or eggs
I get I bring from the village."

She kept on smiling but his face fell. She had gone down
on one knee and was holding out her hand to Cat. Cat kept
his distance, wary of strangers.

Beard said ruefully, "Is that how it is in the country now?"

I said, "More often than not. Don't pay to keep a cow
unless you can keep a couple of dozen. Nor hens except in the
hundreds."

"Then if we're going to eat we have to get to town."

He turned away slowly. She got to her feet and matched
her step to his as if they were dancing together, but she
glanced back, still smiling, and said, "Thanks anyway,
Mister."

Then he stopped, turning toward me again.

"We couldn't get you to drive us downtown?"

"All I've got is a bicycle."

"Oh . . . Well — sorry I troubled you."

They started on across the yard and I saw her tuck her
hand in the crook of his arm and tip up her bright face to
him, talking. I let Cat in and was pulling on the door to close
it when he called:

"Mister? . . . You need anything we can bring back for
you?"

". . . No, I — how you going to get down there?"

He shrugged and his grin came back.

"Walk. We don't have a bicycle. Only a motorbike that's
suddenly gone crazy. Must have got soaked. Should have
left it under cover, only one place seemed about as wet as
another."

"You staying at the house on the hill?"

He nodded.

"It's my family place. I'm Larry Sturtevant."

I said, "So? Can't be a very comfortable place to visit."

He said, "Comfortable? No way!"

Her smile grew into a laugh, and she said, huddling against him, "But it's what we've got. That is, it belongs to Larry's grandfather. And we're not visiting. We're going to live there. We're going to start fixing it up. So we're your new neighbors. My name's Lisa. What's yours?"

Something about that girl tore me apart. I wondered why, for she was obviously as happy as a duck on a millpond.

I wrenched the door open again, and heard myself say, "Come back here. I'm William Crowley. I didn't know you were Sturtevants. Crowleys and Sturtevants have been neighbors for three hundred years. Come in and have a cup of coffee."

"Coffee!" she squealed.

"Yea, man!" he rumbled.

She snatched off her jacket, tossed it through the door ahead of her and then stood on it, vigorously rubbing her feet. He joined her in this exercise. If the first I had seen of their dancing was a tango, this was a softshoe.

"I don't know why you're doing that," I said. "Except that you seem to like to. This way, when you're ready."

Leaving the hall door open behind me I went back into the kitchen and pulled the spider and coffeepot to the front covers of the stove, was relieved that the sliced oatmeal started sizzling again. I didn't want to put in more wood because I thought I would toast some strips of saltfish as soon as the fire got down to coals. I was trying to get my mind on familiar chores because inside I was all of a quiver.

"We did it before stepping on your beautiful carpet," said Lisa's gentle voice behind me. "If we'd known we were going to step on a carpet, we'd have worn shoes so we could take them off."

"It's just a rag carpet," I told her without looking round. "Kate made it out of old clothes. A little wet wouldn't hurt it."

"Anyway, our feet are clean," she said, "and that's lucky. wow! See how white the boards of this floor are, Larry. How do you keep them so white, William?"

"Seasand," I said, and went into the sinkroom for cups. They clattered on the saucers as I brought them to the table.

Larry and Lisa were standing close to the stove. I had to push between them to turn the oatmeal slices.

"That coffee's got a mighty fine aroma, man," he said. "And this heat! I tried to get a fire going in the fireplace last night but it smoked so we had to put it out."

"Birds' nests in the chimney," I said. "Hang your jackets behind the stove to dry."

Lisa asked softly, "Who was Kate, William?"

Had she guessed from my voice that Kate is not here? Or from the look of the kitchen that it has had no woman care lately?

"Kate Crowley," I said. "Bart Crowley's wife. They brought me up. This was their house. If you've begun to dry off, sit down."

I pulled two chairs out from the table. Quite a way out, because that was what Lisa would need. She was going to have a baby. As far as I knew, she might have it within the hour. I poured their coffee, took the cover off Kate's red block sugarbowl, and pushed the can of condensed milk toward them.

"Oh, Larry," sighed Lisa contentedly, "is this heaven?"

He grinned at me, took a long drink, kissed her nose, her lips, and her chin, and said, "If they serve coffee in heaven."

"You're going to have some with us, aren't you, William?"

"Soon as I get this saltfish browned. You folks want any? I don't know as you like saltfish and fried oatmeal but it's what I'm having for breakfast."

"We shouldn't take your food," said Larry. "It's enough to take coffee and fixings that you've pedaled all the way up here. Must be five miles to the center, isn't it?"

"We'll get him more," said Lisa. "If there's enough right now, William, we'd love some. I never ate either but I'm sure we'd love it. And then we'll go downtown and get you some more."

"There's enough," I told her.

But when I flipped the oatmeal slices and fish strips onto their plates I knew something was lacking. She must need the vegetables they had come here hoping to get. I had no vegetables fit to eat, as I had told them. But I remembered a kettle of sauce I had made yesterday from the last of the Northern Spies. She was feeding Cat bits of fish. I put a bowl of the sauce on the table, poured my coffee and more for them, and sat down at the window end of the table where Bart used to sit. They were where I usually sit, where Kate always put my plate. Bart at the head of the table, Kate at the foot, near the stove, and I between them. I wished with all my heart Kate would open the door and come in and sit in her place, ready to take over calmly, as I knew she would, whatever might happen. I couldn't eat much.

They ate, as Bart used to say, as if this were their last meal before starting out West in a covered wagon that was all loaded and the horses pawing at the door. Between mouthfuls they kept touching each other, smiling at each other and at me. Sometimes they said a few words, but mostly they talked with their eyes.

"Feel better, baby?" . . . "Feel *marvelous*" . . . "Any more applesauce?" . . . "Just enough for you. Unless William wants it." I shook my head. "Is the coffeepot empty?" . . . "I'll see." . . . "Wait a minute. Sh-h. Hear William's clock tick."

Every time she spoke to me or about me she called me William. Now that her hair was drying out it was turning up at the ends and had little moving lights in the darkness of it. I thought the lights must be reflections from her bright face. His hair, drying, became almost red. I remembered the red streaks in the last Alexander's grizzled beard, and that Hoddy had a red topknot when we used to play together before his folks sent him up to Massachusetts to school.

Finally I could stand it no longer.

I asked Larry, "Now what about that motorcycle? Think you can get it going, or don't you?"

He gave himself a shake and thrust out his underlip with a puff that made the short hair across his forehead spread into a fan.

"I doubt it. Ashamed to say I'm no mechanic. Bike's three years old and it's had hard use. We went to Florida on it Christmas. Before that —"

"You *both* went to Florida on that thing?"

"Oh, William, it was fantastic," Lisa said dreamily. "I'll never forget a mile or a minute of it. I get good vibes just thinking about it. We left the snow behind us, and assignments behind us, and everybody we knew behind us, and the road unrolled, and the sun kept coming up and going down, and by and by there were orange groves. You see, we were at home all the way. That bike is the only home we've had together until now. Being on it is so — peaceful."

She got up and began stacking dishes and taking them to the sinkroom, Cat rubbing against her ankles and winding in and out between her feet.

I was bound I wouldn't be distracted.

"All the more reason it ought to run, if it still will," I told Larry. "If you can't fix it, you ought to get somebody out here from the garage to look it over."

"You're probably right, sir." *Sir!* "We'll see about it as soon as we get down there."

But he seemed in no hurry at all. He was watching Lisa, and they were smiling at each other as she came and went.

"No need to *go*," I said. I thought afterwards I may have sounded as if I were snapping at him. I wanted to let my mind wander as his was wandering. I also wanted time and quiet in which to come to terms with the fact that now I was sitting where Bart had sat at every meal all the time I was growing up and all the years afterward, as long as he could get to the table. Now I was there and another young fellow, a Sturtevant, sat in my place. Had I ever looked to Bart as Larry looked to me? Lovable, innocent, helpless? But I thought *somebody* should concentrate on essentials right now, face the facts, exercise a little self-discipline, and do something. "There's a telephone in the entry. You can just as well call Wesley's garage and see if Brian can run up or send somebody."

Lisa had come back and was leaning against him, her arm around his neck, her fingers twisting his hair.

"But *why*, William? We have to go anyway for groceries and —"

I pushed back Bart's chair, went to the stove, and looked

into the coffeepot. It was empty and I had known it was. I had seen Larry drain it and noted that he had set it over on the cover of my hot water tank.

Still looking into it, I growled, "Because the sooner the thing is running the better. You're too far from everywhere here to be without wheels. Brian might have it fixed before dark if he starts soon enough. And if he's coming out, nobody has to go for groceries. If you want me to, I can call your order in to Elaine Pease at Nationwide, she'll send the stuff over to the garage, and Brian or whoever he sends can bring it when he comes. I'll call the garage, too, if you say so."

"Well, how about that, babe?" Larry asked, turning his chair and pulling Lisa onto his knees.

Cuddled there, she smiled at me.

"Oh, that would be beautiful, William. Would you? Because we don't know those people so we couldn't ask favors of them. But they'll do it for you, won't they? I can see you don't have the slightest doubt. Larry, we're going to have to learn to be good neighbors, and somehow repay everybody. You see, William, where we've lived nobody did much for anybody else, and nobody thought you could owe anything but money."

I figured the chances were that what they were going to owe me was money, before this day was over, but I didn't care. I thought once they had some food and transportation I could stop worrying about them; and anything this cost me would be worth it.

"Make out your list," I said.

I tore off a piece of brown paper bag and gave them a pencil from Kate's blue china vase beside the clock. Lisa was back in her chair, pulled very close to his, and she did the writing. Her bent head was against his cheek, and once he gently bit her ear, most of his face hidden in her hair but his eyes twinkling at me.

I called Wesley's, some woman answered and yelled for Brian, told him what I wanted, and laughed heartily. "He says is Bill setting out to be a Hell's Angel? Says he'll be out there in about an hour to see what's up in Punkintown. The old Sturtevant place, you said? Across the road from you? Okay, he says he knows where you are."

He ought to. Brian Wesley grew up on this road. After his folks died, he tore down the buildings for material to use in the house he built next to his garage in town. Nothing but a cellar hole now where the Wesley house stood, and the Wesley fields have all come up to bushes.

They handed me their list and I read it to Elaine and asked her to send the order right over to the garage for Brian to bring up. She said it would be there in fifteen minutes, and I hung up.

Lisa said, her smile anxious, "You didn't order a package of saltfish, William. It's the first item on the list but I'm sure you didn't say it."

"Saltfish in packages isn't saltfish," I told her. "I buy a whole salt cod every fall and hang it in the cellar. I've got enough of that left so Larry can go down and cut you out some, if you want it. Time of year now when it ought to be eaten up."

"Oh, William, you're a kind man. All I know of to do for you right now is wash up the dishes. I'll try to think of something else soon."

I was already thinking of something else. The birds' nests in the Sturtevant chimney, the leaking roofs; and I knew there was not a stick of furniture in that house. It had all

Next of Kin

been sold at auction right after Grace Sturtevant died twenty
years ago. No Sturtevants came. They had a lawyer from
Eaton handle it. Bart bought what he could for Kate. I knew
if I had time it would come back to me what we hauled down
the hill in a dumpcart that night after the auction. But I
didn't have time.

I wanted to light my pipe as I always do after a meal and
as Bart always did, but I said to Larry, "While she's washing dishes, we'd better go up to your place to see how much
rain has come in. Somebody ought to be there when they
come from the garage. I've got part of a roll of polyethylene
in the shed chamber. You can help me haul it out and carry
it up. May keep out some water."

He said, "Beautiful! I'd sure like to buy it. But it won't
take us an hour to finish these dishes. Lisa can help me
carry it up."

I knew he didn't want to leave her. Probably she ought
not to be left. But I didn't want her carrying an end of that
roll, either. I had had Eli bring it to me to be used as a re-
placement for storm windows when old frames rotted out.
But I had not needed much of it last fall. It was pretty hefty.

I said, "If a ceiling has to be covered — and I don't doubt
it will — you'll need another man. She'd better stay where
it's warm and dry. I'll fix it so she can let you know if she
needs you."

I went into the bedroom, got a red bandana out of the
bureau drawer and told her if she closed that into the top
of the back door, with the flap outside, we could see it from
Sturtevants' and he would come right down.

She smiled at me and said, "You're sweet, William. Leave
it right there on the table."

I wondered what good he would be to her if she did need

help. Then I thought that if we should see the red flag I would tell him the name of the nearest hospital and where to find the ambulance service number; and I felt better. I would have felt better still if I could have given her the name and number, but how could I do that? I put on my jacket, said I was heading for the shed chamber, and went, leaving the doors open behind me.

It must have cooled off some in the kitchen before he followed me. And as we crossed the road I had all I could do to keep him from making me drop my end of the roll, he turned so many times to wave to her.

That was the first time I had been inside the Sturtevant house in two years and it was even worse off than I thought, but it is too late tonight for me to describe it. Before I go to bed I want to see if I can put my hand on what I copied out of the diary Sophie Sturtevant kept the first year she was married to Orestes. Maybe it will be quieter around here tomorrow than it has been today.

Saturday, May 13

It wasn't. Larry and I had cut pine boughs with a dull axe we found in the shed up there. I tied a piece of rope to a bundle of them and rammed them down the chimney from the top. Then we dragged them down through into the fireplace, swept up the mess as best we could with more pine boughs, and built a good fire. They had put their bedrolls beside the only fireplace Justin Crowley didn't brick up and plaster over as soon as Adams Sturtevant died. (Sophie says in her diary that she told Orestes "with all the conviction I could muster" she would break off their engagement if he went all the way with his sister Aphrodite who had a feverish dislike of ashes. Sophie told Orestes she would never go to live in a house which did not have a single fireplace. She wrote in her diary that she was not afraid to say it because she was sure he knew she was incapable of carrying out the threat. She was only afraid she would be forced to admit it, that he would not think it necessary to humor her. Whether or not he regarded it as necessary or, if he did, for what reason, he left an open fireplace in one of the two parlors; which room, Sophie wrote, Aphrodite promptly closed up and it was not opened again, except by a maid going in to dust, until the wedding night of Orestes and Sophie. So that is how it came about that Larry and Lisa had a place for a fire, after we got rid of the birds' nests in the chimney. But they don't know that.)

About that time Brian drove up. I went out and introduced Larry to him. Once they started work on the motorcycle I went back into the house with the groceries, measured the parlor ceiling, and started cutting sheets of polyethylene though all I had to do it with was the jackknife I always carry in my pants pocket. The lathes were bare in two big sections and I couldn't judge how soon more plaster would fall, but I was nailing polyethylene along the edge of the room when Brian and Larry came in and said the motorcycle was running.

Larry said, "I'll go over and get Lisa now and she can help us put up that stuff. Shall we lock your door when we leave?"

I nodded.

"Where's your key?"

I took nails out of my mouth and told him, "In the door.

Bring back the key with you. Bring up a pail, too, from the cupboard under the sink. And as much of that saltfish as you can use. Cut it out in strips and wrap it in newspaper. Any newspaper you can find."

He left, but Brian still stood there grinning at me.

"What are you up to, Bill? Think poly's going to hold up the roof when it falls in?"

"I don't figure roof's going to fall in tonight. Fella pay you?"

"Not 'till tomorrow, hey? Yup. Paid me."

"May stop raining by then. Look around the shed and the stable, will you? See if there are strips of anything out there long enough to go across this room. Two will do it, if they are long enough."

He came back with four strips of molding we spliced into two. While he held them up I nailed them into place. Brian is a tall man and for some reason the ceiling in that room is lower than the others up there. Sophie spoke of that in her diary. She liked a low ceiling. It was what she had been used to at home.

As we worked, Brian asked, "That young squirt a Sturtevant, you say?"

"Hoddy's grandson, I guess. Your father knew Hoddy when they were boys. We all used to play together."

"Don't say. Where's that Hoddy now?"

"How would I know? Last Bart heard from any of them was more than fifteen years ago."

"What makes you so sure this is Hoddy's grandson?"

"They say the place belongs to his grandfather. And he looks like 'em."

"Even if he is and does, what's it to you? What reason have you got for going to all this bother for any Sturtevant?"

"None, I guess. Except Bart would do it if he could. . . . Besides, I'd do as much for a cat on a day like today, and so would you. . . . There, it's hitched. Much obliged, Brian. Make it up to you."

He shrugged, grinned, glanced around the bleak place, and observed, "As Granny would have said, 'How are the mighty fallen!' See you around, Bill."

The motorcycle coming up the hill exchanged horn blasts with the truck going down. The rain was slackening off.

Larry and Lisa ran in and stood hand in hand, backs to the roaring fire.

Lisa's face was radiant. She said, "wow! . . . Oh, *William!* It's *beautiful!*"

I told her I didn't know where she was going to put her groceries but they were in bags behind the door. I told Larry he ought to get into the village first thing Monday to pay for them at Nationwide, and if they wanted power turned on they ought to have the Light Company check first to see if the wiring was safe. Then I told him to bring the pail and we'd go see what condition the old spring was in. A tree had fallen across it but we chopped out the mid-section, and skimmed off the bark so he could fill the pail. I don't know whether the water is fit to drink but I hope so. Nobody can live long without water. Then I came home.

Tuesday, May 16

Yesterday morning I was out digging around the rose-bushes when they bounced down the washed-out Sturtevant driveway on the motorcycle and headed toward the village. I thought she would have been as well off going bellybump down Tanner Tom's Hill on my old sled in January. She had both arms around him and her cheek pressed against his back, and their hair flew out in the sun like reddish-yellow and black flags. As far as I could tell neither of them looked in this direction. They couldn't have seen me anyway because I was down on my knees behind the bushes. About as soon as the grinding sound of their motor died away I went into the shed chamber and began hunting around. I was still there, maybe a half hour later, when they roared into my yard, and I looked down at them from the door I had rolled back to let in some light. There is only one window in Bart's shed chamber and it is at the far end.

He made for the kitchen with a carton as soon as he jumped off the motorcycle and, finding it open, went in. But she knelt on the grass and was picking bluets.

I said, "You'd better get up. Ground's still wet."

She tilted a shining face.

"Oh, *there* you are, William! What you doing?"

"What Kate called congering. She used to tell me, 'Don't you dare conger amongst my things.' "

Lisa laughed.

"Whatever it is, okay if we do it, too?"

"I wish you would."

"Larry! William's up over the shed! He says we can come up. How do we get there, William?"

"Through the shedroom. He knows the way. It's where we got the roll of poly yesterday."

She ran into the house. A minute later they ran up the stairs.

"wow!" cried Lisa. "What a neat place!" Neat it was

not. "wow, we're right up under the roof! See that beautiful spiderweb across the top of the window. Oh, Larry, I'm getting the best vibes!"

She hugged him and kissed him. I had known, from her voice, that that was coming.

"What are vibes?" I asked.

Larry grinned over the top of her head.

"Short for vibrations. You get them from being near somebody or something you like. Good ones make you feel great. Like you could tear down the world and build a better one."

"And she gets them from spiderwebs?"

Lisa answered me, leaning back from Larry, her hands still clasped behind his neck.

"Partly from that spiderweb, William. Partly the brown beams; they're so solid. Partly from what looks like a square shaft filled with tiny whirling sparks that runs from the door to you. And from the dark lumps of things piled all around the walls, and the musty, dusty smell. But mostly from our all being here in it. If we weren't here, it wouldn't be the same at all. . . . How come we're here, William?"

"Because I happened to think there might be some old furniture moldering away that you could use while you're at Sturtevants'. I knew there was a pine table you could eat at and a few ladderback chairs with doubtful seats; we could tack some canvas over the rush. But I was looking for a bed —"

"Oh, we've got sleeping bags, William. We don't need a bed."

"That's lucky because I can't find a bed. Nothing but this old horsehair-covered couch. It would open up to be a bed, though, if anybody wanted it to."

"I'd like a bed," Larry admitted.

ABIGAIL E. WEEKS MEMORIAL LIBRARY
UNION COLLEGE
BARBOURVILLE, KENTUCKY

"You *would?*" Lisa cried. "You really would like a bed? You don't think the bags are fun any more?"

"Sure they're fun. But a bed would be fun sometimes too . . . You really would lend us your couch, sir?"

"Lend you anything you want that's up here. None of it's been in use for twenty years or more. Come see what you can find."

Lisa squealed softly, "Hey! It's Christmas!"

A minute later they had pounced on the dark lumps around the walls like a couple of squirrels, diving into trunks and barrels and shouting triumphantly over every old cup or plate, rusty saucepan, or ragged patchwork quilt they found. I kept wondering what Kate would have made of such a display of excitement over things she had pushed back under the eaves only because they had "some use left in them," and were "too good to throw away."

While they were still scrambling I picked up a double armful of stuff they had dug out and exclaimed over, took it downstairs, and piled it in a corner of the kitchen. I saw they had brought me milk and eggs so I started up the fire to heat the oven for baking muffins, and when they came down I was scrambling the eggs.

"We'll eat first and then start carrying up what you want at the house," I said. "I take it from this food that you went in to pay Elaine Pease while you were in the village."

He said, "Sure did."

Lisa, pouring milk, said thoughtfully, "She's a doll. I like her. The way her eyes snap you expect her to bite your head off, but what she says is kind. She told us her mother was born up this way."

I nodded. "On the old Watson place. Alta Holmes, her mother was. The family moved into the village when Alta wasn't more than a dozen years old. She married Clyde Pease down there."

"You know all about everybody who ever lived here, sir?" Larry asked.

"More about some than others. Something about most of them."

"Elaine doesn't — isn't married?" Lisa asked, sipping from the glass in her hand.

"If she'd married," I said, "her name wouldn't be Pease."

" . . . No," said Lisa softly. "It wouldn't, would it?"

We ate and again left her washing dishes, with Cat rubbing around her bare ankles, while we started for Sturtevants' with the couch. Before night everything they had found that they wanted was up there, and so was she, and they said it was their turn now to feed me, so I took an iron kettle and spider outside, cleaned off the rust with sand, and in the barn found an old stove grate and some bricks they could set it on in the fireplace. Then while vegetables cooked and they tore up greens for salad I tacked some of Bart's grain bags over the broken seats of the ladderback chairs.

Whatever it was they cooked I never tasted anything like it before.

"What do you think, William?" Lisa asked anxiously. "Do you like it?"

"Takes some getting used to," I answered. "Pretty high-flavored. . . . Yes, it's all right." Bart used to answer Kate that way when she tried out on us some recipe she had cut from the newspaper. After a minute I took a big drink of water, safe or not, and said, "I figure we'd better swap meals often, so my intestinal tract will gradually toughen up and yours can get some rest now and then."

Larry grinned and said, "I'll buy that."

Lisa laughed softly and said, "Oh, William, you're —
you're okay."

When we finished, she asked if I hadn't brought my pipe.
I said my pipe was never beyond my reach, but I hadn't intended to pollute their air; I hadn't seen them smoking and
thought it likely they disapproved of it.

"Not for anybody who has done it as long as you must
have and stayed as healthy as you are," Lisa said. "Just for
those who don't know how it would affect them."

"Besides, one thing we have here is excellent ventilation,"
grinned Larry. "So light up, sir, and enjoy yourself. You've
earned it."

I moved my chair by the fireplace, as Kate had trained
Bart and me to do at smoking time. They were still at the
long, drop-leaf table, cradling their coffee mugs in their
young hands, rubbing cheeks, and smiling at me. I could see
them only vaguely by flickering candle and firelight.

After a few blue rings had floated up the chimney, I said,
"Suppose that table is glad to get home?"

"Home!"

"It came from here. Bart bought it at the auction after
Grace Sturtevant died and we hauled it down to our place in
the dumpcart. The chairs, too. That was more than twenty
years ago. I think Bart bought stuff because he didn't want it
all to leave the neighborhood. People came from as far away
as Boston to that auction, but the bidding was high only on
the very old, elegant furniture and dishes and there was a
lot of that. Bart said he didn't have to pay much for what
he got, and maybe Kate could use it. But Kate had all she
needed. She didn't need much. We stored most of what he
got from here in the shed chamber and it has stayed there
ever since. Until today."

Larry asked, "Who was Grace Sturtevant?"

"Orestes's wife. Born Grace Hasey. They were your great-grandparents, I s'pose. Orestes was married three times. First to Sophronia Watson, and they had one son, Alex, and a couple of daughters. After Sophie died (Orestes was forty-two then) he went away for nearly a year. His sister Aphrodite came to look after his children here. Aphrodite was an old maid, always lived on the home place until Orestes got married, then she went to Cambridge to stay with Chaucer; he was a professor at Harvard. Then Orestes came back and brought a new wife with him, a New York girl. She and Affie didn't get along, so Affie left. Then Orestes and his wife had two daughters, Maude and Jessica, and finally the New York girl left him, went back to New York, people thought, and after a while they were divorced. By then Orestes was in his late fifties but he married Grace Hasey from Hasey's Hill. She had been nurse and governess at Sturtevants' for Sophie's Alex who was a cripple. Grace and Orestes had one child, your grandfather, born in 1901."

"Just — a — minute," Lisa begged.

They exchanged a long look.

"Sounds as if he were reading it from a book, doesn't it?" Larry asked her.

"It's printed in my head," I said.

Her gaze came back to me.

"*Orestes?*" she asked. "*Aphrodite? Chaucer?*"

I had to laugh at her tone and expression and I don't laugh much.

I said, "They had a brother Plato, but he died in the Civil War; all three boys were in the Union Army. Nobody here was surprised by the names and soon got used to them. You see, their father, Adams Sturtevant, was a great scholar.

They said he could read before he was three years old, and he read constantly all his life — which was only sixty years. People who worked up here said every room in the house was lined with books and that while his children were growing up he used it like a library — came to it from a studio his brother Hancock built for him up in the pines right after he built a house down by the road for their brother Franklin and his family. Adams could give all his time to study because the place became his for his lifetime when his father, Holdfast, took up the law. By then it was some five hundred acres of timber, grazing land, and cultivated land, with a great apple orchard, a sawmill, a big dairy herd, flocks of sheep, a dozen or so fine horses, oxen, and so on. And Franklin ran it for Adams, with help from Adams's wife, Roxy — she was a smart woman — and from the neighbors around; everybody here worked for Sturtevants at least part of the year. Hancock never married and was an architect; lived with Adams for quite a while and then built a strange little house with pillars for himself overlooking the millpond. They were all devoted to Adams. Everybody was. I guess you could say he was revered, much as his grandfather had been for different reasons. All of Holdfast's sons but the oldest, Washington, graduated from either Harvard or Yale, but Adams was the one, people said, who honed his education to a sharp edge and used it and never stopped adding to it. Nobody but Sturtevants had ever gone to college from here and in those times all but a very few went to work as soon as they were old enough to leave the district school; but they thought if they had gone to college they could have done different afterwards than Franklin did; thought he might have been a better farmer than he was if he had spent on his father's farm those ten years he was away at school. And they thought a good carpenter had no need of an architect, knew Hancock was no carpenter, and made quiet fun of such things as useless pillars on a little house beside a Maine millpond. Nobody here was surprised that Hancock's house and Franklin's house and Adams's studio collapsed into their cellars while what the first Alexander Sturtevant and his neighbors had built on this site in 1680 was still solid. . . . This room we're in was part of that Alexander's house."

"This room?" Lisa whispered, staring around her, trying to pierce the shadows. "In 1680?"

"Adams Sturtevant was my — great-grandfather?" Larry asked, frowning.

"Your father's great-grandfather. See, after Adams came Orestes, then Horace — your grandfather — then Horace, Jr. And now you."

Larry grinned at that, and shrugged.

"Still sounds like something I might come on in a reference library where I was looking for something else."

But Lisa said, "Not to me, babe. It grabs me. I mean, it really grabs me." She was hunched forward, her elbows on the table, her chin in her hands, and her eyes fixed on me. "*Adams,* William? Adams and *Washington* and *Franklin* and *Hancock?*"

"Holdfast Sturtevant was a stalwart American patriot from his first memory to his deathbed. His wife wrote in her journal that his last words were, 'God save the Republic.' They had daughters Betsey, Martha, Abigail, and Dolly as well as the four sons. You see, Holdfast, born in 1785, heard a great deal as a boy about the War for Independence and what his father, older brothers and neighbors had thought and done about it. This made a strong impression on him, and he had supreme confidence in the new political system, became a lawyer, held many local and state offices, and was in Washington, serving in Congress, when he died in 1870. He was eighty-five years old then."

Larry shook his head.

"How do you know all this, sir? How do you keep it straight?"

"The names," Lisa whispered. "Just the names for now, William. Do you remember any more names? Holdfast . . . Did Holdfast have brothers? Sisters?"

I made a chuckling sound and knocked out my pipe against the bricks.

"Well, now Holdfast's father, the Continental soldier, was the third Alexander Sturtevant in this country. The third Alexander was a very devout man, a greatly gifted and inspiring preacher from his youth. Those of his sermons that are still around — his wife, Caroline, had many of them printed and bound — show that he was a Calvinist but by no means a purist or a bigot. He talked a lot to God, but he also believed in listening to God, rode horseback all over New England to storm against the treatment of Quakers, against all intolerance of any sincere religious faith, declaring over and over that the Devil was not in the people accused of being witches but in those who persecuted others or sought to prevent them from worshipping in their own way. People who knew him best described him as a Christian. From what I read, maybe you would call him a Jesus-person. Anyway, he drew the plans for, gave the land for, helped to build, and was the first preacher in the only church we ever had here. He didn't call it a church. He called it a meeting-house. . . . But you want to know what his children were christened. Well, Noah was his first, and Noah had brothers

Matthew, Mark, Luke, John, and Holdfast, sisters Mary, Martha, Piety, and Mindwell. . . . And that's far enough back to go tonight. I'm getting sleepy."

I stood up.

"William," Lisa said. "You're incredible. Where did *you* go to college?"

"College? I went for part of a year down east to a little Baptist college named Bates. Then I came back to Bart and Kate and the Crowley place, because everything is here — or has been — that I want to know."

By then I had reached the outside door but Lisa called, "Wait a minute."

She ran after me into the dark front hall, put her hands on my chest, and stretched to kiss me on the chin. It was as high as she could reach unless I bent down, and I didn't bend.

Thursday, May 18

I didn't see hide nor hair of them all day yesterday. I was all the forenoon and all the evening writing down what happened here and at Sturtevants' the day before. But it was a brisk, bright day with a smart breeze so in the afternoon I rode my bicycle over to Eli's to find out when he figures to plow for me. Flo was frying molasses doughnuts and gave me a paper bag full of them to bring home.

This morning I was up before six o'clock — thinking about the doughnuts; I find I can't eat them at night late years — but when I stepped out of the bedroom Lisa was sitting on the grass by the back door with Cat in her lap. Cat knew enough to get out of the heavy dew and the blobs of what we call snakespit, and onto a warm spot. Lisa heard me and smiled and waved and called, "Good morning, William," softly through the open window as soon as I glimpsed her. She does everything softly. Even her squeals are soft. I pretended I didn't hear or see her, until I had been to the sink and washed, and used a comb from the tin case under what Bart used to call "the courtin' mirror." Whenever he spoke of it, he rolled his eyes and grinned at Kate, and she always said, "Don't you leer at me, Bart Crowley."

Then I went to the door and said, "Well! . . . What brought you over here this early? Run out of coffee?"

She stood up, still cuddling and stroking Cat, looking over Cat's pointed ears.

"No. I'm sorry, William. I know how early it is, and I know how late you were up last night because I saw your lights go out. Larry is still asleep. But I've been awake two hours and I didn't sleep much before that. I'm sure it will only take you a minute to tell me, and I can't stand not knowing any longer. *What were the third Alexander's brothers' and sisters' names* — if he had brothers and sisters — *and what Sturtevant names do you know before that?*"

I leaned against the door-frame.

"So far," I said, "we've done it all backwards. Now let's start at the beginning.

"First in this country there was Alexander Sturtevant, born in Scotland in 1646 and sent to this country as an English prisoner-of-war. Of the boatload of prisoners nine were men he had not only fought beside but had grown up with. Once on this side of the water they were obligated, bound out, indentured to work seven years at an ironworks to pay the costs of their passage. Then they all came here together and, as soon as they could, bought adjoining pieces of land to start a community. Some got married to girls they found in this country, but Alexander waited until the sister of one of them, Elizabeth Maxwell, who had been only eleven years old the last time he saw her, was eighteen and could cross the ocean to become his wife."

"The first Alexander . . . and Elizabeth," repeated Lisa softly. "Now their children, please, William."

"All but one of their sons were named for men who came here with Alexander. Their first-born was Robin Maxwell, the following sons Dobbin Crowley, Thomas Watson, William McIntire, Daniel Hasey, James Martin, and finally — at Elizabeth's insistence — Alexander. Their daughters were named for the wives of men in the community — Lydia, Mary, Margaret, Ann — except the daughter whose mother died at her birth. It is said that Elizabeth did not expect to have another child after her son Alexander. She did, but didn't live to know her. Her husband named their last daughter Elizabeth." I could, as Kate used to say, have bitten off my tongue as soon as I heard my words. I added lamely, "The first Elizabeth was forty-six years old when Alexander was born, almost two years older when she died. . . ."

Lisa's eyes never stopped shining.

"And the third Alexander was the son of?"

"James Martin Sturtevant. That Alexander was the devout Sturtevant, so —"

"So he had Noah, Matthew, Mark, Luke, and John, and —"

"Holdfast."

". . . Oh, that name grabs me. I mean, it really does. . . . And sisters Mary, Martha —"

Gladys Hasty Carroll

"Piety and Mindwell."

She shrugged slightly and smiled.

"Not names for today. . . . William, just one more question. How have you found out so much about the Sturtevants?"

"Bart talked a lot about them. Older Crowleys have always talked a lot about Sturtevants, and younger Crowleys have always listened. Besides that —"

"And you are the youngest Crowley. The — last Crowley?"

"Bart was the last Crowley by natural descent. Bart and Kate took me in before I can remember. If they knew who my parents were, they never said and I never knew. I am a Crowley by choice."

"Oh, William — what a great choice! Theirs, and yours! . . . It's great when you can choose. . . . Thank you, William. You can get your breakfast now. I'll go and get Larry's."

I said, "Take him some of Flo Martin's doughnuts. She gave me enough for all three of us."

She put Cat down on the step, caught the bag I tossed to her, and ran. I held open the screen door to let Cat in. Lisa had not stayed to hear the "besides that" which has been what I have read the French would call my "raison d'être," especially these last ten years.

Monday, May 22

Tonight I was reading and taking notes at the kitchen table when there came a tap on the windowpane. I turned, pushing my glasses lower on my nose, and there were their faces pressed against each other and against the glass, framed by the dark. I swung my arm for them to come in. We never used to think of locking a door. I still never do when I am in or near the house, until I go to bed.

I had not seen them for two days, though I had heard their motorcycle rampaging; and I felt at once that something had changed. It was obvious in their outward appearance. They wore expressions of triumph and what looked like new clothes. Larry had on creased, muted gray plaid trousers, and a short-sleeved light blue sport shirt, open at the neck. Lisa wore a brief, deep pink dress with a matching, sleeveless crocheted jacket and her hair was tied back with a scarf in the colors of stained glass windows. Both were wearing shoes when they came in but kicked them into a corner so quickly I did not see what style of footwear it was.

I was still in my chair and Lisa danced over and kissed the top of my head.

"Surprise, William!" she cried . . . "We got married!"

I took off my glasses before I answered.

Then I said, "None too soon, I take it. Sit down and tell me more."

He sat down on Bart's couch and there was room enough for her beside him but she sat on his lap.

"Well, you should know more, dear man. Because you had a lot to do with it."

"*I* did?"

"You told us all those great names Sturtevant children have had. Larry says he never heard them before, so of course I never did. Larry is the only Sturtevant I ever met, and he says he never heard anything much about any Sturtevants. So we didn't know whether we wanted to be

Sturtevants or not. For quite a while we thought it might be just as well as any other way if I stayed Lisa Gallico. Not that I get any vibes from being a Gallico, but who uses last names anyway? Still you do need one for licenses and passports and credit cards and birth certificates. I know I had to sign 'Lisa Gallico' Thursday when we popped in to get the marriage license. We still weren't sure we were going to use it. The license, I mean. But I'm not Lisa Gallico any longer. I'm Lisa Sturtevant!"

She was excited and chattering like a mother bird. Larry just sat there beaming.

She said I must have known before I left Sturtevants' the night I had supper up there that those names I reeled off were really grabbing her. She had kept Larry awake until all hours talking about them and trying to make him remember the ones she had forgotten. The next day she kept at him to agree that they would come down here that night to get the gaps filled in and find out more about the people who had those names; but she couldn't get *to* him. He said they were making nuisances of themselves. By night they were both so mad they wouldn't have been decent company for anyone, so they just stayed there and fought until he went to sleep. But she couldn't sleep.

She drew back from him and pushed his face so far to the side I thought his neck would crack. Then she cuddled him and kissed him.

"Are we a nuisance to you, William?"

"No. Go on."

"See? Didn't I tell you, babe? He *likes* us!"

She said that over their doughnuts and coffee the morning after I told her about the prisoners and how the first Alexander waited seven years for Elizabeth to be eighteen and sail across the ocean to marry him, she told Larry where she had been and what I had said. By then Larry was in a better mood so they spent that day "cracking out all the Sturtevant pieces and putting them together again."

"Seemed like it was, you know, *meant*," said Lisa. "I wasn't eighteen until a month ago. Before that I couldn't have married anybody without what they call parental consent, and I wasn't about to get any consent but Larry's to marry him. And lately we'd been too busy with other things to even think about it much. Once or twice Larry asked, 'How about getting married, kid?' and I always said, 'Why?' To which neither one of us had an answer until you gave us one, William. Yes, you *did*, so don't raise your eyebrows. You offered us a family we could belong to without being involved with them, and showed us that names mean something and are important to history. We saw that without a name and a history our house would be just some tumble-down old house, and that without a name a person would be lost, sooner or later. Totally."

I thought she had jumped to at least one wrong conclusion but figured this was not the time to argue about it.

Of course, once they really made up their minds to get married, they had to think about the ceremony. Larry thought any justice of the peace who wasn't busy would be fine, but Lisa bet all the earlier Sturtevants had been married by church ministers, so she wanted to be married by a minister.

"Not only that," Larry put in. "She was hung up on its being a minister with long hair and a beard. Preferably blonde. She thinks blonde is spiritual."

"Either a blonde or a black," said Lisa. "I didn't want anything halfway about this marriage."

So they rode over a good part of the county Saturday, knocking at rectory and parsonage doors and talking with ministers and priests, some of whom were kind and some of whom were brusque, but even the best of whom seemed hesitant. And the only ministerial long hair they saw was red; not very long at that, and he had neither beard nor moustache, just fairly decent sideburns.

"They kept saying in various ways, 'But, you see, I don't know you.' Why did they think they had to know us to marry us? We're people."

Late in the afternoon she decided that the trouble was their clothes. They were not getting anywhere in jeans and ragged shirts. So they stopped in the next small city they came to to buy her a dress.

"She bought two," said Larry.

"I had to," Lisa declared. "One to get through to them in, and one to get married in. Any of those men we'd talked to, if he agreed to marry us today and I went back in the same dress he might change his mind! So I got a real demure dark blue cotton to pay calls in, and this one to get married in. D'you like it, William?"

She got off Larry's lap and spun round.

"Very pretty," I said.

She sighed.

"I *know* it was extravagant, babe. But any day now there'll be enough material in each of them to make me two dresses. Only I can't sew. Well, anyway, I'll probably never wear a dress again as long as I live."

She went back to him.

Well, anyway. . . . She wore the dark blue out of the store and right away realized that to walk beside that Larry had to have some real slacks and a decent shirt, so she made him get them. She wanted him to get two sets, but he balked.

"He can be so stubborn, William!"

"That's Sturtevant coming out."

She squealed merrily.

Now it was obvious they both had to buy shoes. Finally they went to a McDonald's for double hamburgers and shakes and were clearly the best dressed people there; also the most absolutely ravenous.

But this was not really final.

On the way home they stopped in the village at a parsonage where the door had been locked and the garage empty at noon. An old lady let them into the minister's study and an old man talked with them a long time, and then told them if they would come back at 8:00 tonight he would perform the ceremony.

"Oh, William, he is *such* a dear! Almost as dear as you!"

"No beard," said Larry. "No moustache. No hair at all, as a matter of fact. I mean, the guy's, you know, like bald."

"He's black," said Lisa pensively. "He's blonde. He has a halo. I saw it last night and again tonight. A soft pink halo. Like William's roses in the sunshine."

So at last the marriage thing was all settled, they came home and wow, did they sleep. But Lisa had been up early to wash Larry's shirt — because it might have a drop of hamburger juice on it — and hang it on a bush to drip-dry. What luck it was such an absolutely mind-splitting day!

"All of a sudden, she's hung up on washing," said Larry. "She washed all day long today."

Lisa squealed again.

"First I washed the sheets you let us have and our blankets, because it might turn cold enough for a blanket tonight, and the next time we used bedding would be our Wedding Night. Then every single thing we were going to wear except our new shoes, my new pink dress and Larry's new slacks. I didn't dare put his slacks in water for fear they'd shrink, and you can see they're already absolutely skin tight. . . . Then us! We heated water in everything we could find and man, did we scrub in it while it was still practically steaming! After that, in nothing but towels, we ran down to the spring and threw buckets of cold water on each other. For a minute it was a terrible shock. Then it was beautiful. Like I always imagined sauna baths. We kept dipping and throwing and jumping and splashing and shouting — I think it was just about the most fun thing we ever did, don't you, babe? A gutsy thing!"

"I liked it," Larry agreed quietly.

"But not even you heard us, did you, William?"

I shook my head.

"It is so great of that spring to keep running out into that hollow down between the hills. People there feel like the first people on a new planet. Like a new Adam and Eve, only you've found out somewhere else what happens if you eat apples, and you're never going to touch another old apple. Ugh! You know there are some apple trees down there, and now all they've got on them are some blossoms. I pointed at them and told Larry, "No, no!' He laughed but he knew what I meant and before we left he said, 'Might as well pick them if we can't eat them.' So he picked all he could reach, and they were my wedding bouquet. . . . Back at the house I fixed Larry a little supper but I couldn't eat. *Weird* how excited you feel before your wedding even if — oh, it was such fun bringing in all the clean stuff from the bushes. It smelled so good! We made up the bed and then we dressed.

I had thought once about using some perfume somebody gave me last Christmas, but I forgot."

"You didn't need it," Larry said, rubbing his nose against her hair.

"No. . . . And then we went to the village and got there just as it was growing dark and the streetlights were coming on. So still and peaceful. People rocking on their porches. The same little parsonage was still there. The same sweet old lady let us in, and she and another lady a bit younger stood with us while the black-blonde man with the halo said the words — and I must say you get great vibes from words like that, even if they're not said for you, and these were said just for us — and then he shook hands with us, and touched my cheek with the corner of his little prayer-book, and the old lady kissed us both, and the younger old lady poured tea into the thinnest cups you ever saw and passed around a plate of little cookies with pink sugar crystals on top. Oh, it was a good scene. Then we said good-night, and came straight here to tell you, and now we're going home."

He stepped into his shoes. She picked up hers and stood in the doorway swinging them, her face faintly flushed, her eyes on me as if asking, "Aren't you going to say something?"

I cleared my throat.

"This is good news," I said. "Happy wedding night!"

Larry grinned, said, "Thanks, sir," and stepped out into the dark.

But Lisa was still there.

She said, "It will be, William. We know it. . . . Even though Adam and Eve shouldn't have eaten that apple, God has to be loving and merciful because he let *some* good come out of it. . . . If they'd never made any mistakes none of us would have found out how to solve problems."

I nodded.

She followed him into the dark.

Then her face came back out of it.

"William, some day will you tell us everything you know about the Sturtevants?"

"It would take more than one day," I said. "But I'll think about it."

There was the pop, cough, and growl of their motor in my yard, and the small round red gleam of their tail-light rolling up the hill until it stopped and went out.

I was alone with Cat, who had come in as they left.

I was thinking about it. . . . I am thinking about it.

I'm thinking, "You can't help loving people like that. But what else can you do about them? You have to be so *careful*. They need the attention of other human beings. Everybody does. But, whatever they may lack, they have something peculiarly their own that is new and rare, almost unbearably precious and terrifyingly fragile. Above all, this quality, this response, this whatever-it-is must not be lost to them and so to the world, or even slightly damaged; yet it is as delicate as a wild flower, or a pink thread, or a child just born."

I'm thinking of the baby Kate had here when I was six years old. It was the only one she ever had. It lived only three days. They said it was strong, just very little. They told me it was my brother and would get bigger until by and by it could play with me. But suddenly it began to bleed, and an hour later it was dead. I never told anyone how often I dreamed this had happened because when a breeze caught the door as I went out of Kate's room I did not keep the door from slamming shut. I doubt I have ever entirely stopped fearing that my carelessness, my noise, my just going where Kate's baby was had killed it.

Wednesday, May 24 . . .

Yesterday as soon as I could get around to it I pedaled over to Eli's. I knew well enough he wouldn't be there for he was to plow for the Carpenters the first of this week, but I told Flo I just wanted to leave word for him to try to save a whole day for my place because I'd made up my mind to plant a bigger piece than usual. Flo was the one I went over there to see. I needed to talk with a woman. Flo may not be the best housekeeper in the world but she is goodhearted and strong as an ox. She has had seven young ones and they're all still alive and looking after themselves now. She's easy-going, takes things as they come, but when she lays hold, she doesn't let go. She made me sit down to dinner with her, and then we talked most of the afternoon, off and on, while I put some braces under her cupboard shelves, planed a mite off the top of a door that wouldn't shut, tightened some doorknobs. She says Eli keeps putting off what needs doing in the house. Before I left I did the chores — brought in her wood and water and milked for him. Eli still keeps four cows for the manure and because, Flo says, neither one of them can stand the taste of pasteurized milk and she still makes out her own butter and uses her mother's recipes that call for buttermilk and sour milk. It has always given me a good feeling to pull up a stool to a cow, grip a

pail between my knees, press my forehead against a warm
brown flank, and hear the piping song of thin streams of
warm milk hitting tin. Flo filled one of her canning jars from
the last pailful and wrapped it in newspapers for me to take
home in my basket. No better supper in the world than a big
bowl of crackers and milk at this time of year when you can
eat it out on the steps, looking across your land and figuring
just where the plow will start its first thrust in a few days, to
turn the silky green under and the velvety black soil up.

This morning I went to the village to do a few errands
and got Elaine Pease to one side to ask her if more than one
minister down there was bald. They have three old Protes-
tant churches as well as the newer St. Anne's. Elaine showed
no surprise. That store is the town's information center. I
heard her tell somebody once, "People come in here with the
darnedest questions. You wouldn't believe what we get
asked!" She said no, she guessed old Mr. Standish was the
only one. So I asked her where he lived and she told me and
I pedaled over there and he was home and we had quite a
talk. At the end of it we shook hands and he said, "Whenever you think Mrs. Standish or I can be of any help, don't
hesitate to give us a ring. I can't drive any more because of
poor vision but we've kept the car and Helen's sister drives
it, so she would bring us out any time if you call us. Our
three boys are grown now and all living at great distances,
so we count more and more on nearer young people to fill in
the empty spaces. I have an idea you feel much as we do,
Mr. Crowley."

I didn't trust myself to speak. I just nodded.

He nodded, too, and said quietly, "I'm glad you have
them. How God satisfies our every craving, if only we accept
the nourishment He offers!"

I was back here by noon and not long after that Lisa and Larry bounced down the hill and into my yard.

"Honeymoon over?" I asked, from where I was looking over seed by the barn.

"Well, one phase of it is," Larry sang back. "And we're out of food. You want anything from town?"

"No. I've just come from there."

"Anyway, you don't have to plan supper," said Lisa. "Because you're coming up to have some of ours. At seven o'clock sharp."

"It's your turn to eat here," I objected.

"Never mind turns. We're on our way to buy steak. Real steak. Larry says *everybody* has steak on honeymoons."

I was tempted and probably showed it.

But I asked, "Are you going to cook it in something that will take off the roof of my mouth?"

"William," she vowed, "we won't cook that steak in anything but heat. It will be up to you what you put on your slice."

I said all I wanted on it was a dash of salt, and I would be there.

They left, and I spent the afternoon plotting my campaign.

The meat was not so tender as Kate's pork-steak and deer-steak used to be, but it had a good flavor and I was glad to set my teeth into it. The only beef I've had late years has been either corned or ground.

As we sat around the table chewing I told them Eli was coming to plow tomorrow and how would they feel about letting me use a good piece of their land that had not been turned over or mowed for twenty years and would be the better for it. They thought that was a great idea.

Larry said, "Maybe he'd plow enough so we could plant something, too."

"I thought's likely you might want to. You can have the end towards your house and I'll take the end towards mine."

"wow," cried Lisa. "We'll have our own fresh vegetables! Can we grow Boston lettuce and tomatoes and endive? Can we grow eggplant, sweetie? You know how I adore eggplant!"

Sweetie said, "I don't know. Can we, sir?"

I said I had some seed catalogues they had better study over. And I told them that Flo had offered to ride down tomorrow with Eli to cook a boiled dinner at my house for him and me.

"Bart and Kate both always said Flo was a master hand at a New England boiled dinner. There'll be a mountain of it, and you're welcome to come and eat with us if you want to."

"Oh, FUN. But I'd have got dinner for you and Eli if you'd asked me, William."

"Well, Flo offered. And while she's there, she's going to finish my house-cleaning. Can't see I'm ever going to get around to it this year."

"I'd do your cleaning, too, William!"

"Well, come and clean with her if you want to. Plenty of work for two good women."

"Mmm. NICE. This Flo probably knows a lot I don't."

That she does.

"Maybe I can — *learn!*"

That she can. If she will. And I figure she will.

"What am I going to do that day?" asked Larry. "Besides eat?"

"Eli and I'll think of something," I promised him. He has a lot of learning to do, too, if he is fixing to stay here.

Across steaming coffee mugs Lisa said, "William, are you going to begin telling us everything you know about the Sturtevants? . . . When I asked you before, you said you would think about it."

"I've been thinking about it," I answered. "I've thought a lot about it."

Then I told them what I had been thinking.

First I told them the "besides that" — how I had found out more about the Sturtevants than Crowleys had told me. That the first families here had been diary-keepers and instilled the habit into their descendants for several generations, and that after Grace Sturtevant died I had read not only all the Crowley diaries Bart had in a trunk in the attic, but whatever was still in existence in the neighborhood that Martins, Haseys, Watsons, McIntires and others had written. I had also studied old atlases, old deeds, old census records, and copied off sections and made notes. While Bart was looking after the Sturtevant place, I had taken the liberty of going through boxes up there which hadn't been auctioned off because all they held was old papers, and of reading letters and diaries which had been pulled out of chests-on-chests and bonnet-top secretaries and strewn over the upstairs floors. I said that perhaps I could be sued for this intrusion, but it seemed that nobody but me had any thought for this historic material and I took only information and only to preserve it; that is, I never brought any of the papers, letters, or diaries home but spent many months here, all told, copying off whatever I found that was still legible and of interest. I said it was my intention, if I lived long enough, to put this information together in orderly form; but it was a gigantic task to set down all I knew about the Sturtevants and the Crowleys and so far very little of it had been done.

I ended with an ultimatum.

I said, "You seem to be interested in what I know, and maybe it would be easier, take less time, to tell it than it will to write it. Maybe if I tell it to you, you will preserve it and pass it down, even if I don't get it written. But I'm not one to do something for nothing. I'm now at least as interested in you as I am — or you are — in earlier generations. If I tell you about the Sturtevants that have gone, will you tell me about the Sturtevants that are here, everything you know about them, from the beginning?"

They sat staring at me.

"It's a fair bargain," I said firmly. "I satisfy your curiosity. You satisfy mine."

They exchanged glances.

"Will you tell yours first, William?" Lisa asked.

"I'll tell you about the first Alexander and Elizabeth. Here. Tonight. *If* you will promise that tomorrow night after the plowing you will be at Crowleys' for a supper of red flannel hash made from the leftovers of Flo's boiled dinner and afterwards tell me separately about the first years of your lives. Where you were, who you lived with, what happened to you that you remember, and how you felt about it."

There was another silence.

Then Lisa said, "I don't know if we could, William. We've never talked about those times. Even to each other. We've — I guess we both want to — forget —"

"The first Sturtevants and their neighbors didn't want to forget. You might have thought they would have, but they didn't. If they had, I'd know nothing about them to tell you. They'd have been dead long ago. But because they believed in knowing themselves and being known by others and building on what they knew, they are still as alive as they ever were. At least, they are to me. . . . You could promise to try, couldn't you?"

Lisa whispered, "Babe? He's a meanie, but — you know he may be right? And I *have* to hear about Alexander and Elizabeth!"

Larry said, "Okay. . . . We'll try, sir."

So Elizabeth came in.

I put it that way because that was the way it seemed to happen. I don't know what I said about her. I saw her entering the room with no awareness of us; and with her coming it was her room.

Later the small and the growing Lisa and Larry did the same in Bart's and Kate's kitchen, each time bringing their own surroundings and associates with them to be superimposed upon and so to blot out what had been there a minute before. This series continued for many nights, though not for as many as a thousand and one. Having lost track of the dates of the succeeding scenes, I shall record them here dated according to the calendar in which they were actually lived rather than that in which they were repeated.

The First Alexander and Elizabeth (Maxwell) Sturtevant; Year of 1698

The door from a back room opened and she hurried in, her arms filled with white linen which she thrust between the curtains of the big bed in the corner before crossing to rake up the dying coals on the hearth and pile on dry wood from the stack against the wall. A tall, spare woman far gone with child. As the wood flared up her face became visible through the dusk; huge but sunken dark eyes below a high, pearl-white forehead in a face once heart-shaped but now gaunt and thin-lipped for lack of teeth. She pulled the ribbons of her white cap and snatched it off, and the massive coil of hair on the top of her head was coal black, though the smooth long curls in front of her ears had the color of the cap and its ribbons. But as she drew the precious English bone pins from the coil, heaped them on the narrow mantel between the brass candlestick and the heavy, olive-amber flask which held three cat-o-nine-tails, brushed back the curls, and began to braid white into black she was not thinking of her hair. Nor of her face.

Another door opened and Alexander came in carrying a rushlight. Its standard was nearly as tall as he. He set it down near Elizabeth and stood watching her make her braid and fasten it with a scrap of blue yarn from her pocket. As she finished, she smiled round at him with a touch of mischief in her smoldering dark eyes.

"I'm putting ee out, that I know, Alex. But ee must find me a big kittle for the crane here and fill it to the brim. There will be need of water and maybe no time to heat it after Liddy comes."

"Ee do not put me out, dear one."

When he brought the kettle she had pushed aside the bed curtains and was making the bed, leaving the blankets turned over the foot for the fire to warm them and take out whatever dampness there might be.

When he came back with two wooden buckets of water

from the spring, she had unhooked her dress and stays, unbuttoned her waist and petticoats, untied the drawers, stood for a minute by the hearth rubbing her thin bare arms, and now was covered from throat to toes in a pink flannel gown. But she still wore her thick-soled shoes and could feel her black home-knit wool stockings slipping down around their tops.

He filled the kettle and stood uncertainly beside her, shorter than she, and looking younger though he was a dozen years older. A stocky, square-shouldered Scot with ruddy cheeks as clean-shaven as a king's and shrewd blue eyes narrowed by anxiety.

"Do ee think it will be soon, lass?"

"I canna say. One time it has been long. Another short . . . Have ee forked the meat for tenderness?"

"It is some time since ee sent the lads for Liddy. Shall I go to see what keeps them?"

"Ee need not. Young Polly would be afeared whilst ee was gone. Lads could find the way to Liddy's in the wee hours of a moonless night. Liddy will come. They wait to — come with Liddy."

"A pain caught ee then, lass. . . . My bonny lass . . ."

"It did nothing. Only stopped my breath. Have ee forked —"

"Ee does not think Liddy may be down with a sickness and canna come? Or fears the Indians, with only the two lads? Dob is no longer there or he would come with her."

"Ah, no. Dob is no longer there. Poor Liddy. But she will come. If she couldna, the lads would have been back to bring the word."

"But — if she come not, lass?"

"Young Polly will have to help me. And ee will have to

dish up the meat and the msickquatash and the groun'nuts.
. . . Oh, — what an hour to come to my time!"

"What do Young Polly know of birthing? Canna I help
ee better?"

"Ee knows ee cannot help me, Alex. Ee knows good men
of the town have been indicted more than once for acting as
midwives. No, leave — *leave* me, Alex. If I call — call for
Polly, send her in. And ee — *fork the meat now* and be
ready to see to the youngones when — when the Indians
come in. The lasses — more than any our Liddy that the
younger ones look to — may be — be afeared of so many.
. . . *Go,* lad!"

She stamped her foot. He picked up the buckets and went
back into the kitchen, not quite latching the door behind him.
She let the pain distort her face, ran to the bed and held tight
to one of its posts with both hands. By the time she dropped,
panting, on the side of the bed the door had swung open far
enough so that she could see Alexander and Young Polly
Martin bending together over the spit from which the meat
hung above the log fire. She smiled to herself with a trace of
irritation. One as helpless as the other! Young Polly was
only fourteen, and just a month away from her mother's
directions.

Elizabeth's children were all occupied. The youngest,
Daniel, had not yet missed her, for his big sister Liddy had
fed him and now was rocking and singing to him in a tune-
less, senseless chant about Danny Boy. He was growing
sleepy and soon would be tucked into his crib in the middle
bedroom where Alexander would sleep alone in the big bed
tonight unless he let small William crawl in with him. She
could not see William, but she knew where he was. He had
hardly left the window since the Indians took up their

positions on the garden wall. The twins, Mary and Margaret, had little Ann between them in the wing chair the children had called the "arkettyvine" ever since their father had asked why it was always full of children and their mother had answered, " 'Tis their Ark of Divine Safety, 'twould seem." The twins were writing letters of the alphabet on Liddy's slate, and telling Ann the names of them. Robin, the oldest, was not at home. He had left before daylight that morning for Port City with an oxload of logs and would be gone at least two days, perhaps longer, for Robbie was twenty years old now and his mother had suspected since his last trip that someone or something in Port City had caught his eye. Elizabeth sighed. She wished he would turn to one in the home neighborhood; perhaps wait for Young Polly as Alexander had waited for her. Or there was Liddy Crowley's youngest girl, Catherine, almost eighteen and unbespoken, yet a comely lass enough and a born mother, making two mothers in that fatherless family since the good Dobbin died of lung fever a year ago.

Elizabeth tipped over on the bed, bunched a handful of sheet and pressed it into her mouth to stifle a groan. Then she got to her feet again. She had not yet taken off her shoes — good Dobbin Crowley had made those shoes — was not sure she would be able to reach down to them — where was Dobbin's Liddy — would that meat never be done. . . . The kitchen door must be closed. She must get to it and call Young Polly, and Young Polly would come in and close the door behind her. . . . She could see her now pulling pans of cornbread back from the fire. . . .

She moved toward the open door, her steps dragging. But suddenly she felt much easier, though very heavy, and on the way she stopped by the window to look out at the Indians.

There they sat on the stone wall, with folded arms, in the dusk as they had been by daylight, ever since she had told Noah she would cook the meat they had brought if they would go away until dark when it would be ready, that there was not room for so many of them to wait inside. Noah had seemed to understand though he had always been welcome to come in when he was alone, and it was the food he had eaten at the Sturtevant table which had led him to urge this band of strangers whom he had met while hunting to bring their deer to Elizabeth for cooking as soon as it was bled and dressed out.

"Heap good," Noah had said at the door, with one foot on the carcass as if to keep it from bounding away. "Friends hungry. Me hungry. You hungry. You cook. All eat." He licked his fingers in anticipation.

Noah was what they called him, because he lived in a region back of Danny's Mountain which he called Sasanoa. His name was long and unpronounceable for Scots. He had emerged from his Sasanoa not long after the Scots arrived and in due course become their teacher, showing them how to plant corn and how to use it, revealing the nourishment to be found on trees and bushes, in brook waters, and even to be dug wild out of the ground. He was apparently a kind of hermit Indian, not often seen, but always friendly when he chose to appear. Nobody feared Noah — but who were these six young strangers he had encountered in the woods? Elizabeth had preferred to accept them on Noah's recommendation, though she could not maintain that she had much choice. Word of massacres of white settlers in neighboring towns along the coast and on the banks of big rivers had reached the Sturtevants, the Crowleys, the Martins, the Haseys and the others many times in recent years. But Noah and his new friends had gone away at once at Elizabeth's request, as far as the garden, and still sat there on the cold stone wall. It was late March and there were patches of snow in places the sun had not reached.

She *must* call Young Polly now, to come and close the door and get these shoes off.

But at that moment she heard the outside door open and Alexander's voice call, "Tha meat is done, my lads! Come ee in and sup! . . . Well, *Liddy!* It is a blessing from the Lord to see a grown woman's face this night. Elizabeth is in the West Room there. Go ee straight in and see how she does."

So it was Lydia Crowley, widow of Dobbin, who closed the door, who by the candlelight from the pierced lantern she carried helped Elizabeth back to her bed, took off the thick-soled boots and long black stockings, laid the lady down, lit the candle on the mantelpiece . . . and within the half of an hour, during which Alexander, seven of his children, and seven Indians, waited on by Young Polly Martin, chewed the meat of an eight-pronged buck, dipped corn bread in its juice, and savored msickquatash from pewter spoons, the Widow Crowley wrapped a clean, oiled babe in a homespun blanket and left him in a cradle by the fire while she attended to his mother.

"It is another bonny lad, dear," she said, her hands busy. "What will ee name this one?"

"Oh-h-h," breathed Elizabeth. It was good to feel free to moan, alone with Dob's Liddy. But where was Alexander? Always the babe's first cry had brought him to her side.

Gradually she became conscious of loud singing of old Highland lays in the kitchen and realized that the concert had begun some time back. The feasting was over then, at least for Alexander and the older sons. Alexander had pushed back a little from the table, tilted the chair on its back legs, and roared out familiar words in a familiar tune. Dob and Tom, grinning, had lifted their heads from their trenchers and joined in. Now she could hear her daughters' soft voices and William's flute-like soprano among the deeper tones.

Elizabeth smiled. Thus Alexander had contrived to obscure any sound which might come from the room in which she lay. He was a good man, she thought, with ever a quick wit.

"Ee asked me the bairn's name, Dob's Liddy," she said softly. "Alexander and I have long known if it should be another lad, he would bear the name of Jamie Martin. You well know it has been Alexander's hope to have nine sons, one for each of those who came with him from the old country. We still have only six." She sighed. "And I am afeared the sands are running out."

"Six will do, dear," said Dob's Liddy. "Alongside tha four bonny lasses. Ee had a care to name three of them for the women whose men ee have not been able to so honor. 'Twould seem to me ee made a list and have abided by it."

"We did so," whispered Elizabeth. "And do not forget that after the first bairn named for my brother Robin, the second is for your good Dobbin. . . . And when the first lass came she was named for ee."

"Crowleys do not forget," said Dob's Liddy quietly, wiping the birth-sweat from Elizabeth's face with a warm cloth. "But ten will do, mark me. Even ine husband should be content with ten. I would be afeared for ee to bear again. Mark me, Elizabeth."

Elizabeth was doubtful, too. But in her new-found comfort of body, her spirits rose.

"Our Jamie we have, still in all," she said. "Before ee goes home tomorrow, Liddy, Young Polly shall run up the road to tell her father. Sarah, methinks, will not take it ill, neither."

"No more she will. Proud all the Martins will ever be of your Jamie. Now try to sleep a mite and then take him to breast."

But in the kitchen the songs had ended. There was the scraping of the legs of many chairs and benches across wide pine floorboards and the moving about of many boots.

Alexander was saying, "We have all feasted well on what ee and ine friends brought us, Noah. It is good of red man to share bounty with white man. Now may the Great Spirit be with ee through this night and all the nights to come."

He was saying that it was time for the Indians to go. But then came silence.

"Papoose," Noah said finally. "See papoose."

". . . Papoose?" repeated Alexander. "Why, our Danny has been asleep some time but if ee come as stilly as ee would take ine canoe across lake water —"

He opened the door into the middle bedroom where Danny lay in the crib beside the bed in which Alexander and Elizabeth had slept the night before.

But Noah did not move.

"No," he said. "Small papoose." He pointed toward the closed door to the West Room.

So Alexander had not succeeded in his ruse. Highland lays had not obscured that first cry from Indian ears.

Alexander could not think what to answer.

It was Elizabeth who said, "Be ee quick, Liddy. Raise up my head. Then open the door wide and go ee quickly back to the cradle."

The door opened. Elizabeth looked through it at the littered kitchen, crowded with startled children and red men and white. Alexander looked through it and saw Elizabeth, came quickly to her side, followed closely by Noah and a file of six strange young Indians.

"Prithee, was ine good venison done tender, Noah?" Elizabeth asked, smiling, her hand in Alexander's. "I am sorry I could not stay to serve it up to ee and ine friends."

"Cook good," Noah said. He looked round at his companions. "She cook good."

"Uh," some of them said; and some said nothing.

"Papoose," said Noah. "You got papoose?"

"In the cradle there," said Elizabeth. "Very small papoose. Don't touch papoose. White papoose break easy."

The Indians stood in a semicircle around the cradle and Dob's Liddy.

"He will be called Jamie," said Dob's Liddy. "Maybe some day we name one Noah."

"Uh," said Noah.

He reached inside his leather shirt and brought out something in his hand. This he dropped on Jamie's counterpane. It shone red in the firelight.

"Rock," he told Dob's Liddy. "Cut out with tomahawk. For papoose now."

" 'Tis prutty, Noah," she said. "The bairn can teeth on it."

"Noah?" said Elizabeth softly.

Again he stood beside Alexander, much taller than Alexander.

"Ee is a good neighbor to us, Noah. We thank ee."

"Cook good," he replied, and to his silent companions, "She cook good."

He licked his fingers and went out. The others followed him through the deserted kitchen. Young Polly was on her knees by Dob's Liddy, sobbing in Liddy's lap, while the Sturtevant children stared at her, and Dob and Tom grinned.

"Pull eeself togither, lass," said Dob's Liddy, low, rubbing Young Polly's shaking shoulders briskly. " 'Tis over now. All is well. And the lads are a-laughing at ee!"

"And ee now," said Alexander to Elizabeth. "Is all well with ee?"

She pressed his hand and smiled.

"Ee has ine Jamie Martin," she whispered.

"Another lad!"

"Another lad it is! Go show him his father's face, — no, wait you! Listen!"

On the still-frozen ground of the garden there was a rhythmic stamping of feet to a hoarse chant.

Young Polly raised a terrified face, shrieked, " 'Tis a war dance they be doing!" and burrowed into Dob's Liddy's black skirt, covering the back of her capped head with both hands.

"Father — Father —"

"The lass speaks nonsense," Alexander told his daughters sternly. "She is not to be blamed for she is tired and overwrought. But what she speaks is nonsense. This is a serenade. For ine mother and new brother."

He went to the window and Dob and Tom joined him there. A half-moon was rising and by its light they could see Noah and the strange Indians, each energetically stamping his own circle as he sang.

A little later the sound began to die away and Alexander raised the window.

"Rise you up, Young Polly," said Dob's Liddy, sharply. "We must cover the cradle lest the bairn feel a draught."

"We thank ee, lads!" called Alexander. "We all thank ee! Now white squaw and white papoose must have a stillness for sleep."

"Cook good," Noah answered. "White squaw cook good."

Alexander waved his arm and closed the window.

"*Next,* now, white papoose must eat," said Dob's Liddy grimly. She uncovered the cradle and lifted out the child. Alexander crossed the room to look at him and Dob and Tom followed sheepishly with side-glances at Young Polly. But the little girls made a circle around the figure crouched in the chimney corner. There was always a baby, but Big Polly shrieking, being scolded by Father — even though he did say she was not to blame — and now sniffling and mopping her face with her apron?

"While ee eats," Dob's Liddy told the small bundle she was placing in the curve of Elizabeth's arm, "ine father can sit by. I will hie myself to see what of all this good cooking is left for ine mother. When she has fed ee, she will need nourishment herself, I'm a-thinking . . . NOW! The rest of you put yourself into that kitchen, one and all. Young Liddy, ee get Ann straight off to bed; Mary and Margaret can help ee. Tom, ee see to settling William. Dob, ee take a hand to help Young Polly with the cl'aring up, and see ee do the heavy part. She is wore out and most shook to pieces with this night's works."

The last one through the door left it open behind him.

Dob's Liddy was continuing, "Soon as the food is put away and the dishes scraped into the hogs' pail, ee will go to ine bed, Young Polly. Dob and Tom will do the washing

up — a proper job for gre't lads like them — and Young
Liddy and the twins take on the drying. Come! Get about it!
Stir ine stumps, all of ee . . . Now let me see what's here I
can get a bowl of broth from —"

Alexander closed the door and brought Dob's Liddy's
chair close to the bedside, watching silently another new
babe held to breast, half-opening his eyes, letting them fall
shut again, Elizabeth's thin hand behind his head, drawing
him closer, two fingers of her other hand pressing dimples
into his cheeks until his mouth began to open and then in-
serting the nipple between his lips. She did this several times,
both of them making small, unintelligible sounds which were
strangely sweet.

At last she raised her eyes to her husband with a sigh of
relief.

"He's taken holt," she said triumphantly. "A good holt."

Alexander nodded, proud.

She lay back on her pillows and seemed half asleep. The
only sounds in the room were of a stick dropping into the
coals, a few sparks snapping, and the faint, intermittent
sucking.

Alexander bent forward and put his arm lightly across
Elizabeth.

"Don't ee sleep, dear lass . . . Dob's Liddy will be bringing ee broth."

"No. Fear not. I wunna sleep whilst I have ine wee Jamie
Martin on my arm."

"Our Jamie, lass."

"Aye."

"A stout lad, think ee?"

"A stout lad, aye. All, all stout lads. Seems ee give me

only stout lads and lassies to carry, Alex. Never yet have we lost one, do ee ken?"

"Not one, my bonny."

"I pray to tha good Lord we never will, whilst we yet live. Some women stan' it. I doubt I could."

"And no more will ee have to. All will live and flourish."

"Ee is a good man to us, allus, Alex. Such a fine house ee had ready for wee Jamie to come to, and all done since Danny Boy got here. I mind how it was when we had only two rooms, the gre't lads sleeping in the haymow in summer, overhead close to the rafters in winter, and climbing to both by a ladder. . . . As many still do."

" 'Tis a good house now we have. I thank the Lord for it."

"What did Noah bring wee Jamie?"

"I dinna see, lass."

"It glowed red. Look for it in the cradle, will ee?"

He found the trinket and brought it to her on his open, calloused palm, holding the candle close to it.

" 'Tis prutty," she said.

"A big chunk of the red glass we sometimes see embedded in ledges here. I canna recall ever coming on it back home. Noah did well not to break it when he hacked it out."

"Master prutty," she said again, and smiled.

Then Dob's Liddy came in with a bowl of venison broth she had crumbled corn bread into. She took the babe and he roused and whimpered, so she sat in the low chair and soothed him on swaying knees, while Alexander stood, feeding Elizabeth from the bowl.

When he went away on tiptoe, the light from one candle showed his best-beloved asleep in the big bed with half-drawn curtains, his new lad asleep in the hooded cradle, and Dob's Liddy nodding in her chair beside the hearth.

As he closed the door, the candle flickered and went out. Only the coals of the fire remained.

Lisa Gallico; Year of 1959

She had just outgrown her crib. It had been her father's when he was a child, her grandmother told her. The crib was a fenced-in place. To lie in it was to look out between posts like those of the railing of the stairs she had just climbed, only these posts appeared to have been made by gluing many spools together, end to end, and stained dark and varnished until they shone as long as there was light in the room. The fence in front used to be closed as soon as she climbed in; now for some time it had been left down so that she could get up easily without help if she needed to go to the bathroom in the night. But she could still reach down and clutch the spools along the side of the crib which was next to her grandmother's big bed, and she could see the shadows of the other spools on the pale pink painted walls until the light went off. It even seemed to Lisa that she could see those shadows in the dark.

Only tonight the spools were no longer there, and Lisa lay for the first time on her new junior bed which had no fence. It had short, thick legs painted pink but she could not see them after she lay down. The room around her, thus suddenly exposed, looked large and bare, having no furnishings except the two beds, two oak dressers, a stand between the beds with the lamp on it and a book bound in black leather which was turning brown in spots and along the edges; and on the walls two small pictures in heavy dark frames, each of a head which had a circle above it. But they were different heads. Her grandmother had told her that one was Jesus Christ and the other his sainted mother, Mary; and that, like the crib, they had been in the room where her father slept as a child. They were still here, but the spools were gone. Lisa had outgrown the spools.

She had already said her prayers. She was watching her grandmother methodically place a small yellow wool jumper on a hanger, set a small pair of low brown laced shoes under the foot of the junior bed, and gather up a handful of short white socks, underthings, and yellow cotton blouse for the laundry hamper. Finished, her grandmother moved toward the lamp.

Lisa sat straight up, quickly.

"Don't turn it off yet, Gramma! They haven't come! They'll come!"

"Your father is not home yet. Late as it is, he'll expect you to be asleep when he gets here."

"Mommy, then. Where's Mommy?"

"In her room. Dressing to go out."

"But she'll come. Leave the light on, Gramma. Mommy'll come before she goes out. She'll — she'll want to see how I look in the new bed."

"*That's* possible," said her grandmother. She sounded even more grim than usual.

Then Lisa's mother, whose friends called her Syl, was on the stairs. Lisa could hear the swishing of her skirt. She looked in with a happy face framed in hair the color of gold which was cut very short and curled all over. There was no circle around her head.

"Well, sweetie-pie," she cried. "If you don't look adorable in your new bed! You know what I'm going to do? I'm going to get you a new nightie. A pink one. Or would you rather have pink pajamas?"

Mommy was beautiful. Her neck and shoulders were white and beautiful. The cloth of her long blue dress looked as soft as the sky. Lisa wanted to feel it. Still sitting straight up, she lifted her arms.

Mommy ran across the room, laughing, and took Lisa's hands in hers. She was wearing a glittering necklace and, as she bent it swung forward and touched Lisa's chin. It felt cold.

"Careful, honey. Don't muss me. I'm all ready to go make a speech. Just you imagine a big room full of people eating dinner, and then somebody standing up to say your Mommy is going to make a speech!"

"Why can't I go with you?"

"Why? Because it's nighttime, lamby-pie. Little girls have to sleep at nighttime."

"Don't you ever make a — a speech in the daytime?"

"Once in a while. And when you're bigger I *will* take you. I promise, pet. Now I must run. Any minute someone will be calling for me —"

"Who will be calling for you?"

This was Lisa's father's voice. He stood in the doorway. He sounded hoarse. Lisa had not heard a man's voice since he said good-night to her last night. Last night she had slept in his crib.

He sounded angry. Lisa stared at him past her mother's soft, fuzzy, furry golden head. His eyes looked tired. There were gray streaks in his thick black hair. A lump began to grow in Lisa's throat. Her grandmother had gone into the deep closet to put away the yellow jumper. Lisa heard wire hangers scraping on a metal rod.

Her mother let go of Lisa's hands and straightened. Her face had changed. It was not a happy face now.

She said, "One of my friends. Claire Boutillot, to be exact. Jerry will be driving us. It is Guest Night at the club. I didn't ask you this time. You have refused two years in a row. Everyone is beginning to understand that wherever I go, I go alone."

She pushed by him and disappeared. There was the swishing again, and then silence.

Half turning toward the stairs, but still in the doorway, Lisa's father asked suddenly, loudly, hoarsely, "If you will not go where I go, is it reasonable to expect me to go where you go?"

There was no answer.

He completed the turn. His back was toward Lisa. He began to move away. Her grandmother was coming out of the closet.

"Daddy!" Lisa cried. "Daddy, see! Mommy bought me a new bed!"

He turned again slowly. His eyes narrowed as if trying to pierce smoked glass. He was not really seeing.

He said to himself, "Mommy bought . . . and bought . . . and *bought*."

"Because I'm getting longer, Daddy! I'm too long now for your crib."

He made a great effort. She could see him make it.

"Oh, yes," he said, wearily. "Well, this bed seems long enough. This one ought to hold you until you're grown up."

He turned again toward the stairs. A car started up under the window.

From somewhere on the stairs he called back, "Mother? Has the child said her prayers?"

"Of course she has," his mother answered. "*I* saw to that. Now I'll take up your dinner."

With a sigh, she turned off the bedside lamp and followed her son.

Nobody had said good-night to Lisa. Nobody had held her close. Nobody had kissed her. She lay in the dark in a big, bare room, with no fence around her, no spools to clutch, not even the shadows of spools to look for in the darkness.

Everyone is beginning to understand that wherever one goes, one goes alone . . . One is alone in the dark, on a dark sea . . . One sobs, and no one hears the sobs, for no one is listening . . .

Larry Sturtevant; Year of 1959

He was nine years old and had been at York School in Connecticut only a few weeks. Before that he had gone to schools where he did not sleep, but was driven to them on schoolday mornings and driven away from them after lunch to whatever house or apartment he was sleeping in at the time. There had been at least two schools before York, maybe more. In those schools there were girls as well as boys, and they had played together. In those schools he had mostly played. In the summers since he was six he had gone to camp in Vermont. There were only boys at camp. He went there in a train from New York and the coach he rode in was filled with boys going to camp. At the funny little station in Vermont they all got off and climbed on buses. He had learned to swim and dive and paddle a canoe and even sail and ride horseback. He slept in a tent at camp.

At York his schoolmates were all boys.

It was evening in late October and the beginning of Study Hours. Study Hours would be over when a bell clanged in the hall.

Study Hours for Larry's group were held in the reading room of Wintergreen Library. It was a big room with a vaulted ceiling, arched, stained glass windows, and oak paneled walls. There was a log fire blazing on a big hearth, and there were many heavy, dark tables, each with three green-shaded lamps in a row in the center and eight cane-seated chairs around it. There was a boy in every chair.

As Larry sat looking around him, his nearest companion nudged his elbow and Larry turned his face to the left.

From the far end of the room the Master said quietly, "Weston! Don't annoy your neighbors."

Weston looked down at his book.

The Master walked almost soundlessly to their table.

"What is your preparation tonight, Weston?" he asked, low.

"History, sir."

"History! The history of what?"

"Of the early Greek period, sir."

"And yours, Sturtevant?"

"English, sir. We have been assigned an essay."

"Topic?"

"An autobiography, sir."

"What is an autobiography?"

"The story of one's own life."

"Very good. Get on with it, both of you."

Behind the Master's back, the boys exchanged shrugs and impudent grins. Then Weston pushed his glasses higher on his nose and began to read. Sturtevant penned "My Story" at the top of a sheet of thin white paper.

Where does life begin? Larry tried to remember.

They had told him that his mother died before he was a year old. He could not recall who had told him that or what it meant to him when he heard it. By then he had had at least one other mother, maybe more. Every once in a while he and the other children were called into the dining room where his father introduced a pretty lady as "your new mother," told them to kiss her and then to go up to the nursery — later called the schoolroom — where Frannie (or Jane or Heidi or Lana) would give them their supper. It had made no difference to Larry, except that he thought the kissing part was silly and was always glad when it was over.

Sometimes when there was a new mother there were new children. Some children were younger than Larry and some older like the one who kept telling him she was his own sister. She told him that when she wanted somebody to be a father to her dolls and nobody else would. Sometimes he did, for a little while, but he thought dolls were silly. That girl's name was Isabel. He never heard of anyone else named Isabel. She went to camp summers, too, but a different camp, of course; a girls' camp; and was now at some girls' school. It suddenly occurred to him to wonder whether any of those other children had been as surprised as he had been by paper napkins when they first went to camp. The Janes, Lanas, Heidis, Frannies had never put napkins on the schoolroom table. Larry was glad he found out about napkins and what you were supposed to use your fingers for at the table before he came to York, so when some of the other new boys who hadn't were being taught, he could snicker with the rest.

Did your life begin when you got a new mother? He

could not remember that any of his had changed anything for him. His father introduced them, and then he took them to Europe or somewhere far off, and of those who came back with him, all but the last one had soon gone away again. She might be gone by now. Some of the children went with the mothers, and some of them stayed around. Some of them were still around, as far as he knew; or maybe living at a school somewhere. Larry didn't know. He was at York, and Prince and Ogilvie slept in the same room he did. Prince and Ogilvie were great guys . . .

Did it begin when you first went to school? He remembered very little about those first schools. In one of them the teacher asked every morning, "What do you want for dessert for lunch?" and every morning the shriek of "ICE CREAM" nearly split the ceiling. Larry could not remember when he was not bored by ice cream. He supposed he always had been. But it didn't matter. Frannie or Heidi or whoever was in the kitchen with Cook would sneak him a plate of cake or a soup bowl of last night's dining room pudding with brandied sauce as soon as he got there. All the maids made a fuss over him. He thought it was silly but it was a way to get cake or pudding. It was all right, except when they tried to pull him onto their laps.

Did it begin when you went to camp? But that was not *life,* at camp, was it? You just learned how to eat right, and how to swim, dive, paddle a canoe, sail, ride a horse. . . . Sometimes they put on a play for the parents who came in midseason — not Larry's, because they were on summer vacations — and once Larry was a pirate in a play. He wore a funny hat and was told to swagger. He liked the swaggering.

Maybe your life really began when you first went to a

school where you stayed all the time. But he had not been here long enough to have much to say about it yet. He still had to figure it out — the old brick and granite buildings, the hot fires, the cold showers, the lumpy beds, the Masters, the kids like Prince and Ogie, the kids like Weston, and other kinds of kids.

He looked at the boys around him. What did they know that he didn't? What life had they had? What had they written — or would they write — in their autobiographies?

They were all quiet now, under the Master's eye, but some were beginning to look at their watches. It must be nearly time for the bell to clang. Larry thought some of them looked sad, especially those near his age; he had no idea why. Others looked as if they were planning what one of the old Masters called mischief. Larry wondered what they were planning, and hoped he would find out. He tried to think of some "mischief" he could do in the Free Half-Hour before his group had to turn in. The fire was low and nobody was putting on another log. Surely any minute the bell would clang. He *must* think of something quickly. . . .

The Master was suddenly at his shoulder.

"What of your English assignment, Sturtevant? You haven't written a line in two hours!"

Larry smiled up at him, sweetly.

"No, sir. I'm afraid I can't do it, sir."

"Why not?"

"There is nothing to say, sir."

The bell clanged. There was a rush for the door. Passing the darkened, empty faculty room, Larry reached down to a container of seasand just inside the open door and scooped up a handful which he thrust into his pocket. He could not see the container, and did not need to. He knew exactly where it stood, for he had done this after Study Hours once before. That first night he had scooped up with the sand four quite long cigarette stubs which he and Prince and Ogie had smoked around midnight, leaning far out of their fifth floor window. He might be lucky again. Ogie had been sick after that little bit of smoking and even had to go to the bathroom and throw up. Would Ogie dare try it again? Prince and Larry had often snuck cigarettes from inlaid boxes on coffee tables, before they came to York. A few drags were nothing to them. But Ogie! . . .

Running toward Kent Hall, Larry sifted the contents of his pocket through his fingers. He could feel no stubs this time. Maybe the houseman had just filled the container. . . . Well, at least Larry had sand. Maybe he and Prince and Ogie could find a way to get it into Weston's bed.

James and Melura (Martin) Sturtevant; Year of 1737

The room had changed little since the night Jamie was born there, except that now there was no bed in it and the low chair in which Dob's Liddy once sat by his cradle was now under a window and had been replaced beside the hearth by the wing chair to which James every night repaired with his pipe immediately after supper, while Melura put the young ones to bed and Young Lovey Hasey and nine-year-old Lizzie cleared away the dishes and scrubbed the long table in the kitchen.

He was there now. The wing chair, with its high back, narrow seat, and new striped dark red and dark blue home-spun covering fitted him well, for he was tall and thin, with a thin ruddy face and narrow blue eyes. He had always been told he had his mother's build and his father's coloring; but he had no memory of his mother, only of Marm, his father's second wife who had been born Lydia Watson and later became the Widow Crowley. . . . This was the chair he and his brothers and sisters had called the arkettyvine. Marm had told them they did so because their mother had spoken of it in the hearing of her older children as the Ark of Divine Safety. Marm had always been talking to them of their mother. . . . But James could not remember her, only what he had been told about her. He remembered Marm who had cuddled, scrubbed and dried him, buttoned his shirt and tied his boot laces, fed him and dosed him, scolded and praised and spanked him until Young Alex and the one she called Little Dear were old enough to need such ministrations. Then she had told him he was old enough to climb into the wash tub on a Saturday night and scrub himself, old enough to do his own buttons and tie his own knots, too old for cuddling and spanking and ready for switching. But she had continued to dose him as long as she lived, to praise him on the rare occasions when she thought her praise had been earned. And always until he was ten — or perhaps twelve — she had found a way to get him alone and cuddle him in secret, soon after she had dosed him or reddened his bare legs with the stinging green willow she seemed always to have ready for the prompt meting out of justice.

He chuckled now at the memory.

Melura was silhouetted for an instant in the doorway between the middle bedroom and the parlor, on her way with a candle to look in on Old Alexander whom James had helped to bed before it was dark under the table. His father had reached the great age of ninety-one, had his gruel by the kitchen hearth at twilight, while Melura sat across from him nursing the baby, and thus before dark, like the babe into its cradle, Old Alexander was tucked into the canopied bed in which he had once slept with Elizabeth — never with Marm who had remained Dob's Liddy to him even after he married her. The canopied bed now stood in the end bedroom which had once been small but then been doubled in size for his use at the time James and Melura married, soon after Marm's death. At that time Little Dear was still at home and slept where Marm had always slept, with the door ajar between her room and her father's, to keep him company; and James had built on a big shed and carriage house and finished off a fine room in the top of it for himself and Melura with a stairway to it from the kitchen.

This had made the Sturtevant house, James and Alexander felt, suited to serve as a garrison for the women and children from smaller houses round about in case of threat of an Indian attack such as had from time to time all but wiped out settlements not twenty miles away; and so it came to be and was still called the Sturtevant Garrison. But the house had never been needed yet for that purpose, nor had James and his father expected that it would be. Noah had disappeared from his Sasanoa some years ago now, and none knew what had become of him, but Sturtevants and others did not feel that he had died, only that he wandered somewhere among his wandering brothers, telling them that Elizabeth cooked good and urging them not to take out their resentment against white men upon the people of this friendly settlement.

Alexander had said to the Minute Men toward the end of their meeting in this room for the planning of the additions to the house and the registering of it as a garrison, "Ee ken t'will have better protection than palisades and gun-holes

under the eaves, for all 'neath its rooftree. The night Jamie
was born Noah dropped his blessing into the cradle where
he lay. Take down the Red Stone, lad, and pass it round the
circle."

As it passed, glinting, from hand to hand, Alexander had
said, " 'Tis Noah's prayer to his Great Spirit . . . Knowing
his Great Spirit is strong . . . Stronger than evil . . . Noah
prayed for us . . . 'Tis Noah's promise . . . So long as ee do
as ee would be done by . . . So long shall no harm come
anigh ee . . ."

James glanced up now at the Red Stone, still lying on the
mantel. Though he and two more had teethed on it, and
though later Marm had let him and Alex and Little Dear
play with it, rolling it from one to another across the big rug
she had hooked and laid there, she had been firm that it must
always be safely back on the shelf above the hearth before
the youngest of them went to bed at night. Melura, in her
turn, had never allowed her children to play with the Red
Stone, only to look at it in the palm of her hand and sometimes to hold it in their hands or press it to their cheeks, or
lay it on a pillow when they burned with fever. If the child
recovered, Melura said the Red Stone had helped to bring
her back from the gates of Heaven. If she did not, Melura
said staunchly, through her sobs, that it had eased her in.
Melura shared much with Alexander, and faith in the powers
of Noah's red stone was not the least of it.

When Alexander's Little Dear — Elizabeth — married
and went away, Alexander had seemed strangely distraught
and a few days later took a bad spell which bade fair to be
the end of him before long. So James and Melura and the
only lass they had then had moved from the shed chamber
into Little Dear's room and been there now for ten years,

ears alert even in their sleep for any untoward sound from the babe beside them, from Father in the room on their left, from the small lassies who had once slept in the room on their right but slept there no more, or from the bigger lassies up chamber with Young Lovey snoring softly among them. . . . All lassies, every one, for fourteen years. Another Elizabeth, another Lydia, a Caroline, a Paulina, a Margaret, and an Abigail. The Paulina they had lost when she was five, and the Margaret at the age of three, of black diptheria . . . Two years ago now. The wonder was that all the others had survived it, and the new bairn Nabby had come since.

Melura sighed and then, looking in at her James, was filled with thankfulness and smiled. He did not see her, being lost in thought. She had just peered under the hood of the cradle and seen Nabby rosy among the blankets. Now as soon as she had looked in on Father and perhaps pulled an extra coverlet over him — for it was January and the wind howling like banshees around the chimneys — her day's work would be done and she would bring her sewing and sit near James. He might not see her even then, though the candle hanging from the back of her rocker to light her work would also light her face; but her James was a master one at thinking, which was natural enough, he having much upon which to ponder; family spread out through the countryside around him, buildings to be kept in repair, seed and fuel to be got in, field land to be fertilized and cared for and extended, the logging-out and the new boards to be sawed, cattle and horses and sheep and hogs and fowlkind . . . All depended on her James. James was the center of his world and hers, the hub of their universe. Why should he always see Melura? Let his mind go whither it must. It would be

enough for her to be where she could see him. In good time
he would notice that she was sitting nearby plying her needle.
When he did, it might surprise him, his bushy eyebrows shoot
up, a smile come into his eyes, and he would exclaim,
"Lass?" After that she might tell him that when Young
Lovey came back near nightfall from a visit home today she
had vowed she heard a wolf call; had come into the kitchen
all of a flutter and out of breath. James would laugh and
say, "Be a fleet wolf that catches Young Lovey when she
takes to her heels."

Melura went on her way and James did not know she had
paused in passing. Yet, in some way it did not occur to him
to try to fathom, he had been brought to think of her.

. . . Strange how much like Marm Melura was, though no
closer relation than her niece. It must have been that likeness
which made him notice her among all the other children of
the settlement who came to learn to read and write and
cipher in this room, with Dan, Jamie, Alex, and Little Dear,
when Liddy kept school here, having been sent to Boston by
her father to learn how. He could remember being astonished by Liddy's becoming such a stranger the minute she
faced the rows of children sitting cross-legged on the floor,
and comforted by finding in front of him Melura's small,
square shoulders, and the straight white parting down the
back of her head to the slender white neck between two
tightly plaited red braids. He had thought long before that
that Marm's neck was too small for the size of her head,
and he had wondered that it never broke from the strain on
it when she scolded him fiercely. On his first day in school he
wondered if Marm's gray hair had once been red. Like
Melura's. . . . Years later, when he began to court Melura,
he learned much about her that he had never seen evidence

of in Marm and supposed Marm had never been nor had. With children — first her little brothers and sisters, and now with her own — Melura was almost a counterpart of Marm; so much so that James listened with amusement when she scolded them, but was careful to let no sign of amusement appear on his face. With a man — not only with James but with his father too, and with her father — Melura was unfailingly all he had a right to ask of her, always welcome as a candle in the dark, soft as a blossom from the garden, quiet as a brook flowing through level ground, yet quick as a lightning bug and strong as woodbine. Surely Marm had not been all this to Alexander, else he must have loved her as he had loved Elizabeth. . . . But had she been, perhaps, to Dobbin Crowley?

Father . . . What did he think of these winter nights as he slid off into sleep? Did he recall his childhood in Scotland, of which he never spoke, his family there, and his losing battles for the Covenant of which he did not speak neither and never had? James had had to learn from books, quite lately, of the Scottish rebellion against the Crown. His father had always lived and talked as if his life began when he set foot on these acres and with Robin Maxwell, Dobbin Crowley, Thomas Watson, James Martin, Daniel Hasey and the others put up two-room cabins into which they could bring wives and beget children. He talked of waterways and saddle paths, of felling trees and digging out the roots, of great stones dropped by glaciers which had to be moved to make cleared land for planting and for grazing; of Danish cattle brought over aboard ship and landed on the riverbank and driven up here in mudtime; of raging blizzards and barn raisings; of lightning setting fires which buckets of water could not put out and which blazed until all was consumed, unless a rain came, heavy enough to quench it; of what Noah had taught them about the gathering and preparation of food from the wild, and about the curing of hides for clothing, and how the house was full of Indians the night James was born. Did he even remember now, in his great age, that he had once lived on another continent?

Suddenly James wondered if his father knew of a second spot on the place where a spring might be bubbling not far beneath the surface. So far the one he had dug out had served, but with all the stock James was accumulating the demand on that one source was heavy. He must soon be on the lookout for another. What his father could tell him might well save him much in time and steps and digging. Though Alexander had not been beyond the door-rock for a year now he still knew every foot of his land as if he had walked it yesterday; every rise, hollow, boulder, ledge, tree, and driven stake. James must remember to ask him in the morning. Father was always brightest in the morning. As the day wore on he drowsed frequently; but when alerted he still knew more of how to house and provide for a big family on a clearing in the wilderness than any other man now in the settlement had yet learned. Marm had told James this had been true from the beginning, and Dob Crowley would have been the first to say so; that it was always Alexander who proposed and his neighbors who, seeing the wisdom of his propositions, followed his lead. Now that he was the last one left of his generation, not only his own sons and grandsons but the sons and grandsons of the men who had come here with him eagerly sought his counsel whenever they encountered what appeared to them to be an insoluble problem or had an important choice to make. Those who did not call him Father called him Grandsir, and all knew now that it was best to seek him out in the morning.

So betimes tomorrow morning, after his bowl of oatmeal porridge, Alexander would be helped in to this chair by the fire, and then James would ask him where there might be another spring.

"Jamie!"

It was Melura's voice. She did not often rouse him so suddenly, nor often call him Jamie nowadays, though his father always did.

He sprang up, and she was running toward him, reaching up to put both small hands hard against his chest, her head tilted back, her eyes wide.

"What is it, lass?"

"He — he —"

"Tell me, Melura," he said sternly.

"Oh, Jamie — I think Father is dead."

He pushed her away from him and hurried into the bedroom.

". . . Father? . . . *Father!* . . ."

Melura had followed. Their voices came back like echoes into the empty room.

"No, Jamie . . . Poor Jamie, lad . . . He is not sleeping. When I came in a-tiptoe to — to cover him a little more, he turned his head toward the candle, and he spoke. He asked, 'Is at ee, lass?' I said, 'Yes, Father. Dinna rouse you now. I'm only come to pull up a coverlet. 'Tis a cold night.' But as soon as I said, 'Yes, Father,' he turned away from me as if not wanting to hear. He lay there listening to something else, his eyes fixed on the ceiling. I was bent over him, tucking in the coverlet, but he dinna look at me, looked past me. It seemed to me strange and I stood a minute there. Until he raised up and said, 'I knew it was ee, lass, come to fetch me,' and then he smiled, such a smile as never before had been on his face since I knew him, and fell back on his pillow with a wee strangling sound . . . I raised him up again that instant but he was gone. I knew as soon as I touched him he was gone . . . Oh, Jamie, lad, I could do naught for Father, for all I loved him so. Let me comfort ee, Jamie. Lean on me, Jamie, or I think the hearts of both of us will burst this night . . ."

The fire crackled on the hearth. A candle flickered on the shelf above it. The two returned together.

James blew his nose.

"That's it, Jamie . . . You'll do now, lad . . . We knew it had to be. . . . could not be far away . . ."

"I must go down to the Crowley place to tell Dob. Then I'll be right back with Dob's Kate to be with you. Dob will ride out to tell Tom, Dan, Alex, Margaret, and the rest. They may not come until morning. We won't need them until the morning. But Dob will come back to sit with us."

" 'Tis always good to have Dob and Kate by."

"It may be some days before we can get word to Robin in Port City."

"Aye."

"And weeks before Lid and Mary know, in Philadelphie."

"Aye . . . But in the morning?"

"We must bury in the old tater-hole. He said when we had the cellar big enough for all root storage, salt pork tubs and cider barrels, the tater-hole would serve as tomb for winter deaths. But he is the first to go in winter . . . When the ground thaws we will put him beside my mother."

"Where he is now, and knew well he was going," said Melura softly. "So his marked stone will be beside Elizabeth's at the Sturtevant end of the graveyard, as Aunt Liddy's — your Marm's — is at the other end beside Dobbin Crowley, though the initials cut into his stone are D.C. and hers are L.C.S. . . . As should be. As all would have wanted it."

"I must take the news to Dob."

"Aye, lad. I'll bring your greatcoat."

She held it open for a minute before the fire, and helped him into it, though its weight was almost beyond her strength to lift so high. Her man was a tall Scot, and no mistake. She made a jump to loop a heavy scarf around his head, and tied its ends under his chin; jerked mittens from the pockets of the greatcoat and held them out to him.

As he drew them on he cleared his throat, preparing for what he would soon have to say to his brother Dob at the Crowley place at the foot of the hill.

Melura said, "Jamie? . . . Jamie, I speak now when it may help you. I am with child again. I know it. And I know this one will be a lad and we will name him Alexander. . . . I know it all as well as I know I stand here before you."

He made a hoarse sound of mingled agony, joy, and disbelief, and took her into his arms at last, holding her in a bearlike embrace, patting her back with a mittened hand. When he turned up her face to kiss her mouth, both tasted the salt of tears.

A minute later Melura was alone in the silent house. She stood by the fire and smiled, thinking of James and of a small Alexander. Then she sighed, remembering what her James had ahead of him tonight and tomorrow, and of the children she had already borne, six lassies in a row, all sleeping now, two of them never to wake in this life. Of the four who would, one's first words tomorrow morning would be,

"Ain't Grandsir up yet?" For Grandsir was always up before them.

But no more. Their Grandsir would be up no more.

She reached blindly, her hand knowing where it would be, for the Red Stone.

Lisa Gallico; Year of 1961

She had been late beginning to go to school because her mother and her grandmother could not agree on which school she was to go to. But at supper the day she was seven years old, when they finished the birthday cake her grandmother had made and the ice cream her mother had brought home, her father said:

"Now Lisa HAS to go to school. I will take her myself in the morning."

Lisa looked from one of them to another, but no one was looking at her. Her father was looking into his coffee cup, her mother was looking at him, and her grandmother was looking at cake crumbs, pressing the tip of her forefinger against one after another and so picking it up to be brushed off with her thumb into her plate.

"Of course I can guess where you intend to take her, John," said Lisa's mother.

Lisa's grandmother rose. This seemed to be getting harder for her to do. She began by putting both hands flat on the table and pushing.

"Come with me, Lisa," she said. "Bring your new books. We'll see which of them you think you can read. Or I will read one to you."

Lisa went upstairs with her grandmother. Her grandmother closed the door, and they began to read at once, loudly. Still voices and tones — not words — reached them from below, until the outside door banged. This shook the little old house. After that, in the sudden quiet, Lisa's grandmother let her choose the dress she would wear for her first day at school.

The next morning Lisa's mother did not come out to breakfast. Lisa set off without having seen her mother, and her father drove her quite a long way in the car to a big brick building with a gilded cross above the door. He went inside with her and told a teacher who she was. Then he went away and the teacher took her to a room where some other children already were.

Except for the other children, school was surprisingly like being at home with her grandmother. The teacher was dressed in black like Lisa's grandmother, looked grim, and saw to it that everything was done as nearly as possible in the right way. She soon said that Lisa should be placed in a higher grade, and the next morning after that Lisa was led by another black-gowned, unsmiling teacher to a room full of different children being taught to do everything as nearly as possible in the right way. Before the end of the school year, Lisa was taken to still another room. The only real difference Lisa noticed as she went along was that the children around her were taller each time she was moved. She supposed that was what was meant by a higher grade, and she wondered why at school people were called high or low instead of tall and short. She also wondered why, after she was moved the last time, she was shorter than anyone else in the room. She supposed this must mean she was the lowest person there. The thought vaguely distressed her and she could think of nothing to do about it but to sit and stand as

tall as she could. This made her shoulders and the back of
her legs ache, and she felt stiff. But if she slumped it seemed
to her the other children were looking down on her, so she
pulled herself up again.

During the summer vacation from school, everything
changed. Lisa's grandmother's doctor said she had to go to
the hospital. This was the first time Lisa had ever stayed
alone all night. The first night she had to turn the lamp back
on quite soon after her mother went downstairs, and kept
getting up and going to the bathroom until the sky began to
get light. The second night she cried so long and so hard her
mother came back upstairs and lay down beside her on the
junior bed and Lisa fell asleep; but when she woke up later
she was alone and there was darkness all around and she
could not hear her grandmother snoring . . . The next night
she began to cry as soon as her mother said it was time for
bed, and would not go upstairs.

"I want Daddy," she sobbed.

"You know he isn't here, honey. He's at the hospital
visiting your grandmother."

"I'm going to stay up until Daddy comes," shrieked Lisa.

Her mother did not reply and after a little while Lisa
peeked through her fingers to see what she was doing. She
was just sitting there on the sofa, looking at a cushion
beside her and stroking it absently.

When she realized that Lisa was quiet she said, "Come
over here, darling, and sit with Mommy. I may have some
good news for you."

Within the circle of her mother's arm, with her mother's
ringed hand covering both of Lisa's, Lisa heard that since
they knew her grandmother had to go to the hospital her
father had wanted to take Lisa on a visit to his brother's

family, her Uncle Dave's, to stay until her grandmother was
well again. Her mother had not been sure this was best. She
wished her mother — Lisa's other grandmother — were
still living and Lisa could go to stay awhile with her, for that
grandmother had been gay and loved good times and known
just how to make a child happy; but that grandmother had
died before Lisa was born. Lisa's mother had never met
Daddy's brother and his family, but Daddy had talked with
them by telephone from the hospital last night and they had
said they would be glad to have Lisa come.

"So since you are feeling lonely here, maybe it would be
best for you to go where there are new things to see and
think about. Would you like to?"

Lisa said, "I don't — know."

Lisa's mother seemed to understand.

"No, of course you don't know, lamby-pie. Any more
than I do. Because we've never been there and those people
are strangers to us, aren't they? Still, there's no way *to*
know unless you go, is there?" Now her mind seemed to be
made up. "If you don't like it there, you can telephone and
I'll come and get you the very next day, honey. But you may
love it, darling! I know your Uncle Dave has a big farm
with lots of animals. Lots of cows, anyway, and probably
many other kinds of animals. Maybe even a pony. I've
always wanted you to have a pony . . . Oh, Lisa, maybe you'll
have a marvelous time! Let's think you will! Let's cele-
brate!"

She jumped up and put on a record and whirled Lisa
round and round to the music until they were both breath-
less. They were hot, too, for it was August. So Lisa's mother
poured glasses of root beer and dropped a scoop of ice
cream in each and they took them upstairs and as soon as

Lisa was undressed, sat facing each other on the edge of the two beds and drank their floats.

Then, without even reminding Lisa to brush her teeth, her mother snapped off the light, lay down beside Lisa, and began to sing a lullaby.

The last thing Lisa remembered of that night was her mother's voice saying softly, "Go to sleep, my ba-aby, my ba-aby, oh, bye . . . And then Daddy will come and I'll tell him we've decided you will go to visit Uncle Dave and he'll be pleased and take you there tomorrow on a plane like a big bird that flies — and flies — and flies —"

Lisa must have been very tired. She went to sleep and did not wake until morning . . .

Uncle Dave's was like some dream she had when she slept with dark spools in her hand, but now could no longer remember. It was a magic world. They told her the name of it was Canada.

Uncle Dave looked like Lisa's father only much younger. (It was not until a long time afterward that she learned he was fifteen years older.) His skin was so dark the sun he worked under could not burn it but penetrated it to give an inner layer of skin a rosy cast that shone through; and he was always laughing, sometimes with a roar, often in a kindly chuckle, and always with a twinkle which danced up to his hairline and down to the corners of his lips, his square white teeth, and his cleft chin. He was very strong. Anything too hard for anyone else to do, Uncle Dave did.

Aunt Teresa laughed a lot, too, and sang at her work in words Lisa had never heard before and did not know the meaning of. She mostly cooked in the kitchen and at the bake-oven in the yard, and everything she cooked was delicious and she was fat. Her hair was as dark as Uncle Dave's, but straight strands of it kept slipping out of the bun on the back of her head and when she pushed them back to hug and kiss somebody — as she did a dozen times a day — they got floury and looked as if she was turning gray. She had big girls who helped her with the work — as Uncle Dave had big boys in the barns and fields — and they mostly swept and scrubbed and washed clothes. Still the bare floors were nearly always sticky, rolls of dust clung to the shoes and bits of wood and long nails and pieces of newspaper swept into the corners by flying brooms, and except for going to early mass, nobody could find anything clean to wear. The best part was that none of these Gallicos seemed to care. They couldn't feel the stickiness or see the rolls of dust for the children, and after a day or two Lisa didn't feel or see it either. And who could provide and distribute clean clothes for so many? Besides the big boys and girls who worked, there were boys and girls who mostly played, and smaller ones who had to be led or carried, and a baby Rose let Lisa rock and sing to as much as she wanted to. Rose said she had already tended two babies and might have another one any time, so Lisa could have this one. Rose was Lisa's friend. They slept together. Marie slept with them, too, but she was older and didn't come to bed until they were asleep.

Lisa's place at the table was beside Rose's. There was a dining room and the table filled it. The chairs were so close to the walls the big ones had to squeeze into them. The open kitchen door was behind Aunt Teresa's chair at the foot of the table and when she sat in her chair she sat in the doorway. Lisa saw all the Gallicos together at every meal. She looked around at them wonderingly in the strange silence which fell when Uncle Dave bowed his head and began the grace. She saw all the many heads lowered, even Rose's and those of still younger ones. Lisa had never heard a man's voice say grace before. Her grandmother always said it, and her father seemed to whisper it, while her mother sat stiffly and waited for them. Sometimes Lisa had whispered, with her father, and sometimes only watched, with her mother; but it was just her grandmother who really said it. Then her grandmother would tap the front of her dress four times, and sometimes her father would tap his shirt, but Lisa's mother never did this so Lisa hadn't. At Uncle Dave's everybody said it but Lisa, and they all tapped their chests; so after a day or two Lisa did the same, sitting beside her friend Rose.

Then quickly, eagerly, they all began to eat; and how they ate! How fast all those heaping bowls and platters the big girls had set out were emptied! Then Aunt Teresa scraped the legs of her chair over the threshold, stood up, and pushed her chair under the table so the girls could get through to fill again the bowls and platters with Aunt Teresa's good bread, good meaty soup, good vegetables from Uncle Dave's fields.

"Look at Lisa!" they said proudly. "See her cheeks beginning to puff out!"

"Came here lank as a sick chicken! Now look at her!"

"She's even getting a fat tummy!"

Lisa knew this was a good thing, from the pride in their voices.

"Soon she'll be as big as Maman!"

"And what better than that?" roared Uncle Dave. "Show me another woman as beautiful as my woman, your Maman!"

He smiled and waved at Aunt Teresa, down the long table, and even his big brown hairy hands twinkled . . .

Then the telephone rang in the back entry one hot evening as they all sat around the yard in the half-light, spooning from thick goblets the wild blackberry ice cream the big boys had churned before supper and packed in ice they had brought from the ice-house in burlap bags and pounded with the heels of axes into splinters. When they finished the churning they had pulled out of the freezer what they called the dasher, put it on a cake pan, and given it to Lisa. A good deal of the cold purple cream still clung to it, but she had asked Rose and the littler ones to share it with her and all too soon there had been nothing left but some liquid in the corners of the pan. Lisa had drunk this from her end of the pan and Rose from hers.

It was good when everyone had his own heaped goblet. Now the ice cream was very hard. As you scraped off each spoonful you looked for bits of blackberries.

At the sound of the bell one of the big girls *plunked* her goblet on the grass as if she did not care whether it tipped, and ran into the entry, stumbling over people's feet as she went.

"She thinks it's Gerry Robichau calling *her!*" shrieked another big girl.

All the big girls laughed and hooted.

"Why?" asked Rose. "Why does she think —"

"Because he smiled at her from the sidewalk after mass last Sunday. Anyway, she *says* he did."

Everybody laughed again. These Gallicos were always laughing, but usually not so many of them in one place.

"She's crazy," said one of the big boys. "Gerry had Carmen Therrien at the dance Saturday night."

"He did!" cried one of the big girls. "Carmen Therrien? Now I can almost believe he smiled at our Ursula the next morning. Maybe Ursula saw what she says she saw. Anybody ought to look good to a guy after —"

But Ursula was calling from the entry, "Father! . . . Be quiet out there, will you? . . . It's long-distance for Father."

Uncle Dave got up as quickly as he could and went in, goblet in hand.

Those still on the grass wondered why Ursula did not come back.

"You don't s'pose she's gone and hid?" one of the big girls asked another. "You don't s'pose she's off — crying?"

"*Crying!*" growled one of the big boys. "Crying because some guy she thought smiled at her from the sidewalk didn't call her up?"

"Oh, shut up, Oliver," the next biggest girl to Ursula said furiously. "You're *such* a fool! You don't know — you don't know — *nothing!*"

Everybody looked at Aunt Teresa. Aunt Teresa was the only one sitting in a chair. Now she was getting up, holding her goblet carefully as Uncle Dave had.

"I'll go see about Ursula," she said quietly. "Somebody look after her goblet. We had two dozen of them when we got married and there's only seventeen left."

They watched her go in. They finished the blackberry ice cream. The big ones pulled the little ones into their laps and fondled their hair, murmured to them, sang low to them. The middle ones wrestled for a while, began to yawn, crawled to the big ones, burrowed in next to the little ones, lay on their backs, watched the stars come out. Everything was still and peaceful.

But finally Aunt Teresa appeared in the lighted doorway and told the big ones to get the little ones to bed.

The next morning, while Rose and Marie were still asleep, Aunt Teresa woke Lisa and led her downstairs. Nobody was there but Uncle Dave, and he was wearing the dark suit he only wore to mass.

Aunt Teresa set Lisa in the sink and washed her, then dressed her in the clothes she had worn when she came; the blue and white checked dress her grandmother had made and later let down the hem on, and the new black patent leather shoes with buckled straps her mother had brought home to her.

While this was being done they told Lisa that it was her father who had telephoned the night before. He wanted her to come home today. So Uncle Dave was going to take her, as soon as she was clean and dressed and had had her breakfast.

That was all they told her then. On the plane Uncle Dave told her the reason why they had to go. Her grandmother — who, he explained, getting out a big handkerchief to rub his eyes and nose and mouth, was his and her father's sainted mother — had died the morning before. There would be a funeral mass for her tomorrow, and of course they would all go to the funeral mass. Then her father and Uncle Dave would bring her grandmother back to lie beside her husband only a few miles up the road from where Uncle Dave lived.

Lisa sat very still and listened carefully, but she did not understand any of it. Did not understand what dying was, nor why it made her father send for her, nor why her grandmother wanted to lie beside a husband Lisa had never heard of before. Least of all did she understand why Uncle Dave rubbed his face with his handkerchief nor why he no longer looked or sounded like Uncle Dave.

She understood nothing that happened for several days after that.

Her father met their plane but he looked strange and had a great deal to talk over with Uncle Dave on the ride home in the car. Her mother met them at the door of the house but she looked strange and was very busy going for groceries and cooking and talking on the telephone. Lisa was put to bed on the living-room sofa that night because Uncle Dave was using the room where she used to sleep. The next day she went to mass with them and afterward her father and Uncle Dave rode away in a big black car and Lisa rode home with her mother. That night Lisa slept in a twin bed beside her mother's. Her mother told her in the dark that her father would not be back for a few days and reminded Lisa that school would begin again in the morning.

So the next morning Lisa went back to school, but it was not the same school. Her mother walked with her to a new school, telling her to watch where they turned because she would be coming home by herself and tomorrow she could go by herself. This school would be much better because it was near enough so that she could go and come by herself instead of having to be driven and picked up.

Lisa liked the new school. Her teacher was young and pretty, wore a short, flowered dress, and had long, polished fingernails. Lisa had never before seen such fingernails. She found herself staring at them until she felt as if she were floating in the air and there was no way to get down and she couldn't move her eyes if she wanted to.

Before the end of the week a boy came to the door of Lisa's room with a note for the teacher. After she read it, she named one of the children as monitor and put her arm around Lisa and took her through the hall and led her out into the September sunshine where her mother was standing.

"Why did you come for me, Mommy?" Lisa asked, as in a dream.

"I came to take you home, honey," her mother answered.

She reached down for Lisa's hand and they walked hand-in-hand along the street, around the turns Lisa had been told to watch.

On the living-room sofa, in her mother's arms, Lisa was told that her father had died. She never saw him again.

Now she knew what dying was. They sent for you, you went home, and nobody was there. . . . She did not learn until many years afterward that her father had taken his own life.

Larry Sturtevant; Year of 1961

He had been dismissed "in disgrace" from two schools because when one of the Masters asked him if he had done something he had done, he said he had, and grinned. The reason for the grins was his pride that they had not caught him at it, that the only way they could find out was from one of the guys who knew and would tell (which, to their credit, none of them ever had, as far as he ever heard) or from his own say-so. Both times these grins had apparently been the final straw. It did not trouble him that, when asked, guys who had broken rules with him looked first insulted, then very solemn, said they certainly had not, and therefore were not "disgraced" and could remain in school. Rather, it amused him. He had seen to it that they were not caught.

Now, if they wanted to stay in this stupid school, let them. As for him, he had done about all he had found to do there, most of which the Masters had never even asked him about, and he was bored; he would welcome a change; any change.

When he got back to New York someone showed him the letter the school had sent ahead of him. He never cared enough what it said to make the effort to find out.

Then someone would exclaim, "From the way he looks and from what is in it, maybe he can't read it. Read it to him."

What they read aloud was always boring. It said he had admitted to this and that, or he had admitted to that and this, which could only bring to an end the surveillance under which he had been since shortly after he reached the campus because of the reluctant suspicion, etc. Not only *that,* but when confronted he had shown no regret for his ill behavior, but become actually impudent, etc. And not only *that* but he was failing all subjects, refusing to make his preparations or perform other tasks assigned by the Masters on the ground that he could not, though objective tests showed his intelligence to be above the norm for the school. The headmaster — or his secretary — deeply regretted that Lawrence had proven uneducable at Whichever School. It was hoped (but obviously hardly expected) that another school could be found to which he would be more responsive.

Lately, applications to camps where he had already spent a season were not accepted. There was a great flurry every Christmas about getting forms filled out in the hope that some as yet untried camp would provide the relief of knowing that a tent in which Larry could sleep the following summer had been located and reserved.

But now he was eleven years old and near the end of his first season at Wakela Camps.

Wakela was something else.

At Wakela there were only pup-tents, rolled and tied for carrying on the back or to be tossed into a canoe. Bunks and sleeping bags were in good supply in all of some twenty-five shelters scattered through the woods, along the shore of a lake, and up the side of a mountain. Wakela Camp-Ground was about two miles square. Its land boundaries were clearly marked both with red paint on trees and rocks and with white bandages on trees, white flags on bushes.

There were few rules at Wakela.

If you appeared to answer roll call (announced by a bugle) at 8:00 in the morning you were free until the next morning roll call. If you didn't, whenever you did appear you were sent to bed in the infirmary at the Block House for a minimum of two days.

If you crossed the boundary or landed on the opposite shore of the lake, you were to keep on going for you would not be allowed back.

If you started a fire you could not put out, it would be your last day at Wakela.

Prove yourself a stout swimmer and your own canoe would be assigned to you for the season. You could paint your name on its side and take it wherever it would go, except to land on the opposite shore. When you had put your name on a canoe, no one could use it who did not have the same name on the dogtag around his neck.

Hot meals were served at regular hours three times a day at the Block House. Campers who preferred to eat out could pick up provisions at the Cellar Door between 8:00 and 9:00 in the morning. No other time. A choice between prepared picnic lunches and food for cooking over a camp fire was offered. Cooking utensils, matches, tools, fishing gear, signal horns, waterproof ponchos were for the taking at the Compound, to be returned there after use.

Nobody said you had to return the utensils clean; and Larry didn't.

Nobody told you you had to write letters home; and Larry didn't.

Nobody said you had to do anything different on Sunday than you did other days; and Larry didn't.

Nobody told you you had to change your clothes; and Larry didn't.

Nobody said you had to play games, and Larry didn't.

Nobody told you you had to make friends; and Larry didn't.

Wakela was a keen camp.

Three brooks rushed down the mountainside, spread out in the flat valley, and each spilled into the lake through its own mouth, hairy with marsh grass. One mouth could be seen from the Wakela dock, but the others were near the opposite ends of the lake obscured by great trees and giant boulders.

Nearly every day all summer Larry had been at the Block House for breakfast at 7:30. Every day he had answered roll call at 8:00. Every day, rain or shine, he had been one of the first to appear at the Cellar Door and then at the Compound. Before 9:00 he always had his stuff in his canoe and was standing in it, pushing it out into deep water. He was a scout on patrol, a trapless sourdough, a lone explorer, a surveyor of hitherto untrodden wilderness.

Usually he left the canoe later on a sandspit and strode into the forest with a small pack on his back, keeping on until he reached the top of the mountain and found a hiding place which kept off the wind, if it was blowing cold, or the rain if it was raining. There he lay on his back and watched the sky, or huddled motionless and watched small animals as free as himself, until he was hungry and reached into the pack for his lunch. If the day turned hot, he ran down the mountain to the canoe, dropped his pack, moccasins, and dungarees beside it, piled on top of them whatever he had stowed in the canoe, paddled to the middle of the lake, jumped out and was a porpoise, rolling, diving, coming up snorting, and diving again, often rolling the canoe over and over with him, until he was tired and climbed back in to lie in the canoe, drying off as it drifted, and perhaps falling asleep. When he woke he went back to the shore to load in his stuff and headed up one of the brooks to a clearing where he could gather twigs, build a campfire and fry his bacon or roast his frankforts to put between big rolls he had torn apart to eat with handfuls of lettuce, bites of tomato or apple or orange. There was canned fruit juice to drink, but if there was a spring he drank from that, and sometimes from the brook if he was high up and it ran fast over the white stones. He sometimes saw another camper but if he did, pretended not to, went on without stopping, without speaking. He was careful to spot a shelter before dark, for they had no lights; then went to it only to get a sleeping bag and travel on again, or waited until anyone likely to come to it was already asleep.

In his mind he had spent the whole summer alone with his canoe.

That was where he was now. Lying on the floor of his canoe in a pool of brook water so shallow that the canoe rested on the sand, his arms spread wide and his hands in

the water, looking up through oak leaves at the sky, listening
to the sound of the water and to a birdsong he did not recognize. These were not the summer birds of Wakela, but
strange birds who spent the summer months farther north,
somewhere in Canada, and now were making their leisurely
way south because they knew winter was coming. They would
not be here much longer, either. What were the Wakela
winter sounds? The lake would turn to ice. Would the brook
freeze too? The shelters had only three sides. Would they
be full of snow? . . . Every Block House door would be
locked, even the Cellar Door; and the Compound. Even the
windows would be boarded up. They had told him this when
he said he did not want to go to New York tomorrow on the
train. They had even showed him pictures of Wakela in
winter. All snow and ice and locked buildings. All black and
white. No red canoes with names on them.

He did not want to go to New York.

He thought of running away. He had never crossed the
open but marked boundaries because they had said that if
you did you could not come back. What did he have to lose
if he crossed them now? But then again, what did he have to
gain? He did not want to run away from Wakela. What he
wanted was to stay at Wakela as long as he lived. If he
crossed the boundary, he could never come back. . . . Well,
he hadn't crossed the boundary, and he wouldn't cross the
boundary until they took him in a bus. So he could come
back, couldn't he? If he didn't cross the boundary, and he
didn't start a fire he couldn't put out, and he took back his
stuff to the Compound, and he answered the last roll call
tomorrow morning, he could come back next summer
when they unlocked the doors and brought out the canoes.
Couldn't he?

He got out of his canoe, pulled it to where it would float, stood knee-deep in the water, and with one finger traced the letters of his name on the side.

Suddenly he jumped back in and paddled as fast as he could down brook to the lake and the Block House. He went straight to the office and asked if his name could be left on his canoe through the winter, because he liked his canoe and wanted to have the same one next summer.

The girl at the desk asked his name, opened a drawer in her filing case, took out a card and studied it. He stood looking at her back. He had forgotten to put on his moccasins and the boards of the floor felt hard to his bare feet.

When she turned around she smiled at him.

She said, "I don't see why not, Larry."

That night he ate his first supper in the Block House. He had roast chicken and warm raspberry shortcake. And when the campers cheered Wakela, he could hear his own voice above all the others. When they sang songs, he sang, too, even though he did not know the words.

Alexander, Jr. and Caroline (Crowley) Sturtevant; Year of 1784

Another Yuletide had come and gone, closing the seventh year of the great rebellion of the American colonies against the English King, but still no word that independence had been won.

It was afternoon of a bleak January day, and Caroline sat here at Alexander's great desk, quill pen poised above a fresh page, round white chin cupped in a small, calloused hand. Unable to send letters to Alexander, since she did not know where he was or whether he was allowed to receive letters, she had now written to him every day for nearly two years in this ledger intended for the keeping of accounts. Often before she had found it difficult to bring herself to pen the first word. Today it seemed impossible, narrow her wide blue eyes and pull at her honey-blonde hair as she would.

After a while she reached up to open the glass doors above her and take out several of the small volumes in which Alexander had habitually written every evening of his life, since early boyhood, until he went away. Caroline had read every word in all of them several times in the past two years, for love of Alexander's always spidery hand, but the ones dearest to her were those written since their engagement to marry and particularly those during the years when their children were coming.

So much of Alexander's thinking had always been about the Bible. Caroline would never understand what had turned him to it at a tender age nor kept him always at the study of it thereafter. There had never been a church in the settlement. From the first settlers had been passed down a strong dislike amounting to a horror of ecclesiastical power, as if it were a loathsome and incurable disease from which they had escaped, mercifully uncontaminated, from the Old Country. Here in the New World they were free of it and intended to remain so. Here a man need fear nothing except weakness in his own character, not even his God whose name he often spoke in reverence but who showered him with so many blessings that he could feel only love for such a generous Father.

Yet Alexander in his youth had set out alone every Sunday morning — in summer by canoe and in deep snow a-horseback — to spend the day in the church-house at the head of tidewater. He knew his family and his neighbors watched him go with great uneasiness, were heavy with un-asked questions when he came back, and listened in anxious silence to what he tried to tell them of all that he saw and heard there. So he stopped trying to tell them, and wrote it in his book at night. But after a year he stopped going, not having found what he was looking for, and wrote that in his book. His family and neighbors, greatly relieved, welcomed him back. But now he had a great need to be alone with his Bible. He did his work in fields and woods with the others, but whenever the work was halted he did not throw himself full length on grass or moss with the others, or in winter sit on a log and smoke a pipe with the others; instead he went apart and sat reading his Bible. Every night he found some quiet corner in the crowded house where his older sisters were being courted and his younger brothers were playing pranks on them and wrote in his book what he had read and what he thought about it. Nobody understood what he was doing. Only his mother, Melura, and later Caroline had been serenely unfaltering in the sure knowledge that what-ever Alexander did could not be other than a fine thing to do. He said so in his book, and Caroline liked to read that part.

She liked even more the later parts where he said Caroline not only knew how to run a house but was as capable as any man in overseeing the outdoor work. Throughout his books he referred to the Bible as The Beloved Book and to Caroline as My Beloved Friend, sometimes adding to this in parenthesis the word "earthly." In the early fall of 1765 he had written:

"Have returned this Day from the Vineyards of the Lord to the North, and found as Expected that My Beloved Friend (earthly) has seen to the cutting, drying, and housing of Fodder for the Cattle, there is a good Crop of Potatoes, Corn and other vegetables near ready for the Harvest, Work has gone on Steadily at the Mill, and of the Orchard she had planted last Spring only two Trees have died. My Beloved Friend has, among many Virtues graciously Bestowed on Her by Our Lord, that of Conveying her Wishes to her Helpers and responding to their Efforts which far exceeds my own small Talents in that Direction, She being Well-Known to Them and they to Her. She and her Women Friends have also Brought the Precious Little Ones safely Through a Hot Summer. Our First-Born, Noah, passed his Tenth Birthday in my absence and now begs to take one end of the crosscut saw. Matthew will soon be Nine, Mark Six Years of Age, Luke very Manly at Three Years Old, and John begins to Walk About some, albeit Falling Down a good Deal. My Beloved Friend assures me our Mary at age Eight already takes great Care of Small Martha and John, watching over these Little Ones, she says, like a Mother Hen. I am Solemnly Promised by Mary that she will Make Father some Pumpkin pies as soon as the Sun Comes up Tomorrow. What Joy their Names are to me Whenever I think of Them. It does not Occur to me now what I could Christen Another should it please God to send Another. . . . My Beloved Friend cooked this Night the fine Mess of Troutfish I Brought Home in my Saddlebag. I watched Her at Her Work with Singular Pleasure. . . ."

Caroline smiled faintly and lingered over the last sentence, though she knew it by heart.

She leafed through descriptions in Alexander's spidery script of how he had taken the Lord's message to scattered farmhouses and the isolated cabins of trappers and hunters; how he had found in a coastal town an old woman whose neighbors whispered that she was a witch, and a man who lived in fear and trembling lest his wife be taken from him because she was an Indian, and Alexander had ridden through the town calling out a meeting of all God's people to be held by a spring in a field where the grass had been cut, after milking time on a summer evening. To this meeting the old woman had ridden pillion behind him (how Caroline had loved to ride pillion with Alexander!), and the man and his Indian wife had met them at the spring. Not many others had come to the meeting but on those who did Alexander, in God's name, had placed the solemn responsibility of befriending these dear souls and letting no harm come to them, promising he would be back before winter to see that all was well . . . But first, Alexander noted, he must now ride south to look to the welfare of Quaker friends with whom he had been unable to make contact since mudtime. He asked forgiveness for his inability to cover great distances faster and more frequently and thus to serve oftener and more promptly the needs of his suffering fellowmen. . . . He had entered the birth of Piety in 1768, of Mindwell in 1771, both of whom had been several weeks unnamed in the cradle before their father reached home to christen them. As long as Caroline lived, she supposed, she would sometimes catch herself calling her youngest child "baby."

She replaced the volumes she had removed from the shelf and firmly set herself to writing in her own book but still could not. She tipped back her head to study the bindings of those of Alexander's which she had left undisturbed.

She knew what was in them.

Alexander's new, deep concern about animosities in the towns between those who were called Tories and those who were called Whigs . . . The leaving of Noah, Matthew, and

Mary's young husband, as militiamen, to join the Continental Army, which left Mary and brought Noah's bride, Amy, to have their first babies here with Caroline. . . . The stones tossed against the bedroom windowpane by Matthew one winter midnight. Starved, ragged, he had left a straggling company on their way back to Boston after going with Arnold to defeat at Quebec; he had come five miles out of his way to bring word that Noah had disappeared under river ice on the long march through the wilderness from the head of navigation on the Kennebec and that he had last seen Mary's husband, Arthur, lying deathly ill of the smallpox. Caroline and the girls fed Matthew well that night and Alexander brought a tub and filled it so the lad could wash himself before falling into his own bed for a few hours. While he slept, the women cooked and packed food. At daybreak Mark and Luke brought three horses at the door and rode off with Matthew, now warmly clad, and saddlebags filled with food, until they overtook Matthew's fellow-soldiers not far beyond Port City. It had grieved Alexander not to go as far as he could with Matthew, but he felt he needs must stay to console Mary and Amy. The boys returned next day on one horse, having left two, by their father's instructions, on which Matthew and his fellow-patriots might take turns, as needful, for all to reach Boston where Matthew wrote a letter saying he had enlisted for three years . . . That spring Alexander accompanied disconsolate Mary and her infant to Philadelphia for a long visit to cousins, and she never returned, but married there after a year of widowhood. Amy, however, stayed on with Caroline and married Matthew when he returned in 1778 with only one of his two handsome legs left to walk on. Alexander and Caroline had seen to building them a tidy house on the

Upper Forty. (After they went there to live Piety and Mindwell had missed Noah's little Caroline to sleep with, Caroline recalled.)

While in Philadelphia Alexander contracted to have a gazette posted to him at Port City and it came in by packet nearly every month. In this way he had read of the battles in which Matthew might be involved — though his family did not know where he was — and Alexander wrote references to them in his book. The Declaration of Independence was approved by the Continental Congress in July. By August General Washington's 20,000 men were divided quite evenly among Long Island, Manhattan Island, and the New Jersey shore. Said Washington, "Remember, officers and soldiers, that you are freemen, fighting for the blessings of liberty; that slavery will be your portion and that of your posterity if you do not acquit yourselves like men. Be cool but determined. . . ." Brooklyn Heights . . . Kipp's Bay, the slaughter of rebel prisoners by Hessian Grenadiers, and New York left to the occupation of invaders and the fire of looters. . . . Harlem Heights, where Washington's men outfought the British in a trampled field of buckwheat. Nathanael Greene wrote, "We want nothing but good officers to constitute as good an army as ever marched into the field. Our men are infinitely better than their officers" . . . Crown Point . . . Pell's Point . . . Dobbs Ferry . . . Fort Washington . . . The American forces, now reduced to a few over 5000 "effectives," left most of New Jersey to the enemy and crossed to Pennsylvania, finding they numbered only 3000 when they reached Princeton. An enemy advance on Philadelphia was expected daily. The Congress withdrew to Baltimore. (Mary's new husband was in the field. Where were Mary and her children?) A high-ranking officer wrote,

"The game is nearly up . . . If overpowered we must cross the Allegheny Mountains" . . . McConkey's Ferry, Trenton, and the rebel army captured 1000 Hessians plus a nine-piece band . . . Princeton, where General Washington and lesser American generals enjoyed a breakfast left behind at Nassau Hall by fleeing British officers. Thus the Congress could return to Philadelphia. (And Mary was spared.) . . . New Jersey, having known occupation, was no longer neutral. Had only the British General Howe "seen to it that his prisoners and the Jersey inhabitants were treated with as much humanity and kindness as Sir Guy Carleton exercised toward his prisoners" all might have been very different . . . The British stood to gain by every exchange of well-fed British redcoat prisoners for rebel captives "with miserable, emaciated countenances and shocking accounts of their barbarous usage," no longer fit for military service. It was seen that nothing could be gained except by retaliation, not on the rank and file, but on captured officers. When Ethan Allen was taken to England in irons, the British General Prescott was clapped in jail. Alexander's gazette reported, "His Majesty intends to open this year's campaign with ninety thousand Hessians, Negroes, Japanese, Moors, Esquimaux, Persian archers, Laplanders, Fujie Islanders, and light horse . . ."

Brandywine . . . Chadd's Ford . . . The French general, Lafayette, wounded . . . The Paoli massacre . . . The removal of the Congress to York, Pennsylvania, and the fall of Philadelphia. (Oh, Mary, Mary!) . . . The loss of Ticonderoga . . . Victories at Bennington, Oriskany, Saratoga . . . Rebel troops repulsed at Germantown . . . Fort Mifflin . . .

1778, and all former colonies were drawing up constitutions for their state governments . . . The French declaration of war on Britain . . . The French fleet reached the mouth of Delaware Bay. The British evacuated Philadelphia (Mary?). The French fleet sailed off to Boston for refitting . . . Kaskaskia and Vincennes . . . A Colonel Brodhead, with 600 riflemen, penetrated Indian country on the eastern shore of Lake Erie, along the Allegheny river . . . And Matthew came home to be married by Alexander to sweet, shy Amy, widow of Noah, and now as much a daughter to Caroline as her own. Luke, seventeen, and Martha, fifteen, stood up with Matthew and Amy, as Matthew and Mary had stood up in this same room with Noah and Amy. Mark, two years older than Luke, had by then been gone some months. Was he with Brodhead? What a sad, sad thing that the Six Indian Nations had gone into this war on the side of the British! How Alexander anguished over this as he had earlier over the French and Indian wars, and pled with his God for an explanation as to why those who loved freedom beyond all else on earth could be so riven apart as to war against each other, pled for a sign, for even a crumb of comfort!

Caroline reached into a drawer of the desk and took out the Red Stone which had been given to the babe Jamie by the Indian Noah for whom she and Alexander had reverently named their first-born son, now long ago drowned in icy waters. She sat holding it between her two hands as she had so often seen Alexander do in prayer.

Alexander continued to anguish about the enmity in every village and countryside where he traveled between the loyalists, the Tories, who supported the English king, and the patriots who defied him. There was no division in the home settlement. Scots had long been alienated from British

kings. But wherever Alexander rode he worked and talked
for reconciliation or at the very least for charity and under-
standing on both sides, and many a night he prayed for it
until dawn.

Then the next year the Commonwealth of Massachusetts,
whose contribution to the Continental Army already was
greater than that of New York and Virginia combined,
raised its own funds, troops and ships for an expedition into
its far northeast corner to storm a British fort lately established on Penobscot Bay; Luke was one of the 3000 militiamen transported from Boston and landed there for the siege
which ended when the Massachusetts ships were destroyed
by their own crews after being bottled up in the harbor by a
British force. With all the rebels who had survived —
sailors, marines, and militiamen — Luke was said by one
who came back to have started the 180-mile journey back
through the woods but he had died of hunger and exposure
on the way. Luke had always been the least strong of all
Caroline's children. Once she had hoped as she believed
Alexander had prayed that, if it was the Lord's will, this
war would be over before Luke was old enough to go.

Now Alexander's anguish mounted daily.

That same month there were raids on Connecticut.
Houses were plundered of everything movable, even window
glass, sashes, and women's "buckles, rings, bonnets, aprons,
and handkerchiefs." Fairfield and Norwalk became smoking
ruins . . . General Washington wrote, "Our prospects are
infinitely worse than they have been at any period of the
War . . . A part of the Army has again been several days
without bread . . . For the rest we have not either on the
spot or within reach a supply sufficient for four days . . ."
There was a severe salt shortage. In Morristown, New

Jersey, Washington's 76-year-old housekeeper, fearing the collapse of the Commander-in-Chief, plodded miles through the snow carrying a small basket of Army salt to exchange with country people for food . . . Of his men it was said that they "have a bed of straw on the ground, a single blanket to each man . . . badly clad . . . destitute of shoes . . . Snow 4–6 ft. deep." The quartermaster-general reported that the troops had been unpaid for months, since "The public is insolvent. The treasury is without money, and the Congress is without credit" . . . Still, looting by American soldiers remained punishable by death. However, in quiet areas or periods they were allowed to hire out, if they could, as farmhands for bed and board, and many a Massachusetts private learned to read and write by candlelight in such a farmhouse, instructed by his host-employer. Mark could already read and write. *Where was Mark?*

Victory at Stony Point . . . John Paul Jones, commanding the *Bonhomme Richard,* an old merchantman built over into a man-of-war, and shouting, "I have not yet begun to fight," forced the British *Serapis* to strike her colors; a few hours later his tub sank, but he already held his prisoners on the captured enemy warship . . . "This cantonement . . . at present without meat . . . Sick in hospitals have not a sufficiency . . . Transportation even of the inadequate supply of flour, forage . . . is at a stand . . . Every dept. of the Army is without money, and not even the shadow of credit is left . . ."

Alexander wrote, "It is enough. Thou Knowest, O Lord, I can no longer Bide here with the Sweet Comforts of Shelter, Fire, Food, and my Beloved Friend rarely more than a Day's Journey distant. Even if I can do no More, I must know for Myself the straw Bed with the Single

Blanket in the Snow and the Pangs of Hunger; must share Something of what Four of My Sons have Now Endured; must Do this while it is There to be Done; must do it Before John is Old Enough to go, while he is Still Here to place his Strong Young Shoulder to Wheels His Mother sees Waiting to be turned, to go where a Man must have Two Good legs to Carry him. Guide me, O Lord, ever guide Me. I now feel Most Called to The Prisons. If it be Thy Will, show me a Way through the Lines and into those Beastly Holes where our Good Country Boys Languish and Perish, to be a Solace to Them in their Terrible Trial. If such Cannot be, take me to *Some* Prison, to bring Gentleness and the Knowledge of Thy Promise of True Freedom one day for All who Believe On Thee. I must Go in the Morning. Lord, I now Close this Book for the Last Time, and Pray."

He had gone the next morning. Now the gazettes came to Caroline, and she noted the news in her ledger.

France came in, but was slow to action . . . Most of the military operations were far to the south . . . Reverses at Savannah . . . The siege of Charleston failed, leaving the city in enemy hands . . . Partial rebel victory at Hanging Rock, where a handful of armed rustics defeated trained troops . . . Rebel rout at Camden . . . General Benedict Arnold convicted of treason . . . Rebel victory at King's Mountain, Cowpens, Hillsborough by overmountain men on a 5000-mile march through woods and swamps . . . A French officer wrote, "Those brave fellows make one's heart ache. It is almost unbelievable! For the most part they were almost without clothes . . . only trousers and a little coat or jacket of linen. The greater number were without stockings . . ." . . . Fort Watson . . . Camden . . . Fort Motte . . . Fort Granby . . . Augusta . . . Orangeburg . . . An American officer wrote, "For more than 2 months more than ⅓ of our men were entirely naked, with nothing but a brush cloth around them . . . the rest were ragged as wolves. Our beef was perfect carrion; and even bad as it was we were often without any . . ."

Then the French *Resolve,* after sixty-two days on the way, anchored at Boston with 2,000,000 silver livres in casks. These casks were packed in oaken chests and attached to wagons by iron bands, each wagon to be drawn by four oxen to Philadelphia. Couriers reached the head of the Chesapeake with assurances of transport for footsore soldiers. The gazette told of the safe arrival of the money, and of its display in heaps in the new national bank. Mary wrote of seeing it, how the coins shone, how she could almost taste it. A rebel lieutenant wrote that this was the first hard money any of his lines had yet received. But there was no word of Alexander, or of Mark . . .

The Allied French and American forces assembled at Williamsburg . . . The storming of Yorktown began on October 14, brought capitulation three days later. The next day a rebel captain wrote, "Lay quiet in Our Camp cleaning Ourselves." The news reached Philadelphia in the wee small hours of October 22. Mary heard the call in the thick accent of an old German watchman, "Basht dree o'clock and Gornwallis isht taken!" Celebration began before daybreak in the city and continued for several days. Many panes of glass were broken in the homes of Tories . . . Caroline shook her head and sighed. Perhaps Alexander was in one of those homes or passing among them . . . The best part was that there would now be a big exchange of British troops for rebels held on prison ships. If Mark had been held on a prison ship, would he now be sent home? Caroline tried to remember what he was most likely to eat when he was feeling puny . . .

The French left for home and distant campaigns early the next month, but the war of skirmishes among picket guards went on through the abandonment of Savannah by the British in July. Mark came, hale and hearty, in September. No, he had seen nothing of Father. He was in time to see to the cutting of the marsh hay for bedding for the cattle . . . The last bloodshed of the Continental Army took place in November on James Island when a rebel detachment dispersed a British foraging party . . . On December 14, the British evacuated Charleston. General Wayne and his Continentals marched into the city while hundreds of enemy sails were still to be seen in the harbor, and that night there had been a Grand Ball in a hall decorated with magnolia leaves and white paper blossoms. Only last night Mark had brought Caroline the gazette telling of the great celebration down south in Charleston. It was this she must now enter in her book.

General Wayne . . . sails in the harbor . . . magnolia leaves and paper blossoms . . .

Holding the Red Stone pressed into her left palm, she tried again to set her pen to paper, and again could not. She glanced at the tall clock in the corner and saw that her hand had been stayed for a full hour.

It seemed to her that she was waiting for something which was about to happen, and could only think that it was for Mark to return from Port City with whatever had come off the last packet boat for Sturtevants. He had been gone two days. She trusted he would be home by nightfall for the snow was deep and another storm was brewing. What would he be bringing? A new gazette? Would it say the war was over? A letter from Mary, with pre-Christmas news of Philadelphia? Even — even a letter from Alexander of whom nothing had been heard in nearly a year?

In the room where there was no sound save the ticking of the clock and the crackle of the fire, Caroline had from time to time been conscious of activity in the kitchen — the chatter and occasional trill of song as Piety, now fourteen, and Mindwell, eleven years of age, opened the brickoven door to add water to the baking beans, to stir the Indian pudding, or to put in a pie for which they had just rolled out the crust, and closed it again with a thump.

But now suddenly the heavy outside door opened into the kitchen. The cold from it was already reaching Caroline's feet when she heard Mark's triumphant shout.

"The packet came in this morning! And look what was on it!"

The gazette? Was he holding it up for his sisters to see the headlines? Or was he waving a letter? Which would bring shrieks from Piety and Mindwell and the racing of their feet like those of wild ponies?

Caroline stood up, sliding the Red Stone into her pocket, and moved stiffly, unsteadily to the door.

As she reached for the latch she heard a voice, the most familiar in the world to her, albeit husky, asking, "Where is thy angel mother?"

She opened the door and saw him looking at her over the heads of their daughters whom he held clasped in his arms, and with their son Mark beaming from behind his shoulder. He was gaunt-faced, sunken-eyed, thin as a beanpole, but he was home.

She said, "I am here, Alexander. . . . You have been in the prisons."

"Aye."

"And you have had a long, cold journey. Mark, help your father off with his coat and boots before you put the oxen in. And bring out the arkettyvine. Mindwell, fetch his slippers from my closet. Piety, heat a bowl of gruel." Taking the coat from Mark, picking up the boots, she said, "This is fine raiment, lad."

"Mary found them for me, praise the Lord. I came to Mary in tatters."

"Oh, you have been with Mary. That is good. Sit ye here, my dear. Piety will be quick with the gruel. It will ease your stomach for what now bubbles in the oven."

When she came back from hanging the wet coat and mittens to dry and brushing off the boots, he was sitting by his own kitchen fire with a folded paper on his knees.

He said, "I bring you news Mark says has not yet reached you."

"What news, Alexander?"

She drew a small rocker close to him and read the headline when he had unfolded the paper with bony, shaking hands.

GREAT BRITAIN AUTHORIZING PEACE COMMISSION TO TREAT WITH THE THIRTEEN UNITED STATES OF AMERICA

Raising her brimming eyes, Caroline nodded and smiled at Alexander.

"The thirteen United States of America," said Alexander, huskily. "Oh, beloved friend, we must make a prayer of thanksgiving. What a prayer of thanksgiving must go up the great chimney of this house this night! When Mark comes in from the barns . . . Will all be at home then?"

He looked with some bewilderment around the room,

once so crowded, and now containing only himself and Caroline and two young girls.

She turned to slip both her hands between his.

"John has been helping Matthew in the woods today. Mark will ride over at once to take the word to them. They will soon be here, bringing Amy, little Caroline and the newest Alexander. Then, before we all sup together once more, will be the time for the prayer of thanks. Here is Piety with your bowl of gruel. Drink it down. 'Twill strengthen you. . . . There! Now put back your head and try to sleep a little. The Lord wants you to rest. I know He does."

"Sit by me while my eyes are closed, Caroline."

"I shall not leave your side until you wake, dear one."

A year later their last child, a son, was born, and Alexander christened him Holdfast. By then Alexander and his neighbors had builded him a *meetinghouse* with a pulpit to which he returned every Sunday morning, from wherever he had been, and preached to them of the Father, the Son, and the Holy Ghost. This was a great blessing to all, including Caroline.

See it all as if it were a kaleidoscope which you hold to your eye to study each pattern carefully before you turn on the next. Or as slide following slide in an old magic lantern. Or as reel succeeding reel of moving pictures which you know are in sequence though there may not be time to establish clearly in your mind what the sequence is. Or best of all, let it be a long night of strangely real dreams in which you cross many time tracks, barely emerging from one dream before you slip into the next, finding yourself a different person in another age than in the dream preceding . . .

Lisa Gallico; Year of 1966

She was a thin, dark, solemn little girl, seeming the more so because her mother, whom she now called Syl, was beautifully rounded, brightly blonde, and sparkling whenever they appeared together in public. Year after year, as Lisa went through the grades, Sylvia visited her classroom faithfully, a half-day each quarter, and appeared with other parents at any program in which Lisa participated, or whenever one of Lisa's sketches or paintings was on display among others in the auditorium. At such times classmates of Lisa, who had never spoken to her before, spoke to her.

"Hey! Is that your mother?"

"Yes."

"You call her Syl?"

"She likes me to."

Sometimes the questioner said, "That's cool!" or "She's really neat!" and went away from Lisa to push closer to Sylvia. Sometimes he or she just stared, shrugged, and ran off. Either way they left Lisa as suddenly as they had appeared before her, left her as alone as she had been last week and would be next week.

She and Sylvia had moved to a large city. On the sixth floor of a big apartment house they had a small but sunny, furnished apartment. All the furniture was new and shiny, the color of Sylvia's hair. The walls were painted a soft yellow, had pictures on them which Lisa could not understand, and all the picture frames were alike.

Sylvia had told Lisa why they moved. The house in which they had lived belonged to Lisa's grandmother who had made a will leaving her property in trust for Lisa's education but stipulating that the house be kept for the use of her son, John Gallico, as his home as long as he chose to live there. After his death, the trustees thought it best to sell the house. Sylvia had thought it best, too, as she must live where she could support herself and Lisa. She did not say she was glad to sell the house because she hated it, but Lisa knew this. . . . So now Lisa's small legacy from her grandmother lay untouched in a bank, accumulating interest, because, as Sylvia explained, the will had also stipulated that it could be used to finance only a Catholic education for Lisa, and Sylvia by no means intended that Lisa should be educated by nuns.

Lisa wondered if Sylvia liked to say the words "stipulated" and "stipulation" as Lisa liked to hear them. For some time after Lisa first heard a long new word she said it herself under her breath, and even aloud when she thought no one would hear.

But there was nearly always someone who would hear if she was listening. Sylvia was very careful never to leave Lisa alone. They left home together every morning. The bus which stopped at Lisa's school took Sylvia on to her office. In the afternoon some woman who had been cleaning or cooking in the apartment, or some high school girl, was waiting in the hall when Lisa left her classroom, to ride home with her and stay until Sylvia came, usually about five o'clock, but often not until eight or nine, and sometimes not until so late that Lisa did not hear her come in. Sometimes Sylvia took Lisa to her dancing class on Saturday or sat on a bench while Lisa swung in the park on Sunday, but generally she was away on weekends, and some girl was with Lisa. She nearly always saw at least one movie on the weekends Sylvia was away, sometimes two or three. There was also a television set in the apartment. Once in a while Sylvia took Lisa with her to a ski lodge in winter, and always in summer for three weeks at a beach hotel. Wherever they went, some of Sylvia's friends went with her. All Sylvia's friends were women. Lisa heard them say they could not imagine what so many women saw in men. The women had good times together, laughing and shouting. They played golf and tennis while Lisa sat on the grass and watched them. They swam and dove into the water while Lisa built sand castles. They played bridge in the evenings while Lisa lay drowsily watching and half-listening to them until she fell asleep.

When Sylvia and Lisa were by themselves, Sylvia rarely sparkled. Sometimes she was very quiet, picking at the food on her plate, sitting in front of the television screen but not really seeing it, absently washing dishes or folding clothes. Lisa thought at those times Sylvia was wishing she were somewhere else. She wondered where, but did not ask. Many things Lisa wanted to know she did not ask about for fear she could not bear hearing the answers.

Sometimes Sylvia talked for hours, mostly to and about herself, but breaking off now and then to speak to Lisa.

". . . Lisa, one thing above everything else you must prepare for. To be self-supporting. Once you are grown, never get into the spot where you are dependent on anyone else. . . . If ever you think of marrying, darling, GO SLOW. Men take up with women for more crazy reasons than a woman would ever suspect. . . . Never let yourself get boxed in, will you, honey? Refuse to settle down. Make up your mind you are going to go everywhere, see everything, try out dozens of roles while you're young enough to enjoy it. If you try to settle when you're not ready, it will drive you out of your mind. If you *are* ready, it will be because you're old. Stay young, darling. Promise? It's the only way to live."

Lisa listened and nodded. She wondered what was so wonderful about being young. But she did not ask.

Ever since she left Uncle Dave's, the one thing she had really wanted was to get back there. Now she had just finished grade school. Next fall she would enter Junior High. Sylvia had asked her what she would like for a present, and she had answered that she would like to go to Canada to visit her Uncle Dave.

Sylvia was surprised and puzzled. She had never heard from the Canadian family since her husband had taken his mother there for burial. They had not responded when she sent them the newspaper notice of her husband's death. She had not supposed Lisa remembered them. They might not be living in the same place. She was not even sure she still had their old address. After she had thought about it a few days she asked if Lisa would rather spend this summer's vacation at Uncle Dave's than at the beach, and Lisa said she would.

Perhaps two weeks later Sylvia told Lisa that she had written to Uncle Dave, and Aunt Teresa had replied that they would be glad to have Lisa whenever she could come.

She showed Lisa what Aunt Teresa had written in pencil on a piece of thin, rough, blue-lined paper torn from a pad.

Dear Sylvia

    send Lisa any time. We would All be glad to have her

    still cold for time of year, boys only got last of peas in week ago

    Don't no as you can read my hen scraching, hands stiff til on to noon time i better get this to the mail

Yours truely,
TERESA GALLICO

"Are you sure you want to go, darling?"

"Yes. I am."

"Why, honey?"

"I want to see them all again. And the house. And the yard with the bake-oven. And find out if any more of the goblets have been broken."

"The goblets!"

"They had twenty-four when they were married, and only seventeen left when I was there. That was five years ago. They eat ice cream out of them."

Sylvia thought about this. She was trying to understand but couldn't. She shook her head, smiling sadly at Lisa.

Nevertheless, she and one of her friends decided to spend their vacation in Montreal and Quebec and on a cruise up the Saguenay. They took Lisa with them to Montreal where Sylvia telephoned Uncle Dave's to find out what plane someone could meet at the airport if she put Lisa on it.

Now Lisa was back where she had wanted to be. But there had been many changes in five years.

Uncle Dave could no longer walk. He did not come to breakfast now. Someone took his breakfast to his bed and propped him up to eat it. Before noon two big boys came in from the field and lifted him into a wheelchair by the window. Rose and Lisa wheeled him out to the table for dinner. He could not wheel himself very well because he had the use of only one arm. At the table he asked the blessing on the food, and sometimes he still twinkled but his twinkle seemed to be flickering out like Tinker Bell. The big boys were not the same ones who had worked with him in the fields five years ago. Those boys and all the big girls had gone away. Rose said most of them were married. These big boys were the ones who had been middle-sized. One of them, called Joe, kept winking at Lisa, and once when she was picking nasturtiums for Uncle Dave near the bake-oven this Joe came to help her and pulled her hard against him, pushed up her chin, and kissed her on her mouth. He was laughing but Lisa had never been kissed on her mouth before and it frightened her. She screamed and ran screaming to Rose who was putting the youngest ones to bed. Rose came downstairs with her and told Joe, "Leave this kid alone, you fool," and Joe was mad. Rose was as tall as Aunt Teresa now and nearly as fat as Aunt Teresa used to be though only fourteen. She slept with Lisa as before, and talked every night until Lisa fell asleep about the boys she liked at school, the boys her sisters had married, what it must be like to have a baby, and how she would bring up children when she had them. There were no babies now at Uncle Dave's, and none expected. Aunt Teresa was fatter than ever, touched door-frames on both sides when she went through, had to be supported while getting to her knees and then helped up again; but she worked as hard as ever, her bread and meat and vegetables tasted as good as ever, and when she was in a room alone with Uncle Dave she said things that made him chuckle and her own laughter rang out like a girl's. Lisa had stolen to the cupboard and counted the goblets. There were fourteen left.

She liked everyone in the house except Joe, but she felt no more at home there than anywhere else. She had not felt at home there before, but had assumed she would if she stayed long enough. Now she was sure she never would, no matter how long she stayed. She wondered what it really meant when they crossed themselves. She went uneasily to mass with Aunt Teresa and a truckload of big and smaller boys and girls, and would have stayed with Uncle Dave but —

after Joe — she was afraid of whichever big boy was left to look after him.

The only Gallico she could talk with, not just watch and listen to, was Armand. Armand was two years younger than she, not as tall as she, and quite as thin, but with very light skin, small, pale blue eyes, and roughly cut, almost white, strawlike hair. Every time he came into the house he washed his hands. His hands were always very clean. Sometimes she thought he was almost as much a stranger in the house as she was. She thought he might not be all boy, but part elf. Aunt Teresa said fondly, when the others made fun of his being so quiet and washing his hands so much, "You wait now. Armie is going to be our priest. Armie's getting ready to be a man of the cloth."

Lisa liked his quietness and cleanliness. She was not afraid of Armand. When she wanted to walk in the fields or wade in the brook, she asked Armand to go with her. One day they went to where her grandmother was buried. She saw her grandmother's name on a stone monument and Peter Gallico's name on the stone beside hers.

She said, "I wonder if he was my grandfather."

Armand said, "I guess so. He was my grandfather and she was my grandmother. But I never saw either one of them. Did you?"

"I lived with her. Until she went to the hospital and died."

"You did? . . . Was she a Catholic?"

"She used to cross herself like you do, and go to church."

"Are you a Catholic?"

"No."

"Why not?"

"I don't know. Maybe because my mother isn't."

"Is your father?"

"I don't know. He died."

She found it easy to ask Armand questions. Going with him several times to put flowers on their grandparents' graves, she asked him what it meant when he crossed himself, why people kept bending down a little on their way to the church altar, what they were saying when they held rosaries and their lips moved but you heard no words. She also asked him if their grandparents had lived near here when they were young, if her father had lived here when he was a boy, if he and Uncle Dave had once lived together as Armand lived now with his brothers.

Armand told her what he knew, but there was much he did not know.

He said, "Have you asked your mother?"

She shook her head.

"Why not?"

"I don't know as she knows. She's never talked about it."

"You could ask Pa. I'll bet he knows."

"I can't ask people things."

"You've been asking me."

He smiled at her, chewing on a long spear of dry grass, and she smiled back.

"You're the only one I can. You're different from everybody else. I wonder if it's because you're going to be a priest."

"Maybe I am. Maybe not."

"Your mother says you are."

The big bell hanging by the back door rang out. That meant, "Gallicos, wherever you are, come home! Supper's ready!" Probably Rose was ringing it, having dried her hands on her apron, big strong arms bare to her shoulders and dark hair falling away from her round, ruddy face as she reached up to pull on the leather strap. Armand caught Lisa's hand in his small, clean one and they raced together across the fields to the house.

The last Sunday morning before she would be put on the plane for Montreal, Lisa did not go to mass. Aunt Teresa told her Uncle Dave wanted her to stay with him. He wanted to visit with her, just the two of them, before she went home. One of the big boys stayed too, but Lisa was not afraid because Aunt Teresa told him to stay outside unless Lisa called him.

Aunt Teresa took Lisa into Uncle Dave's room and pulled up a chair for her beside his bed.

"Now don't you wear yourself out, Davie," Aunt Teresa said. "I'll just tuck another pillow under your head. If you need a nap before we get back, Lisa can ease out the pillow and wait in the kitchen for us."

Uncle Dave lay looking gravely at Lisa until all was quiet. She tried to find twinkles in him but there were none.

Then he began to talk to her.

He said he had heard from Aunt Teresa that she had told Armie she did not know much about her father and his family. He said she mustn't mind their telling him what she had said. Armie always told his mother everything that bothered him — "like the rest of us do" — and Armie thought Lisa ought to know whatever she wanted to know about the Gallicos while somebody who had known her father was around to tell her.

He said Gallicos had always been Catholic, and they had lived in this Canadian town for generations. Both his parents — Lisa's grandparents — had been born here. The first Gallico house in this country had been near where the

Gallico cemetery was now. He, Dave, was the first-born child of his parents; John, Lisa's father, their last. There had been only girls between them. Dave had been fifteen years old when John was born. Just as Aunt Teresa now prayed that Armie would study for the priesthood, Dave's and John's mother had prayed that John would. And so he had, but before he had gone far in his studies he decided to marry, which meant he could not be a priest. This was a great disappointment to his mother, but John was not the first man to choose the life of the world. What made his family anxious was that the girl he married was not a Catholic. She was willing to make the promises required for marriage by a priest, but could not become a Catholic herself.

"That was Syl," Lisa said softly, not to interrupt Uncle Dave but just to show she was listening carefully.

Uncle Dave slowly shook his head, and thought for a minute before he went on.

No, he thought the name of that girl was Gwen. He never saw her. None of the other Gallicos ever saw her. John had met her out West and they were married out there and when he came back to see his mother ten years afterward he came alone. He said Gwen had got a divorce from him. After that he wrote oftener than he had before to his mother who was then living alone in the house near the family cemetery. Uncle Dave had married Aunt Teresa and he had built this house. John was traveling all the time, selling books. After quite a few years he wrote that his life had become very lonely and he had married again. That was Sylvia.

John's mother wrote to him, "But, John, how could this be?" Because Catholics do not believe in divorce. Catholics believe that when you marry you are married forever, unless the person you married dies. And Gwen had not died, as far as anyone knew. A person who has been married cannot marry someone else if the first person he married is still living, because the Church considers he is already married. But sometimes the Church can annul a marriage. John's mother asked if John's marriage had been annulled.

He answered no, that he had divorced Gwen to marry Sylvia who was also divorced, and who — like Gwen — was not a Catholic and now he had been excommunicated from the Church. Already he was deeply distressed by what he had done.

His mother was probably even more deeply distressed. His death would have been far easier for her to accept. You see, she feared that when he did die he could not hope to go to live with God. Perhaps there was some way that he could, but his mother did not believe so. She felt she must go to be near her son while he still lived. So she sold her house here and went to the small city where John was working on a newspaper and Sylvia was a secretary, and where they lived in an apartment. In that city John's mother bought a house. John had never worked on a newspaper before, so he had to begin as a reporter, and when Sylvia was going to have a baby and was not well enough to go to an office to work they could not afford to keep the apartment and pay someone to take care of Sylvia. So they had gone to stay with John's mother in her house. That was how it happened that Lisa had lived with her grandmother when she was small.

"Her last years were hard ones," sighed Uncle Dave. "So were your father's. Maybe your mother's, too. Life is hard if it is lived outside the Church. Of course your grandmother was never outside it, and she did all she could to keep your father close to it; and they had you. They loved you very much, little one, both of them. And we can hope that in the end he sought and found forgiveness for his mistakes. We must never blame him for his mistakes, little one. We don't know what powerful temptations he wrestled with. I know in my heart John tried all his life to be a good man."

Uncle Dave was growing tired but she had to ask one question.

"Why did he die?"

He closed his eyes and she saw his lips tremble. After a minute he groped for her hand.

With his eyes still closed, he said hoarsely (she thought his voice sounded as she had heard her father's), "Better not ask, dear. I don't know. I never asked."

The next day Lisa flew to Montreal.

Larry Sturtevant; Year of 1966

He had spent four summers at Wakela. Each of the first three had been very much like the others except that one had more rain. It was a keen camp. Last summer had been different, mainly because it was the last; the maximum age for Wakela campers was fifteen. Knowing this is the last time you will be where you like to be, doing what you like to do, makes a difference. You think about it more than you want to when you are huddled in a cave on the mountain, lie on the floor of the canoe out on the lake, are trying to go to sleep on a shelter bunk. You are even aware of it while eating pancakes in the Block House, answering roll call, getting supplies at the Cellar Door, and picking up tools at the Compound. More after you find out that July has been torn off the calendar on the Block House bulletin board. He began trying to get back from the mountain, woods, or lake two or three times a week to eat his supper at the Block House. He liked the food, and he liked to hear the Wakela cheers and songs. More and more he liked to join in them as he learned them.

That was how he happened to be there one night when one of the counselors, Foss, shouted through a megaphone that a rainy night was a fine night to read so he was going to stay here a while after supper and read by the fireplace. If anybody wanted to hear him he would read aloud, he said. After the campers had pushed their dishes through the hole in the wall, most of them ran off but a few gathered around Foss who had sat down and was opening a book. Larry huddled on the floor in a corner, much as he huddled in a cave, hugging his knees and looking out over them with half-shut eyes.

Foss began to read. The book told about a boy who had lived all his life in a monastery. Now he had to go out and find out what the world was like. They gave him some bread and meat and a little money and he started off through the woods. He could go wherever he wanted to, do whatever he wanted to, except go back to the monastery. He probably didn't want to go back to the monastery anyway. After a while he met a great big rough, jolly man whose name was John of Hordle . . .

Some of the boys had gone when Foss stopped reading. Of the three left lying around Foss's chair one had fallen asleep. The other two woke him up and pushed him outside ahead of them.

Foss stood up, stretching, and saw Larry for the first time.

He said, "Well! Were you listening?"

Larry nodded.

"Like this book?"

"Sure."

"Want to borrow it?"

"I don't believe I could read it."

"Have a try."

Larry stood up and reached for the book Foss held out to him, open. It was very fine print. Larry shook his head.

"No, I can't."

"What year are you in school?"

"Just finished Junior High."

"Public school?"

"Yes. Been to private schools, though."

"Where do you live?"

"Glastonbury, Connecticut. Now."

"Glastonbury! Isn't that the next town to Prime?"

"I don't know."

"Hm . . . Well, tell you what. Any night you want to hear more of this book, find me at supper and let me know. If I can, I'll read some. Like to. Good yarn, isn't it?"

Larry nodded and went out into the dark and the rain with a new warmth and light inside him.

The night before the last roll call, Foss finished reading aloud the book about the White Company. They had stayed up until nearly midnight two nights running. And then Foss gave Larry the book.

He said, "You may want to read it yourself when you can. You'll find bits in it you missed this time."

After Larry got back to Glastonbury his father told him he was investigating a private day school in the next town. One of the Wakela counselors had written recommending it for Larry.

Now it was an April dusk and he was pedaling slowly along a back road between Prime and Glastonbury, following the path his one small headlight laid before him, listening to the peepers in the marshes on either side, and thinking about the kid's book he had just been reading to Cy Cingolani. Cy hadn't come to Hillhouse until after Christmas when the experiment he was doing with his new chemistry set blew up and blinded him. At Hillhouse Cy was listening to Talking Books and learning to read Braille but about a month ago Miss Felker had asked Larry to read to him sometimes. She said Cy wasn't used to working alone so much, and needed some companionship to keep his spirits up. Since then Larry had read to the kid nearly every day. Cy said the stories Larry found in books were better than the ones on records; anyway, they sounded better to him. Since they were often reading when one of Cy's parents drove up to take him home, Larry usually went to the car with him. Two or three times Cy's mother or father had run on about how they appreciated what he was doing for Cy, but they had stopped that now and Larry was glad of it.

Cy was a smart little kid for only nine years old, and he got such a boot out of those stories that Larry kind of enjoyed them himself. He had never read any of them before. Sometimes he wondered if he would have jumped up and shouted every now and then, as Cy did, if somebody had read them to him when he was nine years old; but he couldn't imagine what it would have been like to really know what was in any book before he knew what was in *The White Company,* by Conan Doyle.

That was still Larry's favorite book and he had an idea it always would be. He had read it himself now at least a half dozen times. But he had also read many others. At Hillhouse they had started him out on Talking Books, too, but, since he could see, they had given him the printed books to go with the records so that he could follow along and see how the words looked when he heard them. In a few weeks he found it so hard to wait for the records to grind out the words that he was reading far ahead to see what happened. He wondered if it bothered Cy to wait, as it had him. Anyway, Cy had to get used to it. They told him that some day he would read Braille as fast as sighted people could read print and would type faster than anyone could write. That was good.

Larry thought about running tomorrow. Hillhouse encouraged running. Most of the kids just ran around the playing field as fast as they could. Cy was learning how to do that too. But Larry wanted to be a long distance runner, so every day he ran up the main street of Prime and out into the country. By the first of next month he intended to begin leaving his bicycle at home and running to Prime mornings, running to Glastonbury in the late afternoons. He would then have six weeks to do that before school closed.

After school closed. . . . He had no idea what he would do after school closed. His father was going to Europe the first of July. He said he would take Larry with him if he wanted to go, as a reward for sticking out the whole year at Hillhouse. Larry did not want to go. Being at Hillhouse was its own reward. He would probably hole up somewhere and read all summer. If only everybody would keep off his back. . . .

He turned out his headlight, set his bicycle in the rack beside the other bicycles, next to the motorcycle, beyond the stalls for the three cars, took his books out of the basket, and went into the house. There was nobody in the hall. The last mail delivery was on the carved oak trestle table. He was not aware of looking in that direction. He never got mail. But his eye must have caught the name on the top letter. It was his name. He took that letter with his books to his room and opened it.

It was from Foss.

It said:

Hi, Larry!

What are you doing this summer? Any chance we would get you back to Wakela as a junior counselor? We need a good reliable guy to look after the Beetles on their hikes. If anybody knows the old Campground and how to build and douse a fire you must. The pay isn't much but counselors can get snacks in the Cellar any time day or night.

I've been thinking about asking you ever since Christina Felker told me you're having a great year at Hillhouse. She says you've read a stack of books and I want to find out what they are and hash them over.

Then, funny thing! I had a letter from her yesterday saying there's a blind boy at Hillhouse who wants to come to Wakela because you've told him so much about it. She says she thinks this little guy could cut it if he had somebody around like you to show him the way at first.

Now don't think I wouldn't have written to you if I hadn't heard you might add a paying customer to the list. As I said, I've been intending to check with you for weeks now. Just hope you haven't signed up already to go out West roping cattle or shooting rapids. If you have, can't you get out of it?

Drop me a line, won't you?

ED (SIR NIGEL) FOSS

Holdfast and Sarah (Thomson) Sturtevant; Year of 1823

It was a bright September morning but unseasonably cool. Sarah was pleased, on leading the way into the front room after an early breakfast, to find a fire blazing on the hearth.

"Well, there now!" she said. "Warmth is welcome this early, I declare. Who made the fire?"

"I dropped in a little kindling and a match," said Washington carelessly. "Thought the room seemed a mite chilly when I brought down Miss Emma's boxes. There was a half-burned log there."

His mother nodded, glancing at the neat stack of worn leather and sprigged cloth-covered boxes by the door, topped by a gray velvet cape with narrow trim of soft white fur. Then her eyes went on to Miss Emma coming in from the kitchen in her black silk traveling gown, thin, pointed-toed black slippers with silver buckles. A black velvet ribbon tied back her yellow curls, and she held the hand of toddling Dolly. The older girls, Martha and Abigail, followed as close behind Miss Emma as if carrying a very short train, and the boys — Adams, Franklin, Warren and Hancock — were bumping the girls' backs. Only Washington and his father kept what Sarah considered a respectful distance from the young teacher who had made her home here throughout Summer Term.

"Don't jostle Miss Emma so, children," she said. "She is about to make a long journey and mustn't be worn out before it starts. Find places and sit down quietly so we can all have a little visit with her. Martha, take Dolly on your lap.

Sit by me here on the sofa, Miss Emma. There! Oh, my dear girl, we are going to miss you. In these few months you have come to seem like one of the family."

"Thank you, dear Mrs. Sturtevant. I feel that way, too. But I don't think you can miss me while you have — so many left."

Miss Emma had a voice like little bells ringing. She took a handkerchief with a lace edge from her skirt pocket and caught quick tears falling from her gray-green eyes. Abigail sprang up and ran howling from the room. Dolly wriggled off Martha's lap and ran after her.

"Well, at least we can be sure nobody else is going to make that much noise," said Sarah, "however we may feel." She covered Miss Emma's little hand with hers. "But no one else will take your place with us, dear. Surely not Schoolmaster Henderson who will be moving into your room in a fortnight. We had him last Winter Term, you know. He does nothing but study. Which we should thank the Lord for, I suppose, as he has much to learn."

"Watch your tongue, Say." said Holdfast with a significant glance at Franklin and Warren. "Little pitchers have big ears."

"I'm saying nothing that won't be known to all," said Sarah with a rueful side look at Miss Emma. "Besides, dear, you know I won't have so many left. Your leaving is the beginning of the first big change in our household. Adams leaves next week for Exeter — I so wish Washington had gone there — and the following week Mr. Sturtevant will take Martha and Abigail to Boston to live with Mindwell and go with her girls to the Misses Beaufort Day School. Only Franklin, Warren, and Hancock will be left to the tender mercies of him-who-shall-be-nameless. And only Dolly and Baby Melura to mine."

"I shall remain," Holdfast pointed out.

"And what, pray, do you need to be taught?" asked Sarah.

"It's not yet too late for Washington to go to Exeter with Adams, is it?" asked Miss Emma demurely.

"Ha! What do you say to that, Washington?" asked Holdfast.

"I say it is too late," replied Washington shortly. "I have no wish to go, nor ever had. I had done with school two years ago."

"Wish I were in your boots," growled Franklin.

"I too," piped Warren.

"Oh, forsooth," Miss Emma chided them gently. "Both your right feet would not fill Washington's right boot, and you know it well. You still have much to learn in the schoolroom. Though for the ages of eight and nine you both are doing very well. Especially in American history."

"And so has Washington always done," said Holdfast. "And still spends many an evening studying it. On our surveying trips together up north, he and I never lack subjects for long discussion as we ride or walk or travel by canoe or warm ourselves and eat our suppers by the campfire. It matters little to me what else a man may know as long as he can figure close, handle his tools to advantage, and is familiar with his country's history which is the inheritance on which his own present and future depends. It was to make sure all the children, especially the boys, in our settlement had the advantage of knowing the foundation on which they build that I saw to it a schoolhouse was constructed where they could go for this learning as soon as they were old enough to leave their mothers and stay as many years as they would."

Miss Emma turned limpid eyes on him.

In the months she had lived in this house she had heard much of how Sturtevants and their neighbors had made homes and cleared fields in the wilderness, what Noah the Indian had taught them, and in great detail of the parts the second Alexander, four of his sons and two of his sons-in-law had played in the great War for Independence from the British crown. She had been told how her host, born soon after that war, held tight his first memory which was of the firing of many muskets at the dawn of Independence Day and later the gathering of all the neighbors in the meadow to hear the stories of the men who had fought in that war and a talk from the hillside by his father praising their devotion to the mighty cause and asking God's blessing on this young country; how her host, while yet younger than Franklin and Warren now, read all the old gazettes his parents had saved, the few treasured letters of that glorious period, everything he could find which reported on it, and how, during the last year of his invalid father's life, the boy of ten had sat many hours every day by the bedside, writing down whatever his father could tell him of the war years.

Her host had talked often at breakfast and supper, through long spring and summer evenings, and on Sunday afternoons, to Miss Emma and his family, of these things, and of what he had read of the men and women for whom he had named his children, who had now heard it all so often that they often reminded their father of anecdotes he had left out, such as that of how their grandfather, taken prisoner at Hobkirk's Hill, had nursed in Camden Prison a fourteen-year-old boy ill of the smallpox and suffering too from the facial saber cut of a British officer whose boots he had refused to black. That boy's name was Andrew Jackson.

It was her hostess who had told, as they sat together at their sewing one Saturday afternoon with Martha and Abigail, of how the girls' father and their Uncle John had such a sense of loss over having had no share in the victory for American independence that a family crisis arose when Congress again declared war on Great Britain in 1812, this time to end England's search of American ships and impressment of sailors. The Government called for a hundred thousand militiamen, with a quota of twenty-five hundred for that section of the country which, having long been a part of the Province and then of the Commonwealth of Massachusetts, had lately become the State of Maine. Hope instantly flared in the hearts of John and Holdfast Sturtevant that their turn had come at last to defend their country's honor and win her freedom of the seas. But sober reflection convinced them that both could not go far from home at the same time. Holdfast, at the age of twenty-seven, had a wife, three small children, and a fourth child on the way. His mother, frail now and bedridden, lived here with him and with John who had never married and who at forty-eight was as hardy and active as Holdfast with a much stronger strain of the adventurer, always made moody and restless by confinement and routine chores. Mark had sailed around Cape Horn to California twenty years ago and now was master of his own ship. Matthew was much troubled with gout in his one leg and had no son at home, his Alexander having gone to France to become a painter. The many Sturtevant interests here required the presence of at least one able-bodied man.

"Your age, John," Holdfast pointed out gently.

"I'm no more than half of it and you know it."

"One of us must stay."

"It's you that has the family."

In the end, of course, it was John who went. And who died at the Battle of Plattsburg.

But Holdfast, too, contrived to take part in a local skirmish, having joined a volunteer company organized to guard the harbor of Port City. When one of the many boats built in the Great River to serve as privateers put out to sea and was chased back into the river by a British man-of-war too large to continue the pursuit, and British landing parties attempted to overtake it cross-country, Holdfast was among those who turned them back. Thus he had read with double satisfaction in January, 1815, that the final, famous victory of the war had been won at New Orleans by General Andrew Jackson, the same that Alexander had cared for in Camden Prison, and that a treaty of peace had been signed at Ghent. By then Holdfast had his Washington, Martha, Abigail, and Adams, and it was Franklin who was on the way.

"I know how much this means to you, sir," said Miss Emma gravely. "As indeed it does to all who have the privilege of knowing you. As I pray it does and always will to every citizen of this great country."

"I'm afraid, dear," said Sarah, "it is time for you to go if Washington is to have you in Port City in time for the coach."

"Oh, my soul, yes!" cried Miss Emma, jumping up in a pretty flurry and running to find Abigail and kiss away her tears, cuddle Dolly once more, coming back to kiss Martha, slipping into the gray velvet cape with the white fur trim Sarah held for her and adjusting a rose-colored bonnet over her ribbons, shaking hands with her host, and finally flying into Sarah's arms.

"Oh, *dear* Mrs. Sturtevant, I shall pray for you all every

night. Truly you have been like a mother to me. I have been so fortunate. I am so grateful —"

"You will be with us next Summer Term, dear child? You know everyone here is counting on it —"

"Oh, I want to. I mean to. You know I do —"

Then Washington had come in from stowing away all her leather and sprigged cloth boxes under the high seat of the wagon, and she put one silk-gloved hand inside his elbow, gathered up her velvet skirts with the other, and tripped away on her pointed-toed slippers. Holdfast and Sarah, their daughters and younger sons, filled the doorway to watch her go. They saw Washington hand her up into the wagon, tuck an embroidered linen duster over her knees, and spring up beside her, the reins in his hand. Then and then only Adams let go his grip on the horse's bridle, and an instant later horse and wagon were out of the Sturtevant yard and speeding down the hill into the road, Washington throwing his arm around Miss Emma to steady her as she clung to her bonnet with one hand and waved and blew kisses with the other.

As if a dam had burst, all the children flowed through the doorway and spilled over the hill, trying to keep their teacher in sight.

"You don't think, Say Jane," Holdfast heard himself say, "Washington might have it in mind to marry that girl some day?"

Sarah turned to look at him in sweet, mock astonishment.

She remembered him exactly as she had first seen him, the eldest of her pupils in the old schoolroom here. She had only just finished school herself. He already knew more than she could teach him. He went into town every Saturday to study surveying and higher mathematics with a graduate of Harvard College. One of the first Saturdays, while he was away, his mother had shown her his room and how its walls were lined with books. His mother had hoped and planned and believed that he would soon go to Harvard. Instead he stayed on at home and came every day to the schoolroom, helping her with the children of the neighborhood, himself taking over the history classes, eagerly extending her own small knowledge of history . . . and of other matters.

Sarah smiled at him now.

"I can't imagine, Mr. Sturtevant," she said, "how such an idea as that could come into your head!"

Lisa Gallico; Year of 1969

She was conscious of only one longing, which was to find a place where she could hide and never be found; and this drove her day and night.

She had been glad when the company Sylvia worked for moved to a distant city, taking Sylvia along as secretary of the Board. It would be easy to hide in a city where no one knew her. Sylvia rented a large apartment with spacious closets, and Lisa had her own room for the first time in her life except the first few days after her grandmother went to the hospital. Then she had been afraid of being alone. Now she was most afraid when she was not alone. But even here there was maid service, maids with passkeys striding in at odd hours with armfuls of clean linen for making the beds and tidying the bathrooms, or bringing vacuum cleaners which were soon noisily whirring, or setting to work with pails, brushes, cans, and sponges to scrub and wax the tile floors; and the lights in the spacious closets went on when you opened the closet door, went off when you closed it. If you hid in a closet, you hid in the dark, and in the dark Lisa had nightmares even when she was awake . . . worse ones when she was awake. So when she hid in a closet she took a flashlight with her; but a flashlight circling the white walls of a dark closet tells you that someone is looking for you and the one who is looking is yourself.

Lisa rarely left the apartment except to go to school and for her ballet lesson on Saturday. At school she pressed against the corridor walls, clung to the chairs in classrooms, spent her free periods in the library. At ballet she pretended that she was alone at the barre, that the long line of figures in black leotards rising, falling, taking the positions, spinning, running like blown leaves were her many shadows.

For a long time her most desperate fears proved groundless. No one intruded upon her isolation and if any of her contemporaries attempted to she was not aware of it. She felt most threatened between the outside door of the apartment and the street. In the halls and the elevator there was always the danger of encountering one or more of Sylvia's neighbors; a man in a business suit on his way to his office, women in soft tweeds and cashmere turtlenecks going down to cars which they would drive out to the golf course, women with curled hair coming back in silky flowered pantsuits from afternoons of bridge or the theater or shopping. They always seemed to be smiling and their teeth were too young for their faces so Lisa supposed they were capped like Sylvia's. Sylvia said her caps had cost $2000 but were worth it. If these neighbors saw Lisa their smiles broadened and they said, "Good-morning," or "Hello, dear," in somehow deceptively gentle, insinuating tones as if they loved her, though of course they didn't. Sometimes, on the long ride up

or down in the elevator, one asked curiously, "You're Sylvia's daughter, aren't you?" Many times if someone else was waiting for the elevator or already in the elevator when the door opened, Lisa pretended she had forgotten something and ran back to the apartment or to the street, hoping that when she returned the elevator would be empty. It was lovely to be alone in the elevator, only she could not forget that the next time it stopped either someone would get on or she would have to get off.

Sylvia often went out in the evening and often entertained neighbor couples or her friends from downtown for bridge and supper. Lisa liked those nights. She could go into her room, close the door, lock it, and not unlock it until she was ready to come out in the morning. Sylvia was fully occupied and did not even come tapping after she returned home or after her guests had gone, having been given to understand that Lisa always went to bed early and fell asleep to the music from her FM radio.

It was the times when Sylvia and Lisa were alone in the apartment that were most difficult.

Like Lisa, Sylvia now had only one problem which haunted her. Everything else had been successfully worked out. She had come a long way from the day when she lived in misery in her mother-in-law's bare, shabby little frame house. She was supporting herself and her daughter in comfort which approached elegance. She had a position of responsibility at an excellent and steadily growing salary, was investing in the company, had the respect and loyalty of her business associates, made congenial friends quickly and easily, was satisfied with her appearance, did notably well everything she did at all, was entirely independent, felt completely adequate.

She liked to talk about what she had achieved, to tell, laughingly, anecdotes which illustrated or proved her high degree of success in making a place for herself in the world and building the way of life she had always longed for; and Lisa listened and encouraged her in this prattle in every way she could think of. It kept Sylvia happy. It kept her talking. It postponed the moment which was bound to come when her thoughts would return to her one unsolved problem.

"Oh — I haven't heard what happened to you today, darling."

Or, "Any social events coming up soon on the social calendar, honey?"

Or, "Have you made any new friends lately, Lisa?"

What could Lisa say? Nothing that happened to her would please Sylvia, or pleased Lisa. Her grades were usually good, but grades were not the problem. She did not know, nor want to know, what was on the school calendar. And she had neither new friends nor old ones.

So all too soon the dark, anxious lines were drawn across Sylvia's smooth white forehead and around her full, puckering lips; and the probing began.

"Darling, why do you worry me so? It's not right for you to spend so much time alone. It's not normal. What *do* you do with yourself? A girl nearly fifteen years old should be having fun, bringing friends home after school, going to other girls' homes for overnight parties. Aren't your classmates doing things like that? Just yesterday on my way home I saw four or five girls coming out of a matinee together, all laughing, and I thought . . . Is it that the girls you like are interested in boys and you aren't ready for dating? Honey, that's no reason you can't have *friends!* They can't all be dating, and even those who are must do other things sometimes. Find somebody who likes to do what you like to do, and do it with her. What *do* you like to do, Lisa? . . . Listen I have an idea. It's too bad your birthday is in the summer. Let's say your birthday is next week, and you invite some of the girls to a Saturday matinee. We'll look in the paper and choose what you want to see, then I'll get the tickets. How many tickets would you like, beside your own? Three? Four? I'll go up to five, if you say so. . . . Lisa, answer me. . . . Darling, listen to me. . . . Oh, God, I wish you'd *talk!* . . . Honey, something is wrong, I know it. You're miserable, aren't you? Why? Tell me about it . . . Lisa, can't you see I'm almost out of my mind with worry? . . . Honey, shall we go shopping for something pretty for you to wear? . . . Shall we go to some nice place for lunch Saturday? I've promised to play golf but I can get out of it. . . . Darling, are you crying? . . . Listen to me, honey . . . Talk to me, Lisa . . . Lisa, you have to face it. Another year and you'll be through high school. When you go to college — and you *have* to go to college — you'll be living with other girls. You *have* to learn how to make friends, Lisa. Honey, people are interesting. Try to get interested in people, darling. We can't live on desert islands. What would become of you if you didn't have me? And you won't always have me. You're growing up. . . . Answer me, Lisa. . . . Talk to me, Lisa. . . . You're all I have. Don't shut me out so, Lisa . . ."

Sometimes Lisa hated Sylvia. It was Sylvia who had enticed Lisa's father out of his church, and this had killed both him and her grandmother. But for Sylvia Lisa would never have been born. Yet, after causing all this terrible suffering, it was Sylvia who was successful, Sylvia who had every silly thing she wanted except a daughter just like her.

At other times Lisa hated her father's church. Sylvia could not help being what she was. She was making the best of what she had and building what was for her a good life, in spite of the worst the church could do. It was the church which had tortured Lisa's father and grandmother, and through them Sylvia, all the years Lisa had known them. It was not Sylvia's fault that Lisa's father had been born a Catholic, that he had not become a priest, that he had been married before to that Gwen who had divorced him. Maybe Sylvia had once loved him very much and tried desperately to make him happy until the power of his church, the horror of his mother, and his own agony of spirit combined to convince her that no one woman had a chance against them. Maybe she had not given up the battle until repeatedly shown that it was already long lost, which may have happened by the time Lisa was born. After such a hopeless struggle against impossible odds, could she be blamed for fighting to save Lisa from being caught in any such dark tangle? Shouldn't she be admired? Shouldn't Lisa be forever grateful to her?

At such times what Lisa actually felt was neither admiration nor gratitude but blind, mute pity for her mother, her father, her grandmother, and the girl who had been and still was in the swamp into which they had all been cast. Nothing could be done now or probably ever for the man, the old woman, or the girl. If there was still a chance for any of them it was for Sylvia, who by sheer determination not to be defeated had now pulled all but one hand out into daylight and sunshine. That one hand — her left, Lisa thought — held her back, clutching a teenage daughter who still floundered. It was a pity, a great pity, that one so nearly free of her past could not be entirely so. But for months

Lisa had been able to think of only one way of giving freedom to Sylvia, and the details of bringing this way about were still obscure to her. Even if they had come clear, she was not sure that she would employ them for fear her act, instead of freeing Sylvia, would drag her into a quicksand of guilt and sense of worthlessness and destroy her as John had been destroyed. If that happened, all these years of struggle and suffering would have been for nothing, for no one would have survived them.

No, there was nothing to do yet but stare blankly at drawn curtains while Sylvia begged desperately, relentlessly, "Listen to me, honey. . . . Answer me, darling. . . . Talk to me, Lisa. . . . Lisa, don't shut me out. . . ."

Until one day there came a narrow opening; the all but imperceptible gleam of a very small opportunity.

Madame Maria announced that the next Saturday there would be no ballet classes. One of her former pupils, now a member of the National Ballet of Canada, would be dancing with that Company the following Monday and Tuesday evenings in Vanguard Auditorium at the State University. The guest artist on these programs would be Rudolf Nureyev, the greatest ballet dancer in the world. Lovely Lorraine had not only sent Madame Maria tickets to both evening performances, she had also arranged for any of Madame's pupils who wished to come to be admitted to watch the Saturday ballet rehearsals with the University Symphony Orchestra. Madame explained that this would be a rare treat indeed; therefore she would hold no classes that day, but a chartered bus — or more than one, if needed — would leave the parking area by the school at 9:00 a.m. to take all pupils who wished to go to the auditorium on the University campus. But Madame must know no later than this Sunday night who would be going. Pupils might sign up for the trip after class or wait to consult their parents, but the latter must telephone her office by Sunday evening at the latest to reserve space on the bus.

Lisa half-listened to this announcement as she half-listened to everything she heard at all from within a dream, and went to the coatroom to look about for the shoebag, pants, and jacket which she must have left there an hour before though she had no recollection of it. She tried to remember what they looked like. Were they the plaid pants or the navy knit ones? And the jacket — what color was her jacket?

A girl pulling on a ragged pair of jeans asked curiously, "Don't you dare sign up, either, before you ask your folks?"

"Sign up?" repeated Lisa vaguely.

"Practically everybody else is in there doing it right now. I could yell and scream, I'm so mad with myself that I'm not, too. But fact is I don't dare to. All the time *I* have to ask the old lady. And it's always the same treadmill. She says *she* has to ask the old man. Then *I* have to hang around and wait while *they* argue about the cost and what somebody can't have if they spend so-and-so for this. Who cares what it costs if anybody has a chance to see a national ballet company *with* Nureyev? I mean, what's *money?* But there's six of us kids at home and this always goes on every time any of us wants anything. Every *single* time. It's enough to make you throw up."

Lisa had found her pants. They were the plaid ones. She began slowly pulling them up over the black leotard.

The other girl, swinging her shoebag, was ready to leave. She glanced back from the doorway.

"Like that where you hang out?" she asked.

"No," Lisa answered slowly. "No, I — not really —"

"Lucky you!" said the other. "Well, here I go to beard the lions. At least, this time it can't go on forever. It's got to be settled by tomorrow night, and I'll tell them Madame said so. See you Saturday on the bus — I hope!"

It's got to be settled by tomorrow night . . . See you Saturday on the bus — I hope.

These words kept running through and through Lisa's mind as she hurried back to the apartment, feeling pursued as she always did when on the street. Increasingly she was aware that the words were telling her something, offering her something. And as soon as she saw Sylvia seated at the small desk in the corner of the living room, talking merrily on the telephone, she knew what that something was.

The knowledge must have shown in her face, for Sylvia said, "Have to stop now, darling. My Lisa's just come in." Then she hung up the receiver and asked expectantly, "What is it, honey? What's happened?"

Lisa rallied all her forces to meet the test. Her face felt stiff but she managed a smile.

She heard a croaky voice say, "Well! A girl in my class wants me to go to — to the University next Saturday. To see the Canadian National Ballet Company."

Sylvia did not see the stiffness, only the smile, nor hear the croaking, only the delicious words. Her own face lit up.

"Oh, darling, how *wonderful!* A girl in your class! What's her name, honey?"

". . . Nadine." Lisa had heard Madame call someone Nadine. Perhaps it was this one. "I don't know her last name."

"Nadine! Sounds French! You mean she's in your ballet class, of course?" Lisa nodded. "Then she's sure to be of a nice family. All Madame's pupils are. Darling, isn't this *exciting?* You're going with a friend to see a real live ballet troupe! Now it must be about a three hour ride to the University. How will you get there? Are Nadine's parents driving you?"

Lisa concentrated and explained carefully that Madame Maria was chartering a bus to take any of her pupils who wished to go, that the cost for transportation would be $7.50, and Madame's office must be notified by tomorrow night at the latest if Lisa was to go.

Sylvia seemed to wait for Lisa to continue, but Lisa had gone as far as she could; so Sylvia said, sounding a little puzzled:

"But didn't you say Nadine invited you?"

". . . Not — invited. She — she said she hoped I would be on the bus."

If this was a let-down for Sylvia, she instantly overcame it. As always, she took what she had and built on it.

"Well, that's a start, honey. A fine start. She probably wants to sit with you. In all those hours, you'll really get to be good friends. Then you must invite Nadine over. Maybe she can spend the night with us, and after that she'll ask you to her house. Oh, Lisa, what fun you'll have! I wonder where Nadine goes to school, and if she will be going to college. Just think — you might decide to go to the same college and be roommates! Meantime —"

Sylvia jumped up, caught Lisa in her arms, shoebag and all, and spun her round the room.

"Meantime, darling, you're going to see the Canadian National Ballet Company perform! You and Nadine are going to see it *together!* Won't that be marvelous? I'll call Madame's office tonight and make the reservation. Did you ask Nadine what she is going to wear? No? Well, what do you think you'd like to wear? I think a white blouse and your black velvet top. With those nice checked pants, would you say? Or would that cute, skimpy circular black velvet skirt be more suitable? Or maybe we should go shopping right now for something new that's just right!"

Lisa said she was sure either the checked pants or the black skirt would do. She said she would go now to look at them and choose. She felt cruel to close the door of her room behind her, but she could not wait a minute longer to be alone. An hour or so later she became aware that Sylvia was singing to herself as she stirred and beat something in a bowl. So Sylvia was all right. And Lisa was all right. At last, all by herself, she had given Sylvia a reason to smile and to sing. So much had been accomplished. Now Lisa could go back to her shadows for most of the week to come.

One more week. . . . Then on Saturday, Sylvia would give her a lunch and money for the trip. She would set off for the bus, remembering to look as excited and happy as she could and, in case Sylvia was watching, to look up from the street and smile and wave. She would get on the bus and ride to the campus, get off with the others, and go into the auditorium and sit down and watch the dancing. Then somehow the chance would come for her to slip out. Everybody would be watching the dancing. Nobody would notice when she left. Probably no one would remember she had been there or know that she was not on the bus when it started home. By the time Sylvia discovered that Lisa was gone she would simply have disappeared. Entirely and forever. And Sylvia would be sad for a little while, but she could not blame herself and nobody could blame her. Her daughter had gone with a friend in a chartered bus to the ballet at the University, and did not come back. What good mother could have denied her child this opportunity? How could anyone have foreseen what was to happen? . . . And soon Sylvia would again be building bravely and brightly on what she still had, which was all she had ever had — herself. While Lisa would be where she need search no longer for a place in which to hide and never be found. . . .

But it did not work out that way. Lisa had not foreseen what Rudolf Nureyev would do to her; that he would both pin her to her seat in Vanguard Auditorium and take her soaring — as once Peter Pan had Wendy — into an entirely new, completely free, soothingly rhythmic, intoxicatingly magic and yet wholly real world . . .

When the chartered bus drew up in front of Madame Maria's studio at eight o'clock that Saturday night, Sylvia was on the sidewalk waiting for it, and though Lisa was the last to come down the steps, she came.

"Oh, here you are, darling! Was it wonderful?"

Lisa nodded.

"Which one is Nadine? I'd love to meet her."

Lisa had not seen or thought of "Nadine" all day. She might not have recognized her if she had seen her. For the first time she wished she had, hoped nobody's "old man" and "old lady" had kept anyone from seeing and feeling what Lisa had seen and felt.

"I guess she's gone. . . . Sylvia, it *was* wonderful! It was *so* wonderful —"

"Oh, honey, I'm pleased. Have you had anything to eat except what was in your lunchbox? No? You must be starved! We'll go straight to the Tea Shop. Come along. You can tell me all about it while you eat, darling —"

Lisa could not tell her all about it, or even a very small part of it, anywhere. She had not expected to be able to. She would never be able to tell anyone. But she had it inside her, and now nothing would ever be the same as before.

She realized suddenly for the first time since she had left Uncle Dave's what it was to be hungry. And when Sylvia had ordered the food she thought looked best on the menu, while they were waiting for the waitress to bring it, there were words Lisa could say which were the solution to Sylvia's one rankling problem and to Lisa's, too.

She said, "I made a decision today. I want to go to the University as soon as I can after I graduate from high school. I want to live there. I want to see and hear every program in that auditorium."

Larry Sturtevant; Year of 1969

He had had a good year at the midwestern university which he had chosen to go to because no one he knew had ever been there and it was so far away from the eastern seaboard. Sometimes he had wondered, when he heard a jet overhead, which Sturtevant might be on the passenger list, running over to Hawaii or to London for a week or for the winter; but jets were always very high up and moving at great speed, so he could shrug and forget about it. After responding to a wire saying his father had been lost in a yachting accident off the coast of Chile, he had not written again to the family nor heard from any of them. A lawyer had notified the University that semester bills were to be mailed to his grandfather in California, and money for other expenses continued to be deposited from time to time on his checking account. He had spent the year running and reading, thus made the University track team and excellent grades in English, while barely passing subjects in areas which did not interest him. His average was not high enough to postpone his being drafted, so he had volunteered for two years' service and would report to the Army early in September.

But right now he was at Wakela, carrying supplies from the shelters to the Compound for winter storage, boarding up the windows, stacking the canoes in the boathouse. The kids had been gone several days. They traveled to and from their homes by bus now. Campers' trains no longer pulled into and out of the little station. The station had been moved and become a sporting goods shop. It did not matter to Larry. He never went into town.

Eight summers at Wakela. Four as a camper. Three as a junior counselor. One as a full counselor. He had the same rating now as Foss, at Wakela. But neither of them would be at Wakela next summer. Likely neither of them would ever see Wakela again.

They had talked about this for the first time last night, by the campfire over which they had cooked their supper on the beach. They had talked late every evening all summer, but only about the books they had read, were reading, or wanted to read.

Last night Foss asked through the smoky half-dark, "Want to venture a guess as to where you'll be a year from now?"

"Who knows? Like Vietnam, I'd say. I'm going in next month."

"How do you feel about that?"

"I don't know. It's where the action is."

"That's for sure. . . . Think you could shoot at anybody?"

"Not likely. Don't plan to. The reason I volunteered is

there's a better chance you can choose what you do. I might get into the medics."

"That's a good service. . . . A lot of the guys from the college where I've been teaching have gone to Canada to get away from this war. Two or three have stayed and gone to jail. More, of course, have gone into training or will go when they're called."

"Yeah. Well, it's sure a mess. Think I'd rather get in and do *something* about it than sit back and watch it any longer. If I'd wanted to stay out of it I'd have studied harder at the U — those languages, that math and history and stuff. But seems like I don't mind going if I can make some kid who's sick or hurt feel better."

"That'll come naturally to you. . . . Tell you, I'd like to know how you make out, fella. Wish we could keep in touch. But we may not be able to reach each other with addresses."

"I could write to you at Hoagland from Dix. And let you know where I get sent from there."

"No, that wouldn't work. I won't be at Hoagland."

"Oh?"

"The girl I think I want to marry lives in San Francisco, so I've got to get out there and see. I'm thirty-five years old, man. If I'm ever going to get married, it better be soon. I've got some lines out at colleges on the coast, but no strong bites yet. Some people want to interview me. Should have gone out, probably, as soon as college closed. Instead of coming here. But I'd signed up with the Harrisons. Besides, after all these years, I'm attached to Wakela."

"Yeah. Likewise."

"I think that's pretty clear. I thought that in the course of the summer I might get over this girl. But I didn't. Anyway, it's probably best to make a break. For both of us."

"Yeah. What I've been telling myself."

"A little New England campus is a great place, if you like it. So is the wilderness. But . . ."

"There's a great big world out there."

"Right. And if we never go out into it, we'll never know what's there."

"Yeah. Right."

"Some day we'll run into each other again, Alleyne."

"Yeah. After you've settled a lot of small bickerings."

"By then you'll have little gold spurs pinned to your pants, and be the Socman of Minstead."

"Maybe."

"Still got that copy of *The White Company*?"

"Yea, man."

"I've picked up another one in a secondhand place. Some way, couldn't quite get along without it. Damned good yarn, isn't it?"

"Damned good."

"Whenever I pull it off the shelf, I'll think of you, kid."

"Same here, Foss."

Now it was late afternoon. Larry lay on his back in the old red canoe which still bore his name on its side. He had painted over the letters eight times, but they would never be painted there again. Nobody else would ever use this canoe at Wakela. All other canoes at Wakela now were aluminum. This one had been kept only for him. But it had done him good service. Soon he would bring it in from the lake for the last time. . . . He stared for a while through narrowed lids at the sky, then turned on his side, slipped one hand into the water, closed his eyes, and drifted, half-asleep . . .

Adams and Roxanna (Martin) Sturtevant; Year of 1870

Adams had been gone for three months, but whenever Roxanna came into this room she felt he was still here and she was determined to keep him here at least until Orestes and Sophie Watson were married and Sophie had become its mistress, for Adams, like Roxanna herself, had been heart-set on this union ever since their son Orestes came back from the war.

From the threshold she peered in through the thick lenses of her gold-rimmed glasses, alert for any changes which might have been made during the furore of the house cleaning Aphrodite had supervised during the preceding two weeks. Seeing none, she strode to the nearest window, snapped to the roll the stenciled shade which had been pulled to the windowsill like an over-modest woman's skirt sweeping the floor, and raised the sash.

"Who is there?" asked Aphrodite's ladylike voice, instantly, from somewhere in the rear. Then her light footsteps and, "Oh, is it you, Mother? I didn't hear you ring."

"Of course you didn't," snapped Roxanna. "For the excellent reason that I didn't ring. For heaven's sake, Affie, did I forfeit the right to walk into this house whenever I want to, just because I moved out of it?"

"Certainly not, Mother. Naturally you are welcome any time. It is only that I didn't know you were here, and so I was startled. Why did you raise the shade? The sun is streaming in —"

"Well, calm yourself," said Roxanna. "Welcome or not,

I'm here, and I need the sun to see by. As you would if you had my eyes."

"Oh, is your vision poor this morning?" inquired Aphrodite politely. "I'm sorry."

Aphrodite was on the threshold now, as tall as her father and Orestes and as slender, with much smaller bones. Like a beanpole inside her tight gray bodice and full black and white flowered skirt, thought short, sturdy Roxanna; a beanpole with coiled cornsilk at the top of it, and with long, pale, soft, tapered-fingered hands dangling at her waist like the flippers of an albino penguin.

"No poorer than usual," answered Roxanna. "Poor as it is, sometimes I see more than I wish I did."

"In a bit of a bad humor then?" asked Aphrodite gently.

"That's it," said her mother quickly. "Best to leave me right straight alone until I'm over it. It's hot out and I've been down to the cemetery. Justin Crowley came along with the mail while I was there and gave me a bundle of it. On my way by here I stopped to look at the cinnamon roses Sophie admires so much — they weren't dug up around this spring, were they? Then I thought I'd stop in and cool off before climbing the hill. Now I want to read my mail. There's a letter from your grandmother. So run along to whatever you were doing, Affie, and let me be."

"Would you like me to read the mail to you?"

"No. No, I can manage. I said run *along,* Affie!"

Aphrodite did not run. Her mother could not remember that she had ever seen her run. But she sighed and went, flippers still flapping; and Roxanna closed the door.

Sitting by the window, smelling the roses she could see only as a pink blur, she let all her confused, conflicting thoughts and emotions come tumbling through like water when a dam has burst. Her lips moved, making no sound but telling it all to Adams as she often had before at such times. It had always been safe to say whatever was on her mind to Adams for he never mentioned it again, probably because he did not remember it, having never really listened, his mind being full of more important matters.

"Adams, my dear, I hate to bother you, but I must talk to you —"

The instant she breathed his name the turbulence began to subside, as always.

He looked up from the book he was reading or spun round in his swivel chair from the desk at which he was writing and either took his pipe from his mouth or reached for and slowly pressed tobacco into the bowl with his left thumb, feeling for matches in his vest pocket with the thumb and forefinger of his other hand. His crisp, thick hair and muttonchop whiskers, once fire-red, had turned during the years the boys were at war, and been as white as his eighty-year-old father's five years ago. His mother had remarked on it to Roxanna as they walked together up the hill behind him and his father, coming home from the cemetery the day of Plato's burial. The men still carried their hats in their hands.

"Is it possible, Roxy," Sarah had whispered, "that the loss of a son is even harder on the father than on the mother? Adams's hair is as white as Holdfast's!"

But it was not only from losing Plato to some unknown illness when he was already on his way north for discharge from the Union Army. Adams's hair had turned while he did not know where Chaucer was, when he learned that this first-born was held in Andersonville Prison, and when they visited Orestes in the hospital in Philadelphia where he lay among the dying, trying to get back the use of his arm after a bullet went through his shoulder.

"It's hard enough," Roxanna had answered Sarah. "Depends some on the person's nature, I guess. Adams is one that tells nobody how he feels. It only comes out in his face, never in words. Everything he says, even everything he writes is calm, no matter what. But it stands to reason —"

"I know," his mother had nodded. "He was always like that. The only one of all I had. And the only one of them with red hair, too."

"Now I'm just the opposite," said Roxanna. "I sputter and carry on at a great rate. Not likely to keep anything to myself. Especially when I'm upset."

But she had told no one then that suddenly she could no longer see clearly. She took it for granted that as soon as she stopped crying long enough, her sight would come back.

Now, as always lately in the light — lamplight, firelight, sunlight — Adams's hair shone like spun silver. On either side of a fierce Roman nose from which once-merry freckles had blended into skin browned more by years than by exposure to the elements, he peered sympathetically, inquiringly at Roxanna through narrowed, warm dark eyes, and his deep voice rumbled gently.

"That's all right. Don't hate, Roxy. How can I help you?"

She did not dwell on her knowledge that he would have responded in much the same way in a similar tone to anyone who interrupted his studies to ask for his attention. There had been more of his grandfather, the third Alexander, in Adams with every year that passed, which had increasingly endeared him to his father far beyond any of his other children. Holdfast, the fiery activist, had been inspired all his life by his father who died when Holdfast was ten years old and by this son born when he was twenty-five. Without either of these two, Holdfast no longer had a rudder, and within a few hours of receiving in Washington the wire informing him of Adams's sudden going had slipped senseless to the floor and lain paralyzed on his bed ever since, lucid only at intervals.

Sarah had said, the day of Plato's burial, "Is it possible, Roxy, that the loss of a son is even harder on the father?" Yet Adams, beside the eighty-year-old Holdfast, had stood straight and walked with steady steps that day. Could he have done so if it had been Orestes they were burying? She knew well Adams had been as close to Orestes as Holdfast was to Adams, though for very different reasons. Would Holdfast, even at eighty-five, have had a stroke if the word had come that Washington had died in his business office in Boston, instead of Adams at his desk in the studio Hancock had built for him up in the pines? Or even if it had been Franklin, Warren, or a daughter? No, there was no doubt that, though a parent may believe he loves his children equally, there can be a bond with one that no other is comparable to, a kind of intermingling of vital functions on which the elder is dependent for existence. As it is said that if one of identical twins succumbs, the other is likely soon to follow. Orestes was far from identical to Adams, or Adams to Holdfast, and still . . .

Roxanna looked down at Sarah's letter lying on her lap, and looked away again.

Time for that later. Now she was about to talk to Adams who had just said, "That's all right. How can I help you?"

It was to spare him the result of many such responses that she and Hancock had conspired to provide him with the studio where no one was allowed to seek him out. While there he was never interrupted. In his own natural peace and in perfect quiet except for the brook singing under his window and the wind singing in the tops of the dark, pointed trees, he had studied and thought and put his knowledge on paper to be published in books, magazines, newspapers, to be copied and passed around at committee hearings in the Nation's Capitol, to be incorporated into his father's speeches on the floor of Congress. Since the end of the war, he and his father had been striving to bring truly together those who had fought and suffered on opposite sides out of equally strong convictions. They had felt so alone after the assassination of the President. She remembered how late the two had sat and talked, the night after they buried Plato, in this room she and her neighbor women had painted black the day they heard of Lincoln's death. And black it had stayed until a year ago when Hancock, ailing, had gone down to live with Franklin and she and Adams, thinking of Sophie, were about to move into Hancock's house with the pillars. Then Roxanna and her neighbors had stripped off the black, restored this familiar blue-green to the woodwork and papered the walls with giant, swaying ferns.

"One cannot grieve forever," Roxanna had said firmly. "Old grief must give way to new joy."

But she was still waiting for joy.

She must speak now to Adams. He was listening. He would always listen to her now, for when they were together no one else was there or could come in. She was the only one who could call him back . . . Or could Aphrodite, too? Aphrodite was for the moment mistress of this house and much alone in it. Did she come to this room sometimes, to see her father still at his desk, perhaps write out a letter at his dictation, or find a book he had misplaced?

Roxanna gave herself a small, irritated shake. Aphrodite was so *intelligent* — or thought herself to be — and from the age of eight or ten had assumed she was or was fast becoming everything her father needed in a woman; his willing servant, his amanuensis, the soundingboard for his ideas, his interpreter to the less sensitive and intellectual, his receptionist, his bodyguard. All day while he was at the studio she hovered over its approaches as a mother bird flies close to the nest where her little ones sleep, ready to swoop upon a possible trespasser. Not that anyone ever trespassed on the studio. There was no one in the family or in the neighborhood who would not as soon have shouted raucously during the Elder's prayer in church on a Sunday morning. Still Aphrodite hovered. And even when he had come down to the house for dinner and then withdrawn to his desk and books here, she made it clear that for anyone to go in to speak to him was more than a breach of etiquette, a flagrant violation of her rules unless she had set up an appointment . . . But now, as often before, Roxanna had sent her away, closed the door, and was blessedly alone for a little while with the man she had married, the father of her children.

"Well, Adams, now that it is so close to Sunday when Orestes and Sophronia Watson will be married by Sophie's father in the church your father had built in memory of his father, I hope your mind is as relieved as mine is and as I'm sure your father's is if he is able to understand it when your mother tells him down there in Washington. If he hasn't heard about it when he gets where you are, tell him as soon as you can. So he will know that even though apparently neither Chaucer nor Aphrodite will ever marry, Orestes very soon will, if by then he has not already, and thus it is alto-gether likely that you will have descendants for many generations to come.

"All that worries me now is the future of this house, who will be living in it, and what their lives will be . . .

"Yes, yes, I know no Sturtevant has ever yet made a will dividing this property, and that so far the children of the owner have each time equably made arrangements satisfac-tory to all, providing homes for those who wished to live here to carry on the place and legacies for those who wished to settle elsewhere. And I know you had only money to leave us, the property being still in your father's name. But what is going to happen when your father follows you?

"Yes, of course your brothers and sisters can be depended on to consider that this house is yours to be passed on to your children, provided only that your mother and I have a home here as long as we live. I have as much confidence in their dedication to family tradition as you do. It is, I am sorry to say, our children who worry me. Orestes is about to marry and will want to stay here. Will Chaucer be satisfied with the cash settlement Orestes can afford to make? And will Aphrodite want to continue to live here? It would seem so now, though it is obvious to me that she has a strong dislike of Sophie. When Sophie, who is by no means made of milk and water, discovers that — if she has not already — what peace can Orestes have? And Orestes, enough like you to need peace, is without your love of academic pursuits to withdraw into. Ever since you and I moved out of this house, Aphrodite has considered herself its mistress. . . . I wonder if you observed that, Adams, and, if you did, what it suggested to you. I used to long for you to speak of it, hoping you had in mind some solution to what seemed and still seems to me an insoluble problem. . . . Because a house cannot have two mistresses. And when Sophie comes she will come at least as determined to be its one mistress as Aphrodite is. I might say, in terms a man would understand better, that one of them will have to be skipper and the other mate. Which is it to be? And how long and bitter will be the battle before the ascendancy is established? That is what I want to know."

He answered with a gentle question.

"Was there such a battle between you and my mother when we married?"

"Certainly not. There is no similarity whatever between the two cases. For one thing, she and I were of different generations. I had loved and respected Sarah as long as I could remember. I had always tried to learn from her, though knowing I could never be like her. I certainly did not come here to replace her but to help her — and you. As it turned out, if I replaced anyone it was your father as he was away so much and you were shut away with your books. Sarah knew more about running a house than I did, but I knew more about running a farm and quickly learned to handle business details. Sarah and I were partners, each with our own responsibilities. She was older and wiser; I was younger and stronger. Being what we were, and the situation being what it was, we might have done equally well if she had been my age and your sister, but I am not sure of that. Anyway, Aphrodite is not Sarah, and Sophie is not me, and Orestes will see to everything outside the house. Only the inside will remain for Sophie — and Aphrodite . . . Adams, did we spoil Affie, just because she was the daughter we had feared we would never have? I can tell you and no one else that I do not believe any woman can ever feel at home in a house where Affie lives. I know I never did, after she began to grow up. Did you realize, my dear, how precious every minute of our last year was to me? After Orestes had taken over the management of the place and we had at last a little home all our own? Even though you still spent every day at the studio, and most evenings you came up to this room to work and I suppose Affie waited on you, still eventually every night you came back to me, we had our breakfasts together, I packed your lunch and walked almost to the studio with you, then went back to our house and began planning our supper. I hope you were as happy as I was, Adams. It was the happiest year of my life . . ."

Lost in her memories, she was not aware that he had not replied; and when she looked toward his desk, later, he was no longer there. His swivel chair was turned back to her, as Aphrodite had set it, and there was not a paper in sight; all the books were in place on the shelves.

Roxanna sighed, glanced at the pile of mail on her lap, absentmindedly drew a black wire pin from her thin coil of iron-gray hair, and slit the end of the envelope postmarked Washington, D.C.

Some time later the door was suddenly opened and Orestes swung in.

"Marmee! What are you up to? Sis says you've been in here all by yourself, still as a mouse, for an hour or more!"

Roxanna took off her glasses, rubbed her eyes, put the glasses on again, and smiled at him.

This boy swung in wherever he went, swung into whatever he did, looking as Adams had when he was young, but moving and talking in the manner of Holdfast. Strange he had put off marrying so long! Here he was in his thirtieth year! But he did not look or act or sound thirty years old. Even the war had not aged him. He had come back, if anything, younger than when he went away. The sight and sound of him was now his mother's greatest delight; she prayed every night that if the time should come when she could no longer see him, she would still be able to hear his voice and his springing step. And now he would marry within the week; marry Sophie Watson on whom, while she was still a child, Roxanna had set her heart for him though she was ten years younger than he.

"I stopped in to rest and cool off on my way back from the cemetery. What have you been up to? Seen Sophie today?"

"Should you ask? Isn't that prying? You've made a great point for years of not prying."

She was rising and, on the pretense of helping her up, he pulled her against him.

"I try not to," she answered meekly.

"Well, for a Marmee you don't — much — and that's a fact. So I'll tell you. Yes, I've seen Sophie. We had a rendezvous in the studio. Which Sophie's mother doesn't permit. Presumably because she won't be sure until Sunday that my intentions are honorable."

"And if Gussie has any doubts, whose fault is that?"

"Mine, of course. I dilly-dallied, didn't I? Men aren't supposed to do that, according to mothers, are they? Very well. My shoulders are broad, and the burden will lighten as you all find out what a model husband I'm going to be."

"I'm sure that is so. Whatever Gussie may think."

He patted her back.

"I know that, Marmee. You're sure, Sophie's sure, and I'm sure. That will take care of Gussie's qualms automatically, in time. By the time we're back from our trip, I trust."

"Then you are going away?"

"Careful, Marmee! Don't ask where! . . . Yes, doesn't everybody nowadays?"

"No. And Affie said you asked her to move over with me before the wedding to stay a few days."

"That's because Sophie has a notion she wants us to begin our married life in this house, as most of its other inhabitants have. Sophie's almost reverent about this house. Rather surprising in such an uppity young thing. She isn't reverent about much, I can tell you."

"We have long known her feeling about this house. It meant a great deal to your father. And it does to me."

"More than our feeling for each other, no doubt." He was grinning.

"It all blended in together in our minds. And perhaps in hers."

"You think she wouldn't have me without the house, then?"

"No. I'm sure she would."

"You'd better be. And she'd better be. Was Sis put out because I asked her to pay you a little visit, do you think? I couldn't tell. But what else could I do?"

"Nothing. Who ever knows whether or how much Affie is put out? She acts put out most of the time, to me. You did right. She should be glad to come over since Chaucer will be there anyway. They always have to argue the hopeless state of the world and readjust their philosophies of life when they get together. That takes a while."

"And chances are we'll leave Monday. If Sophie's willing . . . Can't you stop for supper with us? Sis is fixing something."

"No, dear. Thank you. I still have to plan out what I'll

feed Gussie and the girls tomorrow night. I'm slower than I used to be, and I still miss your grandmother in the kitchen."

"Well, then, I'll drop in a minute on my way to Watsons' tonight. Watch your step, Marmee. I'm going to try to get the path smoothed up a little for you before Sunday."

She slipped out the front door as she had slipped in, and hurried home, eager to reread Sarah's letter which she had already read three times.

My dear Roxy,

I write to inform you that there is little visible change in Father. Day and night are alike to him now. He rouses from his sleep only now and then and takes no nourishment but occasional sips of warm milk from a spoon. He has been ready to go for several weeks but seems to be waiting for something, though not clear as to what it is. I believe it is for word of dear Orestes's wedding, so do ask dear Chaucer to wire me of it immediately on his return to Cambridge. Father asks me once or twice every day what I have heard from "all at home," and sometimes tells me he has just had a letter from Adams or from his father. These communications bring him such great joy and reassurance I cannot doubt that they actually occur.

I wish we were near enough, Roxy, dear, so that I could see you and take your hand. You have so lately sustained the loss of your own beloved husband, our precious son, and we could not be with you then, I have not seen you since, and you are only sixty years old, thus I fear I may not be sufficiently aware of the depth and extent of your personal suffering. Your letters do not reveal it, always expressing first your concern about us and then telling us all you can of what our dear young people are doing so that we can never doubt life does go on despite the shadow of death. I bless you every day, my true daughter, and only wish I could be as much comfort to you as you are and have always been to me.

The reason I suspect my own unawareness is that I know how

fortunate I am in having had my husband by me until together we have reached an age when our coming separation does not fill either of us with foreboding or despair. I know, and I am sure Father does, that it is not for long; and I have discovered in recent months that at eighty-five nothing hurts as it once would have. One seems to have been prepared without knowing it for resignation to the inevitable and to feel a lively thankfulness for *any* earthly experience one may still be granted in the goodness and wisdom of God.

So the reason I fear the results of my possible unawareness is that I cannot expect you, at sixty, to be as I am now, and therefore what I am about to say may be very difficult for you to understand and accept. It may shock you, cause you to think me insensitive and cold. Yet I pray that, knowing me so well, you can believe that I am not, despite what may seem to be evidence that I am. For there is something I feel I must tell you, something you — and possibly others; I readily leave this to your judgment — should know at the time of dear Orestes's marriage.

About six weeks after Father's first stroke, you will recall, he had a week or two when he seemed improved, was often lucid for hours at a time. Early in that period it was borne in upon me that Adams's tragic predeceasing of his father had made changes in his father's responsibilities to those who remained. At the first opportunity I spoke to him about this, and for a few days following he often brought up the subject and then decided to make a will, though we both knew there had never been one in the family before and until now he had never considered making one, as far as I knew. But this far from the settlement we all know and love best of any spot on earth, we have seen and heard of much to indicate that it would be extraordinary indeed if, as time goes on, no one who does not wish to settle there ever causes problems, perhaps insoluble, for those who do. Surely the family will be no less close for each member of it having full legal claim to what belongs to him.

Therefore I had a lawyer contact each living co-owner with Father of our acres and what is on them — Father had a complete list in his files — and a satisfactory arrangement was easily made with all, so that as of this moment, he is sole owner. But his will divides his estate so that when it comes into effect, the real property is immediately to be surveyed and a deed written to dear Franklin covering the buildings he now occupies with his family and the acreage nearest to him there up to the amount of two hundred acres, with only two provisions, first that his boundary line be nowhere nearer to the original homestead than two acres away, and second that dear Hancock share his roof as long as he wishes to. At the same time a deed is to be written to dear Aphrodite for Adams's studio and one acre of land surrounding it. The remainder of the real property Father is assigning to dear Orestes, knowing that it has always been his home, that this is what Adams would have wished, and that Orestes can be depended upon to care for it lovingly, intelligently, and with pride in his inheritance. The one provision in the bequest to Orestes is that he make a home for you and me for our lifetimes. Father has also set up a trust fund for me, for you, for our daughters, for Hancock, and for Chaucer and Aphrodite; remaining funds to be divided evenly among Washington, Warren and Orestes.

We both hope, dear Roxy, that this apportionment will seem to all fair and wise, as it does to us. I wished so much that we could consult with you on it, but it would have been difficult to do by letter and Father and I both felt that no time should be lost while he was able to consummate it. In this last we were right for within a few days of signing the papers he had the second stroke.

One more point before I close. I have been two days and nights writing this in snatches. Father is now in a coma, but I will not let myself believe he will not linger until after Orestes's marriage to dear Sophronia and come back enough to hear of it, for I feel it is all he needs to go in perfect peace. You will not, I am sure, speak of this latest development to anyone until after the young couple leave on the wedding trip you thought they were planning. Nothing must mar their glorious day and their first weeks together. It may well be that before they return we shall have brought Father home and laid him to rest close by all those who loved him so much. Washington and Emma are with us now, and will travel home with us when we come.

Then, Roxy, dear, may I stay with you in Hancock's house where you have written you are now living? I have always loved it since I watched him building it. I remember the sunset light on the water, framed by his columns. We went such a long good way together under the same roof, you and I, and nothing could please me so much now as to finish the course, if you can bear with me. I can still care for such a little house, and leave you free for your gardens. Also my eyesight is remarkably good for my years. I can sew for us, and after tea I'll read aloud, if you wish. I remember you used to surprise me by coming in to listen while I read aloud to your children when they were small.

Oh, Roxy, we have so many such beautiful memories to share, and because of them we are still among the most fortunate of women.

I do realize how busy you must be, so do not expect a letter in reply to this to be sent until next week. If, as I pray I may be, I am still here then.

The check enclosed for Orestes brings his grandparents' deep love and warm wishes for great happiness and for him and his bride throughout their life together. Tell him we hope he will spend it on the wedding trip.

When we next meet, Roxy, I shall need you very much. May God help me to make some welcome return to you for the comfort I know your presence will afford me, is the prayer of

SARAH,
Your loving
MOTHER STURTEVANT

Roxanna reached for a tablet, dipped a pen into an inkwell, and wrote as closely as she could to the blue lines on the paper:

Dear Sarah,

With the first reading of your letter of the 17*th* inst. which reached me today, I began to live again for the first time in many weeks. What you have done for me I cannot express in words. Without question you and Father have done what is best for us all, and my relief is immense. But what means most tonight is that you are coming home to me, that we shall live together again . . .

Lisa Gallico and Larry Sturtevant; September of the Year 1971

A brave little hillock reached for the sky behind the dormitory where Lisa had been assigned a room with a desk, a chair, a bed, bookshelves, and a closet with sliding doors. The desk was under the one window and the window looked into the side of the hillock which was ringed at the base with big old hemlock trees. Through this ring she could see steep outcroppings of rock where stunted, scraggly pines and bushes with roughly scalloped yellow leaves clung to the crevices. The hillock either thought it was, or was pretending to be, a mountain; and since Lisa could not see its peak from the window she was easily convinced that it was indeed a very small yet a very tall mountain and that one who climbed it would be above the tree line before reaching the top. If not, Lisa did not wish to know it.

After her first night in this room she woke early and ran to the window. Until now, of course, she had seen the mountain only in shadow, since the dormitory faced west and shut off the reflection of the sunset, and then by the gleam of a small wedge of moon and a thousand stars against which it stood like a dark fortress maintained perhaps by gremlins and other wild wee folk. Now the fort was shutting out the sunrise, grimly clutching its secrets, while all around it light flooded in. In her nightgown Lisa sat at the desk in front of the open window, her chin in her hands, one bare foot trying to keep the other warm, watching the soundless battle, wondering whether she was on the side of the mountain which fought to remain shrouded or on that of the light which was spreading steadily, inexorably, perhaps to teach the mountain and the world around it that it held nothing which need be hidden, had nothing to fear or for others to be afraid of, nothing to lose but much to gain from yielding to penetration.

Though physically apart from this struggle of the elements, as she continued to watch it she was emotionally and spiritually drawn into it, much as once from a folding chair she had overcome gravity and flown with Nureyev; and as since she had crossed limitless spaces while lying on her bed listening to music she had never heard before but now would listen to over and over and over, hearing more in it each time. She no longer felt the cold of the early morning. Now she was the mountain, proud, towering, inaccessible; now the light moving across open meadows, plumes waving, banners flying, silent drums and bugles playing, knowing no obstacle to its steady advance; now the mountain again, withdrawing majestically to a previously agreed upon impregnable position; now the light walking the water of a broad moat, surrounding the turrets, scaling the walls . . .

Just then, from the corner of her eye, she saw an altogether different kind of movement, and turned toward it curiously, almost against her will.

This was a single human figure, clothed only in dark shorts, with a mane of hair glinting red in the spreading light. He was running, but more as a deer runs, Lisa thought, than as a man does. With every bound his hair lifted and blew out behind him. And she could not fail to note that each time he ascended he seemed to pause there, as Nureyev had, though when he came down he was always far ahead of where he had been when he went up.

She heard the tap of each foot as he crossed the clay courts but on the short, wet grass of the playing field he made no sound which reached her. She watched him grow smaller and smaller, circling the base of the mountain at a considerable distance until he disappeared behind it . . .

When her attention returned to the mountain, the battle was over. Light had reached the highest turrets of the fort and flung open the gates. Now Lisa could see patches of moss in the crevices of ledges, and loose white stones lying about like flowers tossed from a basket. She could imagine that she saw small, beady eyes blinking out of tiny burrows.

She looked at her watch, tried to remember what time she had been told the breakfast bell would ring, and went to pull back sliding doors and decide what she would wear on Registration Day. The halls and showers were quiet and deserted as she ventured out and as she came back. When she was dressed, the bell still had not rung, and now she believed she had been told a rising bell would precede the breakfast bell. Since there had been no bell at all, breakfast could not be for at least half an hour.

So she went back to the window. This time she squeezed behind the desk to close it as a brisk breeze had followed the sun up and was billowing the curtains. Then she put her bed pillow on the desk top and sat on it, cross-legged, with her brief wool skirt pulled as near to her knees as she could get it and her hands burrowing into it.

She had a mountain all her own! She was monarch of a mountain! Probably no one else in the world even knew it was there, much less that it belonged to her. It was a secret mountain, but it would always be there, and as long as she had this room it would be hers to watch, to try to under-stand, to talk to, to play with . . . A thread of melody stole into her mind. She didn't know where it came from. She didn't think she had ever heard it before. It grew and pleased her, and she smiled and began to sing it softly, in syllables making strange patterns like those of an unknown but musi-cal language. Smiling, she sang low, swaying on her desk top to the rhythm.

Having decided, on his way back from the river's edge, to run over the hillock known as The Pinnacle, instead of around it, Larry glanced at the brick wall looming before him and wondered what building it was. Two years had now come between him and the little he had noted and retained about the campus from the one year he had spent there; two years which still occupied most of his thoughts and would, he supposed, until he was back to reading again. He had re-turned only yesterday, by motorcycle directly from discharge at Travis Air Base in California, and there would be no classes for upper classmen for a week. So he could run as much as he liked, and get reoriented gradually as he ran. He did not recognize Richardson Hall, a dormitory for first year women.

If Lisa had not been swaying, he would not have seen her, but the movement caught his eye and he slowed down, not aware of caring what swayed but somehow faintly astonished by rhythmic swaying at one of a hundred windows in a red brick wall.

By then it had stopped. Lisa could hardly believe her eyes.

The Runner had reappeared! The Figure was back in her landscape and in the foreground now. She could see the curly, red-gold hair sticking to his forehead, the shape of his nose and chin, his parted lips, the hollows in his neck and shoulders . . . even the grubby lacings in his old track shoes.

Larry blinked. It was uncanny. He would have sworn motion had attracted his attention. Now there was absolutely no motion. Something was there in that window, on a pedestal, like an Oriental idol *in a red pullover*. The eyes looked to him unseeing, like stone eyes.

On impulse he experimented. If it was a person, he was not interested; but if there was an Oriental idol facing a window in some University building, it was a curious thing and he would look for it again when he ran this way. So he tossed back his hair, grinned, and waved one arm at it.

In a breath, whatever it was or had been had wheeled and vanished.

In her haste Lisa had knocked over her desk chair and sat now on the side of her bed in an inner corner of the room, rubbing a bruised ankle and trembling from head to foot.

A bell rang but it seemed at a great distance. Since it was the first bell, it must be the rising bell, so there was time . . . time to try to figure out what had happened . . . what to do about the mountain that was no longer secret and so no longer hers alone . . . Only this was not the first bell. She had been so absorbed that she had not heard the rising bell when it rang, nor the footsteps of those padding past to the showers. Now the feet in the halls were shod, and all crowding toward the stairs and the cafeteria. In a daze, Lisa slung on a leather shoulder-bag and, limping a little, joined them. This was the University. This was her Registration Day.

Orestes and Grace (Hasey) Sturtevant; Year of 1910

It was Spring Week at Sturtevants' and everyone in the neighborhood who could walk was there. This was the annual fiesta, always preceding the spring work on surrounding farms and in farmhouses.

"As soon as we get back from Sturtevants'," Crowleys, Watsons, Martins and the rest had told one another comfortably through the winter as every winter, "I've got to right up the wall under the sou' west corner of the barn. It's bulging," or "I'm going to paint and paper the parlor," or "I'll plow in that seaweed I hauled from the beach last fall and spread up by the ledgehole; see if we can't have a good mess of peas for the Fourth this year," or "I wish you'd go down to the old cellar-hole and dig up some of them lilac bushes to plant by the sink drain."

But first came Spring Week at Sturtevants'.

Men and boys went there every day to plow, or to harrow land plowed earlier, or to plant sections already plowed and harrowed; to sweep down the ridgepoles to the top empty haylofts of the barns; to pick up stones, mend walls, build new fences. Women and girls were there to carry furniture to the broad porches for brushing and polishing and to hang rugs on the lines for beating while others scrubbed floors with seasand, woodwork and windowpanes with Fels-Naptha soap, and swept wet shredded newspaper off carpets; or they shone brass and copper, loosened and fertilized flower gardens, divided and transplanted perennials, cooked, served, and cleared away the noon dinner provided for everyone at long tables built of sawhorses and new boards set up on the front lawns. Men and women too feeble to do much more than get there rocked small babies and watched toddlers whose mothers had all but forgotten them in the excitement of showing and seeing how much work so many pairs of hands could turn out and of being so long so close to other women.

A shout of laughter followed the last of Orestes's tall stories, as he knocked out his pipe and strolled toward the barnyard to hitch the oxen to the drag. It was understood that nobody but Orestes ever drove his oxen. Other men, still chuckling, picked themselves off the grass and headed back to their afternoon work, several with jugs of ginger water under their arms. Some went whistling, some singing to the whistled accompaniment. Some ran, carrying half-grown children on their shoulders and shooing older ones ahead of them like so many chickens. Some drove horses, some mules. Some were still within eyeshot from the house when they bent to take up their tools — sledgehammers, pickaxes, crowbars, bush scythes and sneths — and some disappeared into the barns or pasture woods or over the rolling hills.

The women, through the open windows, watched them, the glint of pride in their eyes almost obscured by fond indulgence.

"I declare," said Eldora Martin, climbing a stepladder to get on with washing the ceiling of the front room, "up here they're all a bunch of youngones. You'd think it was Christmas and Fair Day rolled into one. Only I believe to my soul they like it better'n they would that."

"I wisht I knew how Orestes does it," said Polly Wesley. "Gits George to seem to like hard work, that is. It's a secret I'm in crying need of, a lot of times."

"You must have the same secret, Grace," said Kate Crowley. "You do it to all of us." She added hastily, "Not that anything *we* do is hard. I don't mean that."

"No, but to home we'd likely feel as if it was drudgery, and maybe grunt and groan over it," said Belle Place. "Here it's a rinktum all week long. I'm more rested when I go home at night than I am when I come in the morning. I told Roland last night I felt like going to a dance, and he said if he knew where there was one he'd take me."

"Well, you know when and where there's going to be one, so you just see to it you feel the same by then," smiled Grace Sturtevant from the doorway.

She was reminding them of the coming Saturday night when, as every spring, the old harmonium in the barn loft would have been tuned and fiddlers and drummers gathered around it to play jigs and reels while below men and women, all the young and many not so young, and boys and girls, tripped the light fantastic in streams of light from a hundred kerosene lanterns hung from the beams, and small children reluctantly fell asleep in the haymow across from stanchions where drowsy cattle, chewing their quids, stared out at the whirling figures and seemed to sway to the beat of the music. . . . When at the stroke of midnight tables from the lawn would be set up on the dance floor and laden with sliced meats, homemade bread, relishes, pies, cakes, doughnuts, and tall blue crockery pitchers of iced lemonade and hot coffee; and Sunday would begin with Orestes asking the Lord's blessing on this food and on this neighborhood.

"But I don't know as you will if you keep at it the way you have been," Grace was going on. "At this rate you'll have everything done by Friday and according to you if you stay home and rest Saturday you'll be all tired out before the dance. You know what makes this a rinktum is working all together instead of alone. So slow down a mite, while I go out and see if I can't persuade Alex to come up to the studio and take a nap now there's nothing much going on that he can watch. He's been in the same position for three solid hours and must need a change."

The other women watched her cross the grass, her shadow following, to the great half-chair, half-bed on wheels which was the only place Alex could sit, the only vehicle in which he could ride. The first-born child of Orestes and Sophronia had come to them with something wrong in his back which the best doctors in New England had not been able to make right. Alex had never walked, and now he was going on to forty years old. Before his first birthday his father had made him what they called his little chariot and Sophie had stuffed cushions with goosefeathers for it. As Alex grew Orestes had made a larger chariot every year or two and Sophie stuffed longer and wider cushions until he was eleven. After that Sophie was no longer there. Having borne Jennie when Alex was two and Roxy when Jennie was three, Sophie and another baby died at its birth in 1882. The baby was a boy, and Orestes had the name of Adams put on his little tombstone.

The older women in the Sturtevant front room remembered these things as they watched Grace, and spoke of them.

"But pretty soon it got so Orestes couldn't stand it without Sophie," said Dorcas Drew. "First he sent up to Cambridge for Affie to help him and she left Chaucer and come, but seemed as though he just got more and more beside himself until finally he started off on a trip, leaving the house to Affie to run. Now anybody that knew Orestes knew that wasn't like him. 'Course he had put Justin Crowley in charge of the farm; Justin was a young man then but steady and with a good head on him. Molly Watson was there to help Affie with the housework and the youngones. I s'pose that was how Justin and Molly come to get married later on. But Affie mostly put her mind, Molly said, on Jennie and Roxy; couldn't any of them seem to do anything with Alex, and 'course he needed a lot of help, being in his condition and eleven years old and just lost his mother and his father both. So Molly asked Affie why they didn't try to get Grace Hasey to come to look after him. Grace was seventeen that year, had been two years to the Academy and taught two or three terms of school; Molly thought she might get Alex back to reading, that he used to like to do so much of, instead of just staring out the window or at the wall as he did now, without even letting on he heard you when you spoke to him, most of the time. Affie said she'd be thankful to the Lord, so she and Molly talked to Grace, and Grace talked to Alex and he answered her, so she came and has been here ever since, a good friend to that boy if anybody ever had one."

They watched Grace standing, talking and laughing, beside the bearded man in the chariot, then go to the barn and come back with Bart Crowley, Bart's Bill and Grace's Horace tagging behind them, a barefooted pair of little boys seven or eight years old. Bart had pushed the heavy chariot out there in the late morning. Now he tipped it gently on its back wheels and started it up the hill toward Adams's old studio, Grace walking beside it, talking and laughing, and the little boys tagging along.

"I never could see, though," said Eldora, back on the stepladder, "how she put up with that New York woman Orestes brought back with him after he'd been gone a year.

Nobody else could. Affie couldn't. Within a week after they got here she was back in Cambridge with Chaucer and far as I know she never come here again until they brought her to bury. And it wasn't six months before Molly was married to Justin, starting Bart, and making it plain she was through working out. Can't even remember that woman's name now, but I can see just how she looked riding behind Orestes's sorrel pair. All ribbons and laces and veils and gold rings and bracelets."

"Name was Maude Lattimore when she married Orestes," said Dorcas, wiping down a stenciled wall. "But that was a married name. I never heard what she was born."

"A floozy, I've heard," laughed Belle.

"Judging by the airs she put on, she thought she was royalty," sniffed Eldora.

"Anyway, her first name was the one they gave to their first daughter," said Dorcas. "The one they had the next year. Then of course they had Jessica in '86. Mis' Sturtevant went back to New York to have both of them and Orestes went with her. They used to be gone at least three months so around here folks wondered if she had them or got them out of foundling shelters. But I guess they belonged in the family all right. Maude grew up looking and acting just like her mother and Jessie took after Orestes as much as a girl could."

"Jess wasn't more than sixteen when she went off, was she?" asked Eldora. "And never come back?"

"Seventeen," said Dorcas. "Born in 1886 and went in 1903. Of course that was five years after Orestes's second wife left him and they got a divorce. First divorce the Sturtevants ever had, or anybody in the neighborhood, for that matter. It was three years after he married Grace, that

Jess went. Some folks said she was going to have a baby, but it didn't show."

"A baby?" cried Polly. "Jess? I never heard that. Who'd she marry?"

"Far as anybody knew she wasn't married," said Dorcas, wringing out a cloth, stooped over the scrub pail.

"Certainly never acted married," said Eldora. " 'Course her mother sent her off to some high-and-mighty school soon as she could braid her own hair but minute she got home vacation times she was off on that pony of hers riding from clew to erring, every year taller and handsomer than the year before. I swear Jess grew up into a goddess if I ever saw one. Everybody said so. Rode like one, walked like one, looked like one. Great dark eyes that seemed as if she had a candle lit behind each one, chin strong as a man's, high cheekbones, high color, high forehead, heavy ruddy blonde hair. You never knew where she was going to pop out at you, stepping from a thicket, riding hellbent up a hill, down the choir stairs at church — she played the organ and sang like an angel — or from behind the stove at Wesley's store where generally there was only men and they only in a blizzard. Looked, rode, and walked like a goddess, sang like an angel, and rigged up most of the time like a tramp in a pair of Orestes's old overalls or work pants, maybe a ragged mackinaw he had probably thrown away, felt boots if it was cold, hip rubber boots if it was wet, like enough barefoot if it was hot. But the last year or two she was around here when she galloped into the yard on that pony for every dance, every game-party, every serenade, and every husking bee she was dressed up more, if you could call it dressed up. Generally a red dress, whether it was calico or velvet, with bare arms in summer and a fur jacket in winter, head always bare, and earrings. Kind of like a gypsy. Some said her ears were pierced."

"They said when Orestes put a horse under Jessica he lost all control of her," said Dorcas.

"Do you think he ever tried to stop her from being how she was?" Kate asked. "I've heard my mother say she thought he wanted her to have her way and hoped she'd marry one of our boys and settle down in the neighborhood. And Jess told me that when she refused to go back to school that last year, her father took her side even though Grace felt bad about it. He said Jessica was old enough to know her own mind."

"Well, funny she didn't marry one of them then," said Eldora. "Guess there wasn't one of the lot that wouldn't have been tickled pink to marry her, even the ones that had to settle, after she left, for marrying us. That year before she went, any feller that danced with me plodded around as if he was sleepwalking. Other girls said the same. Fellers were there to dance with Jess and between-times they just waited like cattle to be fed. Queer thing about it, none of us resented it and none of us blamed the fellers. Jess was like a lighthouse in a fog to all of us that year, and it wasn't until some time after she went that it came over us the beacon had been turned off and now it was up to us to get to shore best way we could."

"Nobody ever heard whatever become of her?" Polly asked.

"Grace said once she never has, beyond what Jessica told them when she left — that she was going to New York to visit her mother and Maude and then might take a trip to California. She thought Jessica wrote to her father a few times from California but he never told Grace so, and she doesn't believe he has heard anything from or about her for years," said Dorcas. "Poor Orestes! What a lot of trouble he's lived through!"

"Well, he had Sophronia," said Kate quietly. "And he's had and has still got Grace. There has to be some bitter with the sweet."

"Yes, you say, 'Poor Orestes,' Dorcas," said Paulina Merrifield, another of the older women, speaking for the first time. "What about poor Grace? Come here when *she* was seventeen and been here ever since, taking care of Alex, bringing up Sophie's Jennie and Roxy, doing what she could for wild little abandoned Jessica, having Horace when she was thirty-seven and Orestes sixty years old, and looking after everything including putting on big weddings for both Sophie's girls and then taking Roxy home to nurse for a year before she died —"

"I don't think Grace has ever felt poor, Pliny," said Dorcas. "I think she's always felt rich."

"Well, I guess that's the truth. But she's a saint if ever there was one."

"Sh-h-h," said Belle, hanging curtains. "Here she comes."

"Well, all I can say, Belle," cried Polly, "you're lucky Roly likes to dance as well as you do. If I can get George to move around the barn floor twice Saturday night I'll do well. He'd always rather stand smoking his pipe and talking with men."

"I'll lend you Ralph if you want him," offered Eldora. "He's still proud as a peacock of the jingle in his knees and would rather dance than eat. Which is something to say. But by the middle of the evening *I'll* be ready to sit down and talk to Dorcas. She still knows a lot of gossip I never heard and I aim to get it out of her."

Grace put in her head at the doorway and said, "Your

Billy's a good youngone, Kate. I asked Hoddy if he'd play around up there while Alex has a nap, so he could send word to some of us if he needed to. Horace said he didn't want to, there was nothing to do up there and he supposed he'd have to keep quiet. But Billy said right off that he'd stay, too, and he and Hoddy could be Indians. He said Indians never made a sound. Bless his heart. Such a solemn little boy but always seems contented . . . Now I'll go sprinkle the rest of the curtains. Coming out nice and white, aren't they, Belle? And not a rip in them that I've seen yet. What a hand Minnie is to wash and do up old lace!''

May 10, 1973 . . . Hi. Lisa here.

I know it's absolutely incredible what's happened to us in the year since the first time we appeared in William's diary. Okay, so I don't expect anyone to believe it. It just happens to be the truth that Larry and I have lived not only a whole lifetime in a year, but several lifetimes, beginning before the 1700's.

It all started, actually, that last chilly spring midnight when, huddled under the stadium, rolled in blankets dragged from his bed in the Psi U House, we suddenly made up our minds at the same instant that we couldn't take another day of non-life. We knew something about what living was from those two fabulous weeks during the Christmas holidays when we just rode and rode together, but that was like a survey of a country or a planet where you knew you wouldn't be allowed to stay because you had no visa; also because, as far as you could tell, nobody stayed there; everybody just rode and rode and rode. It did convince us we existed, and that was glorious; and it had filled us with a terrible hunger to get where we could find out if we still existed if we stopped for a week, a month, a year.

You see, neither of us had really lived yet. The only people I had ever watched live were Uncle Dave's family, and the nearest Larry had ever come to life was at a boys' camp with a bookish counselor named Foss. All the rest of those growing-up years we had been in Limbo, and we can tell you Limbo is a horrible place.

This was nobody's fault, you understand. If it had been a condition we could fairly blame on anybody, it would have been vastly easier to put up with and to get out of. We were sure that to have a place to put blame was the reason so many of the kids at college had worked up such hatred of the people they grew up with. We wished we had been so lucky as to have parents who were either too authoritarian or too permissive (nearly everybody we knew thought all his problems had come of one or the other, depending on which kind of parents he had) provided they had managed to stay together without killing themselves or each other, had settled down together with us at the same time some part of every twenty-four hours, and at least one of them had enough interest in us to listen when we talked to them. We used to get disgusted with the other kids and ask them what right they had to expect perfection from human beings. By comparison, we didn't think we asked for much. But it was more than we ever got. And more and more we realize that, under the conditions, we, too, were asking for more than our parents could give.

It wasn't my parents' fault that they made an impossible

marriage, that my father's faith prevented his permitting it to be dissolved, that my mother probably was a woman who should never have married any man, but didn't find that out until too late.

It wasn't Larry's father's fault that he never had any strong roots to put down, having grown up in an artificial society, only transplanted from one greenhouse to another, never forced to draw on and develop his own resources because *his* father was a Sturtevant cut off from all but the Sturtevant money at the age of eight because *his* father (dear old Orestes!) felt his boy must have the best education available in America. Nor was it Horace, Jr.'s fault that Larry's mother died before he had anything to remember her by and all those pretty ladies Horace kept bringing home as "new mothers" didn't turn out to be the mothering kind. Maybe they were like swans with too short a wingspread for the increasing brood. Or maybe Horace's mother hadn't been much for mothering, either, so he didn't know how to measure potential wingspread. Maybe he really tried to find someone who could do what he was constitutionally unable to do.

Anyway, Horace, Jr. is dead now, like Larry's mother and my father, and R.I.P. As far as we know, they did very little living while on earth, and we saw none of it. But they gave us birth, we are now fully alive, and we bubble with gratitude.

Which brings me back to William where I intended to start when I said "Hi."

The story about Spring Week at Sturtevants' in 1910 was the last entry William made in his long series of diaries. He did that during the three days I was in the hospital after Betsy came in mid-August; but I didn't see it until much later when I was taking his dictation of lots of notes on what we told each other afterward and which he hoped to put together, fill out, and enter when he felt stronger.

What a night that was when we circled through the dark of William's yard, blowing the horn and shouting that we were heading for the hospital pronto. He jumped up from beside the lamp on the kitchen table, pressed his face against the screen, and yelled — it was so funny to hear William yell! — something about an ambulance. Larry made another circle shouting, "We'll be there by the time an ambulance could get here," and by then William was on the door-rock, yelling so loud we heard every word above the roar, "Well, don't get mixed up now you're all excited! His name is Alexander!"

This was because we had been arguing for weeks about a boy's name. We wanted to name him William Crowley Sturtevant. William was just as determined that he should be named Alexander. He said later God must have shaken his head over the wilfulness of the young generation and quietly settled the controversy by sending a girl to be named (what else?) Elizabeth and called Betsy.

Of course William never called her Betsy. His Miss Elizabeth, she is.

The day after she was born, he and Flo told Larry they'd never again lift a finger to help us if we took her home to the Sturtevant house as it was then, and before night William had pedaled in to the hospital to tell me. He also brought us a bunch of goldenrod the nurses wouldn't let him take through the door, which humbled him a little but not much. He said well, he might not know about goldenrod (except he liked the color of it and it made him think of me), but nobody better try to tell him it was good for babies to be rained on in the night, or to be hit by falling plaster, beams and bricks, or to drop through the floor into the cellar.

"No, sirree," he said, standing beside my bed and twisting his old straw hat, "when you take Miss Elizabeth out of here you're bringing her straight to Crowleys'."

He went on to say Flo was giving the Crowley house a thorough cleaning, and as soon as she finished the parlor he would set up a bed for Larry and me there. The little bedroom where Bart and Kate used to sleep opened right out of the parlor, he reminded me, and that would be for Miss Elizabeth, whatever use she wanted to make of it. Flo said the floor there ought to be covered with linoleum and he would have that down by tomorrow night. Flo had brought over a crib that morning, and what she called a diaper pail, all as good as brand new.

I said, "Thank you, William. We'd love to make you a visit."

He said, "That's lucky because it may be a long visit. I don't see how we can get even a part of your house fit for Miss Elizabeth before next summer."

On his way out that day he met Larry coming in and told him that before he went home he wanted him to stop in at Wesley's. Seems William had been in looking at secondhand cars and Brian had told him what he thought was the best buy. If Larry thought the same, William was going to get it, and Brian would deliver it whenever I was ready to leave the hospital and bring us along.

"That is, if you figure you can drive the thing once you get the hang of it," William told Larry. "I'll never touch it. But if you can drive it, you can pick up what we need, and get us into the village here when we have to come. It ought to be handy all around. You can't take a baby on that motorcycle and I find pedaling harder on my leg muscles than I used to."

So Bri brought us to William's in a '69 Ford pickup, and William was right that it was going to be a long visit, for we're still here.

William isn't.

Still, he may be, in a way. I usually feel as if he is.

For a few weeks after we came he seemed the same as always except that he was constantly elated. This might have impressed us more than it did if we hadn't all been so elated. It was as if Betsy had brought along an invisible wand and cast a spell on us. Flo came every single day to help me, show me, teach me. There was always somebody devoting one ear exclusively to catch any sound Betsy made. I don't believe she ever waved a fist day or night without somebody knowing it. And we *enjoyed* her so! When she began to smile and crow, every smile or crow brought a glow to everybody's face. We didn't notice that William didn't ride his bicycle any more. Of course he didn't need it now. Larry drove him the few times he wanted to go anywhere. Mostly they worked, either up at Sturtevants' or harvesting vegetables. One day Eli came with Flo and showed Larry how to use the tractor for the fall plowing here. Next day he let Larry borrow the tractor to plow a piece on the Sturtevant side of the road. And he had lent Larry his truck to haul manure for both pieces. William helped Larry spread it. William did come in to rest a while in the middle of the morning and again in the middle of the afternoon, but I took it for granted that was really to check up on Betsy. If she was asleep he always tiptoed in to have a long look at her before he sat down in the kitchen and lit his pipe.

The very first evening after we got here, William went up

to his room and came down with a little box he gave to me, saying it was for Miss Elizabeth and I was to give it to her to play with as soon as she was old enough, but I must keep an eye on it to be sure it wasn't lost, for he wanted it passed on to our other children as they came.

I took off the cover, and I must have gasped.

The small box held a big chunk of shining, dark red glass. "What — is this, William?"

He hesitated, and then said what I somehow knew he must.

"I think's likely . . . it's Noah's red stone."

The very one the first Alexander's friend had cut from a ledge with his tomahawk and brought inside his leather jacket to drop on the infant Jamie's white counterpane . . . The Red Stone Alexander had passed around the circle of Minute Men as they planned to make his house into a garrison, telling them it was Noah's blessing on that house. *'Tis Noah's prayer to his Great Spirit . . . 'Tis Noah's promise . . . So long as ee do as ee would be done by . . . So long shall no harm come anigh ee* . . . The Red Stone which James's wife, Melura, had put on her children's pillow when they burned with fever, that James was looking at the night Alexander died . . . The Red Stone which Alexander, Jr. had so often held between his two hands in prayer, having named his first-born Noah, that America would be led closer to God and that He would show the way to freedom for this young country without war; and which his lonely Caroline had held in the same way as she prayed for his return from the prison camps and that the war might be over before their youngest, John, was old enough for soldiering . . . which Caroline had in her pocket when Alexander asked huskily outside her door, "Where is thy angel mother?"

". . . Yes, but . . . William, how do you happen to have it?
. . . Was it — left in that deserted house? Did you find it
among the crumbling papers and moldy diaries?"

"No . . . No . . . To tell you the truth, dear, I don't know
how Crowleys came by it. The last mention of it I've ever
found among Sturtevant papers was Caroline's. But it was
still at Sturtevants' when Grace married Orestes. She spoke
of it once to Kate and Kate told us about it one night at
supper. Seems Orestes had shown it to Grace then, saying
ruefully that it must have lost its power, if it ever had any,
for he and Sophie had kept it close on to a year under Alex's
pillow, but it neither made him well nor eased him into
Heaven, as Melura was sure it always did. So the night
Orestes started to build Alex's first little chariot he tossed
the Red Stone into his desk drawer where it had lain ever
since. Grace thought privately that the power might be still
there, that it was faith in the power that was lacking. Sturtevants had learned to do so much for themselves they didn't
really feel the need of dependence on the Red Stone. One
time when Hoddy had diphtheria she looked in Orestes's
desk for it and couldn't find it, so she asked him if he knew
where it was; but all he said was no, he didn't know, that he
hadn't thought of it for years. He asked her what she wanted
it for, just a piece of red glass hacked out of a ledge, and she
didn't dare tell him, knowing he would think she was a silly
superstitious woman. And Hoddy did get well. But Grace
told Kate it seemed a great pity if Orestes had thrown it
away, when it was part of the Sturtevant birthright."

"So where was it, William?"

"I can't say where it was when Grace was looking for it.
But quite a while after Bart died, when it got so I could
bring myself to do it, I went through his bureau and his

closet to see what was there that I or anybody else could still get some good out of; and in the back corner of the bottom bureau drawer there was a small pasteboard box with an elastic band around it. DON'T OPEN THIS was printed by hand on the cover and I've never opened it. But one whole side was smashed in and when I picked it up this stone fell out. I don't know whether Orestes gave it to Bart or threw it out and Bart found it. Or maybe it was still in the house after Grace died and he found it one day when he was up there and brought it home to keep it safe until he could give it to one of the Sturtevants. I can't think of any other way he could have come by it. Still none of that sounds like Bart. Or Orestes either. I can imagine Orestes throwing it away, but not Bart picking it up and bringing it home. I can't imagine Orestes standing in the barn or field with Bart, taking a stone out of his pocket and saying, "My folks used to swear by this but it didn't do anything for Alex so it's no good. You can have it if you want it," and Bart saying, "Well, much obliged, I'm sure," bringing it here and hiding it in a box he had labeled DON'T OPEN THIS. Doesn't make sense any way you look at it, does it? . . . Well, no matter. It's here, I put it in another box, and it belongs to Miss Elizabeth and other children you and Larry have."

I said, "Yes . . . Yes, I suppose it does. . . . Thank you, William."

Larry was as incredulous as I was. It seemed like a miracle. I sewed a little pocket for it in a corner of each of Betsy's crib sheets (she doesn't have a pillow) and changed it over each time I washed a sheet. William was pleased.

Much that happened in our first few months here is still incredible to us, and some of the rest seemed like miracles, too. Perhaps it all was, actually.

Day after day was beautiful, and the evenings were always exciting.

In the evenings William told us more about Grace, Larry's great-grandmother.

He said he had always noticed how much good she did everybody by speaking so freely of what they did well and what was nice about them, and that everybody knew this and thought she must be just about the most wonderful woman in the world; still they all seemed dedicated to not "letting on" to her they thought so or ever said so to one another. As if they meant to do her a good turn by not spoiling her.

William said one night, "I do dear hope *somebody* broke down before she died and told her she was a saint; but I don't know. If anybody did, it was probably Kate because they were closer friends every year Grace lived, but it would have been awful hard for Kate to get out anything like that. If nobody did tell her, Grace never suspected it and must have taken quite a start when St. Peter gave her his arm to lean on, walking through the pearly gates."

I wrote that down as soon as he went to bed that night. I was thinking that, as far as I'd heard, if Kate loved Grace she was the only one Kate loved except Bart and William. And I marveled at Kate being able to love her two men so much, so long, so loyally, so unquestioningly while they loved and thought and talked and wrote about so many other people, generation after generation of them, through all those warm summer evenings and all those cold winter nights. I said this to Larry, in bed, and added, "Because there was some bond between Bart and William that she didn't have with either of them. You can tell. And if there was, Kate sensed it."

Larry said, "Right," into my hair. "So Kate must have

gone through those pearly gates just like William says my great-grandmother did."

"I hope she did love Grace because who else did Kate have up there until Bart came? Just her tiny little baby? But Grace had so many to get acquainted and reacquainted with, — all her own and all the old Sturtevants, to say nothing of Orestes and Alex and her other step-children. Do you think she found time for Kate, too?"

"If she found it for everybody while she was here," Larry said sleepily, "why wouldn't she there?"

William told us Orestes outlived all his children he ever had any contact with after they grew up, except Hoddy; and Orestes and Grace saw very little of him. Hoddy entered Harvard Law School when he was nineteen and after that he spent all his vacations abroad; married an English girl when he was twenty. Roxy had died in 1905, Jennie in 1915, Alex in 1918. Orestes began to fail, William said, as soon as Alex was gone, but lived until 1922. He was eighty-two years old then, and William nineteen so he remembered Orestes well, and remembered Hoddy and his wife coming to the funeral. They'd been married only a few months then. His wife was taller than he was, with big blue eyes and short blonde hair and cheeks the color of wild roses. He never saw her again. Word came that Horace, Jr. was born the next year in New York. Hoddy came to Grace's funeral but his wife didn't come with him, nor anybody else. If any of them came to see Grace after Orestes died, William didn't know about it and he thought he would have, because Crowleys — Bart, Kate, and William — were up there a good deal, doing what she needed to have done. By then most of the other ones Sturtevants had depended on had either died or moved away. Grace couldn't keep up the place as it had been, of course. She sold off all the stock, the pastures filled up with pine as time went on, and, best Bart and William could do, more of the fieldland grew up to wolf grass every year, and then to juniper, old roofs collapsed and buildings had to be torn down. By the time Grace went to a nursing home, where she spent the last year of her life, about all she had was the house and that was in only fair condition. It had all got to be just too much for what Sturtevants and Crowleys there were left. If Hoddy ever came to see Grace at the nursing home in Portland — where she said Hoddy wanted her to be; when her doctor telephoned him from the hospital how she was, she said, he asked what was the best nursing home in the state and then said she was to be taken there — she never told Kate so. Bart took Kate to the train many times that year and she rode to Portland and walked a mile or so to where Grace was; this was a long day's trip for Kate and at first she was all nerved up every time she started out, but gradually she got used to it. Grace did tell Kate she got letters from Hoddy sometimes. And Bart did, too, about looking after the place, until some years after Grace died, when he wrote that Horace would be the one to contact now because he, Hoddy, was going to California to live. He never said anything about his wife, and Grace hadn't, so Crowleys didn't know whether she was still living and with him.

"I never heard much about her, either," said Larry. "Maybe she died. I saw a picture of her once. Taken when she was young. Quite a doll. But I don't believe she's with him now. The address I had for him when I wrote for the key was a club in San Francisco. I think it's a men's club. One of those that members live in."

We told William about how the thought of the Sturtevant

place came to Larry on our bike when we headed north from Florida that time. We were still resolved to stick it out on campus until the end of the year. We knew well enough we might never make it, when we were so desperate to stay just as we were then, together all by ourselves, sky over our heads and wind in our ears, far, far away and hidden from everyone we had ever known; but the one thing we were determined on was that we would try; we would find out what was the absolute limit we could stand. We made solemn promises to each other in a church in St. Augustine, among a flower-woman's baskets in Charleston, on a ledge in the Blue Ridge Mountains. . . . But by then Larry had remembered hearing of this farm that belonged to his grandfather and that nobody had made any use of or even seen for years and years; and we thought, "Why not try to get the key to the door?" So the first thing Larry did after getting back to the campus was to go to the office for his grandfather's address to which his bills had been sent since his father died, and then to write there to ask if he had the key and, if so, could we (Larry) have it because he would like to go up there and see the old place.

We told William how excited we were when the key came, and how relieved that his grandfather didn't write a word. There was just that big old brass key rattling around in the kind of box optometrists mail glasses in. It was almost as good as having found it beside a bush or in roadside gravel. We told William how we went to a grocery store and got a little can of polish and polished that key until it shone like gold. Then we put it on a double strand of yarn I was knitting a sweater with and Larry tied it in a hard knot around my neck. It was never taken off after that until he took it off, when we got here, to put into the lock.

I could see Larry was still thinking about the bike. He often is, even now he has the pickup. Says he's never going to turn it in, and I don't want him to. It's part of us. It's even part of Betsy now. Larry says when nobody can get it started he's going to frame it. Actually, he has a real plan for recessing it behind plate glass in the gable end of the old studio when we rebuild that. He says, wouldn't Alexander, Jr. have liked such a bike to do his circuit riding on? How he would have torn around the country then, and into and out of wars, spreading his gospel!

It must have been around the middle of October when we noticed that William didn't go outside much except on the warmest days and then mostly sat on an old milking stool just inside the open barn door. Other days he lay on the kitchen couch, watching me and talking about Betsy. And he never went upstairs now except to go to bed. When he did go he went slowly, both feet on each step. But we must have thought he was just tired from staying up so late, and from being so happy all the time. We never spoke of it to each other until later.

About then he began trying to convince Larry he should write to his grandfather, tell him how we had found the place, what we had done about it so far, and especially that we had Betsy. Larry said he had no reason to suppose his grandfather, out there in his club in California, would be in the least interested in any of it.

William said, "You could be wrong, boy. I never saw much of Hoddy after he was ten years old, but I liked him then, and he's a human being, a Sturtevant, and an old man. It's my guess an old man with his inheritance could get pretty lonesome in a California club, and do a good deal of thinking about how we used to slide down Cider Hill on barrel staves in winter and dive naked off the ledge into the Big Hole on hot days . . . Besides, I take it the Sturtevant place is still in his name. What's going to become of it when he dies? And that bike of yours maybe all glassed in at the top of the old studio!"

Larry hunched one shoulder. He does that when he is getting pushed into a corner. The way we felt about William, it was hard to refuse to do whatever he wanted. Even if there was a good, sound reason.

"Wouldn't know where to write to the old guy," he mumbled. "Didn't keep his address."

"I kept the box the key came in, Lar," I said. "His address may be on the box."

"The box?" William exclaimed. "You did? Where is it?"

I was afraid it might take me some time to find it, but it didn't. The address was there, plainly typewritten on the label. I handed the box to William. He put on his glasses, squinted at it, nodded, and tossed it onto the table in front of Larry.

"There you are," he said. "Go at it."

But Larry shook his head. He wouldn't touch the box.

"Sorry, William. Can't do it. Bound to look as if I'm asking for favors, and I don't want anything of any of them. I'm free and I intend to stay that way. Just want to do what I can for the place before anybody stops me, whoever it belongs to."

"None so blind as them that won't see," said William. "You wouldn't be asking a favor. You'd be doing one — for Hoddy and for the old neighborhood. Including me."

But Larry kept on shaking his head and said he thought he'd better go to bed.

Before I followed him I told William, "I'll see what I can do with him."

So William was the last one up in the house that night. I lay beside Larry and listened to the scratching of a pen in the kitchen. I knew Larry wasn't asleep and must hear it too.

"He's writing himself to your grandfather, Lar."

"Okay, okay," growled Larry. "I don't care who writes to him. As long as I don't."

The next afternoon William asked Larry to take him into the village and he did. I think we both thought that if he didn't William would start out on his bicycle. I expected they would be right back but they were gone almost three hours. When they came at last William looked pale and tired. I took off his tie and gently pushed him onto the couch.

"What were you doing down there so long?" I scolded. "Gossiping with Bri and Elaine and everybody else you met?"

He grinned at me.

"Man has to talk with somebody, once in a while, beside a couple of crazy kids and a babe-in-arms."

I followed Larry into the shed where he parks the pickup.

"You took him to the post office?"

"Yes."

"Where else?"

"To the doctor's."

"The *doctor's!*"

"And then to the drugstore. And then to the lawyer's. And then to the parsonage to see Mr. Standish."

"Oh, what — did you go with him to these places?"

"No. He said every time he got out, 'I'll be right back in a few minutes.'"

We were both worried then. And we were puzzled. We didn't say so, and didn't need to. We just stood there looking consternation at each other.

Suddenly I realized that Betsy might wake up any minute and if she did and we weren't there William would be off that couch and beside her crib in about one second flat. So I ran back into the kitchen.

Betsy hadn't waked. The whole house was quiet except for the low hum of the teakettle. William lay there grinning at me.

"Now I s'pose you've wormed it out of Larry that I had him take me to the doctor's."

"What's the matter with you, William? What did he tell you?"

"Nothing I didn't know before he told me. Says I've got a tired heart. Anything that's been running as long as that has a right to be tired, I told him. What I was there for, I said, was to get something for shortness of breath that's been plaguing me lately. He clapped me on the back and give me a paper to take to the drugstore, so now I've got this." He stuck a thumb and forefinger into his jacket pocket and pulled out a brown bottle. "Ammunition!" he said, chuckling. "I'm going to get up and take one of these pills and right off I'll likely start feeling like a boy again."

By the time we'd had supper his color was back and he seemed quite like himself. While I was rocking Betsy and singing her to sleep, Larry started washing the dishes and by the way they were talking I knew William was drying them, as usual, so I called out, "William, you go lie down. You've done enough for one day."

He promptly appeared at the bedroom door, peering sharply into the dark room and slatting a dish towel.

"Now what kind of a lullaby is that, Miss Elizabeth?
You tell your mother if she doesn't change her tune we're
both going to get mad and racket all night. You tell her
we're going to lie down when we're ready and not before
and if she doesn't hush her mouth, if I ever go into the
village again I'll go on my bicycle and maybe take you on the
handlebars."

The dishes were done when I got back to the kitchen and
he and Larry were sitting at the table, talking.

"First thing to do is set priorities," William was saying.
I poured the last of the coffee and joined them.

"If, as you both say," William went on, "you want to bring
as much of the old neighborhood back as you can, it's going
to take a long time. We've got to be patient and not champ
at the bit, take first things first and do it little by little. This
winter is the time to plan and start getting ready. Being as
you're here, you're in no great need of a Sturtevant house fit
to live in. Not so much, to my way of thinking, as you and
everybody else needs to have that old meetinghouse fit to go
into on Sunday mornings; not near. Thing is, we've got to
get one of them to where it can wait while we get the other
one braced up. Unless you save both of them — the first
Alexander's house and the third Alexander's meetinghouse
— then Holdfast's library, Adams's studio, and Orestes's
barns won't mean a thing. Now what I'm in *hopes* — I'm in
hopes the meetinghouse is so used to hanging there on one
wooden pin that it will keep on hanging until late next spring,
after we've got a new roof over the old part of your house
and new sills under it and the foundation shored up. Then
you can let *that* hang while we look to the meetinghouse. I
was in talking with your Mr. Standish today about the meetinghouse, and he's quite interested. Says he's going to try to

drive out to look at it before snow flies and when he does he'll call in here afterwards and let us know what he thinks."

"I doubt if Mr. Standish knows much about construction," said Larry.

"Of buildings, maybe not," William said. "But I figure he can tell better than we could whether what the third Alexander left us is still housed there."

Now we knew why he had gone to the doctor, the drugstore, and the parsonage. He never admitted that he had called on the lawyer, nor been to the post office.

Though it was a tacit admission of this last when he showed us, some ten days later, the contents of the envelope with airmail and Special Delivery stamps which I had brought him from the mailbox an hour or so before.

By then there had been a significant change. Larry and I had moved into Kate's room with Betsy, and Larry had brought down the furniture from William's chamber and put it in the parlor.

Making up our minds to suggest this to William was one of the hardest things we have ever done. But as every night he put off longer and longer going to bed and then took longer and longer climbing the stairs we knew we had to do it. Every night we fell asleep planning the best approach, choosing the words and phrases we would use in the argument we expected and deciding which would be mine and which Larry's. But it turned out there was no argument at all.

One morning at breakfast I said, "William, it was so cold last night getting up to feed Betsy that we decided Larry will move our bed into her room this afternoon so we'll have some heat from the kitchen. While he's about it, why doesn't he bring your bed down to the parlor? Then we'll all be on one floor for the winter."

William just said, "Sounds like a good idea. I'd been thinking we'd have to set up the chunk stove in the parlor before long. This way we can let that go until around Christmas time, if we want to."

I thought his eyes fairly shone as he watched Larry that afternoon. When I had his bed made up he sat on the side of it, reached up to give the pillow a pat, and said, grinning, "Now we'll be snug as four bugs in a rug."

Dear William!

He hadn't yet begun going in there to lie down afternoons when his letter came, but he went in there to read it, and stayed a long time; didn't come out until he heard Larry come in to lunch. Then without a word he handed Larry the letter and stood by the stove, spreading his hands over the warmth of the lids. I was beside him, frying pickerel Larry had caught in the brook that morning after a heavy rain the night before; he didn't look at me. His eyes were on Larry, but when Larry began to fold the sheet William said, "Now let Lisa read it."

The letter said:

Dear Bill,

Good to hear from you after all these years.

Glad one of Horace's is taken with the old place there. It never meant anything to Horace and it is a long time since I thought much about it. While Mother was alive I used to tell myself that some time I'd spend another summer there, try out the swimming hole, etc. But I never did. Now we're too old for that kind of business, eh, Bill? But maybe Horace's boy has got some of his great-grandfather in him. The Old Man's whole life was always in that farm, as I recall. I used to wonder, when I went down from school, what kept him there, shut away from the world. It wasn't as if he had never seen the world. The farm seemed to me a kind of prison in those days. Now I incline to think we all live in prisons and each man chooses his own, consciously or not.

You can tell Larry I'm having the deed to what is left of the Sturtevant place transferred to him and his deed will be sent to him by registered mail. I have always paid the tax on it and will continue to as long as I live if he will forward the bill to me. I have always felt I did this for my mother, I don't know exactly why. Thus it will be my pleasure if he is willing for me to continue.

I have never seen any of Horace's children since they were small. Some of them I've never seen. I settled out here in the early 1950's, haven't been back East since, and none of them ever came where I am. Still it was a shock to me when word came of Horace's death. He was the only one I had, you know. No wonder this Larry didn't want to write to me. He doesn't know me, and I don't know him. But I lived on the Sturtevant place as a child and I am rather surprised by the satisfaction which comes from knowing that a Sturtevant has lived on it this summer and wants to live on it permanently. I might find this difficult to believe if anyone but you had told me. But you say you know the boy well, and swear by him and his wife, and that is good enough for me. So they have a child, too, and named her Elizabeth. That would have pleased the Old Man. I've heard my mother say that if they had had a daughter they would have named her Elizabeth.

Until you told me, I did not realize that this boy was not staying on at college to get his degree. That seems to me a mistake, but a mistake that can be remedied. If you think best, tell him that if he will take whatever courses he needs to meet the requirements for a degree, he is welcome to send these bills to me also. I was glad to take over from his father the financial responsibility for his formal education, and should like to complete it. Use your own judgment also as to whether or not to tell him that I should appreciate an opportunity to contribute from time to time to the project he is undertaking, if someone will let me know what has been, is being, or is about to be done. Possibly you will feel it is best that correspondence regarding these matters be between you and me. Either way, it would be of considerable interest to me to be informed, and I have all too little these days to quicken my interest.

I should be happy to hear from you again any time, Bill. As I would be to hear from my grandson and/or his wife if they care to write.

May I express here my deep appreciation of the Crowleys' constant kindness to Sturtevants through many generations, and especially of your invaluable service to these young people who came to you entirely unknown and surely in need of what you have given them.

With all good wishes and hoping that somehow we may meet once more,

Sincerely yours,
HOD.

I began to fold the letter. Since William had come into the kitchen the only words which had been spoken were his, "Let Lisa read it now." Over the folded letter I looked at Larry and then at William. After that "Hod," Larry's widened eyes and puzzled expression (with no trace of the cold obstinacy which I had been afraid I would see there) and the pure bliss shining on William's face were the last straw. I burst into tears.

William said, "Now what's all this about?"

Larry, pulling me against him so that I felt his half-indulgent, half-irritated sigh, said, "It's what women do. First."

"I never saw Kate do it in my life," said William. "Not even right after her baby died."

"Yeah?" said Larry, all indulgence now. "Well, this is a Lisa woman."

"I'm crying because I'm happy," I sobbed out as soon as I could. "Because there really was a little Hoddy, and William did go sliding and swimming with him, and out there in his California club he still remembers it and William, and so Larry's grandfather isn't just a signature or an address but a real living, breathing, feeling person. Our Orestes was his own father, and the saintly Grace his own mother, and it's all so — so — so *beautiful!*"

"She'll be all right now," Larry assured William.

"And none too soon," said William, extracting a spatula from under some spoons on the tank cover and digging into the frypan. "Fish is catching on."

I took the spatula away from him and put our lunch on the table. We talked all through lunch, all afternoon, and late into the evening.

By then it had been decided that William would answer Hod's letter and enclose notes from Larry and me. William would tell him his ideas on how we should start on the reconstruction of the Sturtevant house and the third Alexander's church. Larry would thank him for wanting him to have a deed to the place, and say he would think about getting the rest of his college credits but that he probably would not want to take time off for it until he had at least a couple of buildings to where they could wait safely until he got back to them. I would tell him about Betsy.

The next morning when William got up, he said maybe Larry should get the chunk stove set up in the parlor as soon as he could. It was all right there for sleeping but too cold to sit and write and he needed peace and quiet if he was going to fill Hod in on all that was going on in the heads at Crowleys' this winter. So the two of them spent the day on that chore, Larry hauling and heaving and William directing and lending a hand. It was wonderful how warm the wood-fire had the room by nightfall.

That evening, William sat at a table in there and wrote to Hod, and Larry and I wrote to him at the kitchen table. We never saw what William wrote, but I read Larry's note and, as I expected, it was pretty stiff, as Hod's had been. That may be the Sturtevant way in correspondence. I wondered, if Larry had ever written me a letter, if it would have been like that. I can't imagine it, but I don't know. Anyway, the stiffness on his single page set me off and I rambled over four pages, first about Betsy, then about how we found the Sturtevant house when we got there, how we lived in it, and how William made us bring Betsy to spend the winter at Crowleys'. I even told him what I'd thought many times — that we really needed to practice being Crowleys for a while before we tried to go any farther with being Sturtevants because when you haven't really known who you were all your life and want to begin being somebody, it is easier to learn to be Crowleys, with William right here as teacher. Besides, the Crowley way of life is simple. I said William was also telling us a great deal about the Sturtevants, and we were terribly proud of them, but they sure seemed complicated, especially since now there were only shreds of them left here. I also told him Larry and I had gone skinny-dipping off his ledge into his Deep Hole and by another winter we'd take Betsy sliding on Cider Hill.

Maybe you wonder how we began our letters. Well, Larry's began, "Dear Grandfather"; but I started mine:

Dear Hod,

I hope you don't mind my calling you by your nickname. I've always wished I had a nickname. If I had, I'd want everyone to call me by it. Besides, William showed us your letter to him and that is how you signed it. And I just can't think of you as a grandfather. Maybe that is because I never had a grandfather I knew and so don't know what a grandfather is. But I think it is more because when William talks about you you are never more than ten years old . . .

We gave our letters to William the next morning and he sealed them with his into a big, addressed envelope which Larry drove into town to send airmail.

And who do you think was the next to get mail from California? ME!

It was a package with an envelope pasted on top. I opened the envelope first.

It said:

Dear Liz,

Glad to hear from you. If I could write as freely as you do, you might feel as well acquainted with me as I feel I am with you. But I don't have that gift. The best I could think of to do, as a return for your delightful letter, was to go out and buy a camera and a roll of color film and take some pictures of the building where I live, of the roses in our courtyard, of the doorman who lets residents and their guests in and out; and then have the doorman take one of me. Now you will at least know what a grandfather looks like and where he lives. I have put these prints, the camera, and some film into a box and am sending it along, as you may already know if you opened the box first. Somehow I suspect that you didn't. I suspect my new granddaughter is more interested in what I may say than in what I might be sending her. You may already have a camera but again my suspicion is that you do not, else you would have sent me a picture of Betsy, if not of all of you. In any case, I beg you to do the latter as soon as possible.

I shall be writing to Bill shortly and to Larry as soon as I have his deed to enclose.

Bless you, my dear, for your spontaneity. There is no doubt in my mind that you are indeed someone already.

HOD

Hod is a very small man, carefully shaved, with thin, cleft cheeks, squinting eyes, and a willful shock of snow-white hair. He stands there beside a rose bush, bareheaded, wearing a light blue turtleneck jersey, what look like tan chinos, and brown sandals. He seems to be thumping his knee with a rolled-up newspaper. You can almost believe he has never grown since his tenth birthday, in any way but older, and that all this time he has been waiting to be released from some spell. Behind him, what you can see of the facade of his club appears enormous, towering, even menacing . . . Then here is the doorman at the entrance, reversing everything because he is big, burly, quite young, almost filling the doorway in his red uniform, flashing white buttons and white tabs with gold fringe on his shoulders, diminishing the clubhouse from the proportions of a Bastille to those of a county jail. You sense that if ever he tells Hod, "You can't enter here," Hod cannot enter; and if ever he says, "You cannot leave here," Hod cannot leave. It is frightening.

Of course Larry and I took pictures of everyone in the house that afternoon, and William took some of the three of us. To use one of William's favorite expressions, this was done none too soon. It was the last day William was up and dressed. He had always before been out as soon as I had breakfast ready. When he hadn't come by the time we finished eating, Larry went and tapped on his door.

I heard William's, "Come in," and Larry's, "What is it — too cold in here to get out of bed?"

William said, "I guess it is a mite chilly."

Larry said, rattling dampers, "Fire didn't last through the night. I'll start one."

But even after the fire had been going there for half an hour and Larry was splitting wood in the shed, William still hadn't come out, as I tapped on his door and he said, "Come in." He was still in bed, lying on his back, but turned his head to smile at me. He didn't look different than he had before, but he was all over very quiet.

I asked him if I should bring in his breakfast, now the room was warm.

He said, "Just some coffee, maybe. And a piece of toast."

So I took that to him and he said to put it on the stand, beside his glasses, and when it was handy to bring him the picture of Hoddy and my letter from him.

Later I found he had eaten the toast but drunk only a little of the coffee.

He pulled on pants and a sweater over his nightshirt to come out to lunch, but he didn't eat much and went right back to bed. I started making him a bathrobe out of a double blanket that had been Kate's.

In the middle of the afternoon I took in some tea and a cookie.

When I went back for the cup, I said, "You don't feel very well today, do you, William?"

He smiled again and said, "Just lazy. I've been thinking about Hoddy. I wish I'd seen that letter you wrote to him. He was tickled with that, wa'n't he? You written to him again?"

"Not yet. I'll show you the letter when I do. But William,

you don't know what lazy is. Tell me just how you feel and let me call the doctor."

He shook his head.

"The doctor's doing all I need. I've got his pills right here in my nightshirt pocket and I take one every once in a while, as he said. He told me I might have an off day and if I did just to stay quiet until it passed."

"Then you shouldn't have come out for your lunch."

"Oh, that was good for me. I had quite a nap after I got back. Don't you worry. Just go along with your work."

So I went back to stitching on the bathrobe, pleased Flo had helped me get the hang of using Kate's sewing machine.

He came out again towards dark, to watch Betsy rolling from side to side on the patchwork quilt I had spread on the floor. I showed him what I had done on the machine and he seemed pleased but faintly doubtful.

"Well, now," he said, "I never had me one of them before."

I told him it wouldn't have any buttons because I didn't know how to make buttonholes, but I'd make him a sash to hold it together.

He turned down the corners of his mouth.

"A *sash!* What's an old feller like me doing with a *sash?*"

I said, "There are sashes and sashes. This will be a man's sash," and folded my sewing, pushed the machine past Betsy into a corner, and started supper.

He ate better that night than he had during the day, then lay on the couch and we all talked and talked.

After that for several weeks everything went much the same. Every night Larry put a big chunk in William's stove, and before we had our breakfast went in to feed the coals. I hunted up feather pillows I could pile against the headboard of his bed to make him comfortable sitting up to eat his breakfast and to read. He came out to lunch, proud of his bathrobe, swinging the red tassels I'd put on the ends of the sash to make Betsy turn her bright eyes from side to side and wave at them with curled fists; and then slept most of the afternoons, Cat asleep beside him. But he was always out for supper and the evenings, full of questions and plans.

I wrote again to Hod and gave William my letter to read. William wrote to him, bolstered up in bed, his paper supported by a magazine, but didn't tell us what he had written. Hod answered our letters; Larry's copy of his deed came; and when Larry answered he had our pictures to enclose. Hod was touchingly pleased with those pictures and wrote that he was having the best one of William and the best one of "the three Sturtevants" enlarged and framed together. In a way, our lives during those weeks centered around Hod, and in my letters I tried to show him that, hoping he would feel it, and no longer be all alone with that giant of a doorman.

I told William how the pictures from California made me feel. I told William everything, just about, that I thought and felt. I'm not sure anyone, even Larry, ever has or ever will know me as well as William did.

He used to say, "I know what you mean." And sometimes he added thoughtfully, after a minute, "Know *just* what you mean."

I remember he said that after he asked me if I didn't think it was high time I wrote to my mother and I said, "Yes, but I can't. I can't let her know where I am. My mother is impulsive. She's unpredictable. If she knew where I am she might ride in here in a taxicab any day. I'm not ready for that yet."

A few days later he said, as if that conversation had never been broken off, "I've thought of a way you could let your mother know you're all right without running the risk of having to see and talk with her. Couldn't you write to the Gallicos? Either to your Aunt Teresa if you think there is a chance she may be still living, or to one of her children that seems most likely to have stayed on in that town where you used to visit them? They sound like people who would be glad to hear from you, no matter how long it had been since they did. But not like people who would rush to let your mother know they had. Chances are they no longer know where she is, anyway. Put 'Please Forward' on the envelope, and urge whoever gets your letter to answer."

Suddenly I was excited by the possibility of getting a letter from somebody in Uncle Dave's family.

"Why, Sweet William, that's an *idea!* It would be fun to hear from them. Any of them. Even horrid old Joe. Why, it might be as much fun as hearing from Hod!"

"Might be, at that," said William. He added, "And what I was thinking, I was thinking that maybe, in time, you could write to your mother and tell her you're all right, married and all, and send the letter to the Gallicos to mail to her, from some town around there. So she wouldn't know any more than she does now about where you are, or even what your name is now, unless or until you want her to. But it would relieve her mind."

I didn't believe my mother worried about me, rather that her relief had already come from not having to think about me at all.

But I was more than willing to write to a Gallico. And the Gallico I chose to write to was Armand, the boy who had gone with me to put flowers on our grandparents' graves, the one Aunt Teresa had stoutly maintained was getting ready to be a priest.

And so he was!

My letter addressed to him was forwarded to him in a seminary in Montreal and within two weeks I had a reply.

My dear cousin Lisa,

It is a pleasant surprise to hear from you. It has been a long time since you visited us on the farm. I note that you have married, and have a child. May every blessing be yours throughout your life. I should be much pleased if you would send me a recent picture of you and your family.

My father died soon after you saw him last, and my mother last year. May they rest in peace, these two lifelong adherents to the faith.

My mother lived with Joe after the farm was sold, but until the last few months paid annual visits to all those of her children who have made their homes in the vicinity. She was proud of her twenty-seven grandchildren and three great-grandchildren. Several more of both have been added to the roster in the past year.

I am this year completing my studies for the priesthood and hope to be assigned a parish next summer.

Now that we are in contact again, let us endeavor to remain in touch. It is pleasant to know I have a cousin in the States, especially in the State of Maine which I have long wished to see.

I pray for your blessing daily.

> With all kind thoughts,
> ARMAND J. GALLICO

So there are all the Gallicos much as they were, cheerily following their appointed ways, with Armand giving them what little direction they need. It is a growing joy just knowing that, and thinking of them up there across the border; like lying in bed on a very dark summer night and knowing the daisies and buttercups you ran through this afternoon are still dancing in the meadow and if you should get up and run out they would bounce against your bare legs and the dew would feel fresh and cool to your feet. But I am a Sturtevant now, and it is Sturtevants who need me.

During those weeks in the late fall Flo and Eli came often to spend an evening with us, after learning that evening was William's best time of day. William would sit here in his bathrobe and the moccasins Larry got for him so he need not bend down to tie shoelaces, or he would lie on the couch; but he was always the one who kept the talk going. What one didn't remember about what the old ones used to say, about when the older boys came back from war in Europe and took a look around their fathers' farms and went away again, about floods and blizzards and the tornado that blew Albert Hasey's pigpen through his parlor windows, another reminded him of. They were great evenings.

When Flo followed me into Kate's room to look at Betsy, I'd ask, "Do you think I should try again to get William to let me talk to the doctor?"

Flo said, and kept on saying, "Leave it to Bill, Lisa. He prob'ly knows what he wants. Just do as he asks you to."

After the Indian summer afternoon in November when Mr. Standish drove out with his wife and sister to look at the meetinghouse ruins and called in here on their way home — William was still asleep and Larry was up at the Sturtevant place so there was no one to talk to but me — they came again the next week, very late in the day, to talk with William and I made them stay to have supper with us, Larry promising he would drive downtown with them when they had to go, to be sure they got safely home. That evening we all got very excited about the meetinghouse, and Mr. Standish said a young man who was studying for the ministry had lately moved into his parish and we might be able to get him to hold services for us Sunday mornings when the church was safe to assemble in. Mr. Standish said prayers with us before they left, and that night William stayed up late, writing to Hod.

The next time the Standishes came it was evening and they were riding with the Corsons — Jim and Sue. Jim is the theological student. They had come here to live when Sue got a job in the hospital as soon as she finished her nurse's training. We all took to the Corsons on sight. Jim is tall and lean and homely, makes you think of Abraham Lincoln. Sue is minuscule, blonde, looks like some wildflower a breeze would cut down; but she's strong as an ox, as I soon found out. They said they had already been out to our meeting-house and they were excited about it, too. Jim said he would have some free days in the spring and was handy with tools; he would help Larry when they could get together. Flo and Eli happened to be there that same night and Eli cleared his throat and said maybe he could give them a hand as soon as he was through with plowing. Finally we sang some hymns, with Sue leading us — that bit of a thing has a voice like an organ — and Jim prayed and Mr. Standish said, "Now may the Lord be with thee and me while we are absent one from another. In Jesus' name, we ask it."

William said the next morning that he'd had the best night's sleep he'd had in years. As far as I know, I didn't sleep a wink. All of a sudden, I felt too alive to sleep, and it seemed the same with Larry. Still, we felt so peaceful. Like you can imagine Adam and Eve did at first, lying beside each other among the ferns.

Then the Corsons and the Standishes and the Martins got into the habit of coming every Monday night, and when Larry was downtown and Bri and Elaine inquired for William he told them about this so Bri and his wife and their teenagers, Kathy and Une, and Elaine and her widowed brother Ron and his three little boys began to come. Every Monday William looked as if it was Christmas. He just loved seeing his kitchen filled with people, especially people who were his friends. We talked and talked, and then we ate — the women always brought cake or cookies; sometimes somebody brought ice cream, because it was always a treat for William; and I made coffee and cocoa — and at the end we sang, sometimes Jim talked to us and sometimes it was Mr. Standish, and then the other one prayed or asked a blessing. Nobody else said anything out loud but you could almost hear us all saying inside, "Thank you, Lord. Thank you, Jesus."

After a while Christmas actually came. Christmas Eve we hung Betsy's stocking behind the kitchen stove. It was a big sock William used to wear, he said, inside felt boots when he was going into the woods in winter. Together the three of us stuffed it with a big orange in the toe, then a rattle, some buttons I'd strung, soap animals Larry had found in a store, a funny-looking little teddybear I'd made, a small box of blocks William said was the first Christmas present he could remember getting, a bonnet Flo had crocheted, a bracelet from Mrs. Standish with "Elizabeth" engraved on it, and, sticking out of the top, Sue's cloth doll with yellow yarn hair.

Thinking William wouldn't be out in the morning, we

gave him that night what we had for him — two dozen big clear colored prints of pictures Larry had taken, two of them just great of Betsy and the rest close-ups of various parts of the Sturtevant house and the meetinghouse which William had kept saying he only wished he could get up there to check out; and a new bathrobe of a luscious dark red velour so thick that I'd had to sew most of it by hand because the old machine kept getting stuck on it.

He put on the robe as soon as I gave it to him and beamed at us, saying, "By zounds, this one is royal."

Snatching the one he had just taken off so I could wash it (the last time I had, he stayed in bed two days before I could get it dry), I told him it was going to be more royal when I had put on the gold braid that was still waiting in the old wooden piggin I use as a sewing basket. I said:

"But there hasn't been time for that yet, and you just had to have this to wear tomorrow night when the folks come. After I wash it I'll sew on the braid. Man as handsome as you *ought* to have a royal robe, Sweet William."

And I hugged him, and kissed him on his thin brown cheek.

When he opened the envelope that had the prints in it, he sat right down at the table and spread them out under the lamp, studying one after another. You knew from his face how he loved the two of Betsy, but when he began looking at the others he became completely absorbed, as if they were telling him a hundred things he had been longing to know.

Finally he leaned back in his chair, rubbing his eyes, and said, "Well, now, you and I've got to go over these together, real careful, Larry. And before tomorrow night, too, so we can discuss them with Jim and Eli and Bri. And the next day, soon as the stores open, I want you to order another full set for me to send to Hod."

Larry glanced at me. I nodded at him.

He said, "We sent him a set with a Christmas card, William. He probably already has it by tonight."

I had thought we ought to give the first set to William as soon as the rolls of film were developed, to be certain he saw them. It was Larry who assured me, "He'll have Christmas with us, love. What else could I give him for Christmas? And you wanted something to send Grandfather for Christmas. I'll send these airmail in the morning and get another set for William."

William said now, "*You* sent them?"

We nodded. I was afraid this disappointed him.

But he said, "Good!" on an outgoing sigh of relief. "Hand me that other robe."

He pulled a piece of paper from a pocket of it, unfolded it, and pushed it across the table to us. Larry picked it up and I read it over his shoulder.

It was a check for five thousand dollars, made out to William, and signed "Horace O. Sturtevant."

"It's for reconstruction material and any help that has to be hired," said William. "For the meetinghouse or for the house, wherever most needed. He wanted to make it out to you but he didn't dare. Afraid you wouldn't cash it."

I thought of Hod sitting somewhere alone in the Bastille writing that check and padding out, maybe in an elegant housecoat a tailor had made for him, to drop it into a slot in the wall beside the elevator, and looked at Larry. He was looking fixedly at the table, at the empty space between the check and the prints.

Nobody said anything for a minute. There was just the clock ticking. It sounded very loud.

Then William spoke again.

He said, "What do you say, boy? Will you open an account for it down at the bank? Or do I have to send it by you to put on mine?"

At that Larry lifted his eyes and looked straight into William's.

"I'll do whatever you want me to, sir. You know my grandfather. I don't."

"Give me a pen, somebody," said William.

I gave him mine, from Kate's blue vase on the mantel, and he wrote his name across the back of the check.

"Put it where you won't lose it," he told us. "What a mix-up if you had got it into the wash, Lisa. I might have known when you grabbed that bathrobe where it was heading. We'll talk more about this tomorrow. I'd better go to bed now."

He went off, wrapped in red, carrying the pictures, humming. Then I cried, Larry cuddled me, we looked at William's sock full of Christmas for Betsy, we opened the door and stood in the cold, hugging each other, to see the stars; and it was our first real Christmas Eve.

William did come out the next morning as soon as we had the fires going. Our "Merry Christmas" 's woke Betsy and Larry bounded in to bring her out on his shoulder. We put her in William's old highchair in front of the open oven-door, and I got breakfast around her while we all watched her kissing the doll and the teddybear, rubbing the soap animals against her chin, banging one block against another, shaking the buttons, the rattle, the bracelet, and the bonnet by turns, and rolling the orange around her tray. It seemed to me she was almost conscientious about giving equal attention to each item; a bright smile and a crow as it was produced, and then just so much complete concentration on it before she was ready to receive the next. Something is born in babies which tells you, if you will only listen, shows you, if you will only look, *proves* that they have come here from a perfect world.

Later we talked again about Hod's check and it was agreed that when the folks came in the evening we would try to set up an organization for the care of the meetinghouse. If that could be done, as soon as we had elected a treasurer, Larry would open its account with half of Hod's check, and put the other half, for the house, on an account in our three names so that any one of the three of us could draw on it as necessary.

"Quick as that is settled," William said, again on a long sigh of relief, "one of us must write Hoddy about it."

"We all will," I promised him. "All of us that very night. We'll *stuff* Hod's mailbox, Sweet William."

He took a nap that afternoon, but came out for supper in high spirits which kept rising all through a truly glorious evening. That was a night none of us will ever forget.

Everyone was wildly excited about our windfall. At first everyone except the Standishes and the Corsons were simply incredulous. I noticed those four just sat there smiling and nodding as if they had known it was coming but kept the knowledge so the rest of us could have a Christmas surprise. Then William and Eli got to talking about Orestes and Grace and little Hoddy, and Bri and Elaine chimed in with stories they had heard about them, until they came around to agreeing that it was like Sturtevants to move into any breach they knew was there.

"Some way," Eli said, "Sturtevants always knew the rest of us had some things they didn't, and they had some things we didn't, and we was all supposed to go shares. 'Course, one of the things they had and the rest of us didn't was money."

"That's it, Eli," said William, in his red robe in Bart's rocker. "Now you've hit the nail right on the head. Just what all the old ones taught us. You give what you've got to give, when it's needed. You throw it all into the pot and that's what makes a good soup."

We wrote out a constitution and by-laws and formed the Rev. Alexander Sturtevant Association for the Support of the Meetinghouse. We elected William the president of it, over his protestations that he never got far from his bed these days (Eli said, "Long as you don't, Bill, we'll always know where the president is, won't we?"), Larry vice-president ("He can run the errands," grinned Bri), Elaine treasurer ("She's nearest to the bank"), and me secretary.

Then they said the first duty of the secretary would be to write to Hoddy. I said I would, but every single one of them had to write to him, too, the same night I did, even Kathy and Une and Ron's three kids; that I'd made William a solemn promise. They said they would, as soon as Larry and Elaine had been to the bank. I wrote out Hod's address and passed around copies.

Of course we told them what Hod had sent for the Sturtevant house and they seemed almost as pleased about that as with his contribution to the meetinghouse.

Flo said, "Honest, I never thought I'd see that place fit for humans again. Now looks as if 'twill be. Lands sakes alive, that'll be a sight for sore eyes."

Bri said, "I still own one of Pa's old fields up here, you know. Might throw up something on it so we could stay in it summers. Prob'ly the boys would like it, right there on the river. Have a boat. Catch some fish."

Eli twinkled.

"Could be the old neighborhood's getting a new lease on life, eh, Bill?"

They stayed until almost twelve o'clock of Christmas night, and William stayed right there with us.

Maybe he shouldn't have. But I'm glad he did.

After he went to bed that night he never got up again.

We tried to get him to let us call the doctor, but he wouldn't. He said again that the doctor had told him all he had to do was take his pills. So I called Sue. She said she would come out as soon as she got off duty the next day, but she wouldn't have any car because Jim would be at school with it. So Larry went down for her. She brought William some ice cream and insisted the room was not warm enough for him to sit up, so she fed it to him, sitting curled up on the side of his bed and chattering away. He seemed glad to see her and apparently didn't even wonder how she had got there. Then she washed his face and hands (saying, "This is habit. Anybody I find in bed I automatically wash their face and hands"), made up his bed clean as if it were the easiest thing in the world to do, rubbed his back, and said, "Now how do you feel, Bill Crowley?"

William said, "Awful comfortable, Mis Corson."

"Then go to sleep, for goodness sake," said Sue, "and start getting your strength back. You wore yourself out celebrating Christmas, that's what's the matter with you."

But the next day she talked with the doctor when he was on his hospital rounds and called me up to tell me the doctor said William was right, there was no help for him beyond what the pills would do; that he had what is called fibrilla-tion. The doctor was surprised his heart had kept going this long. She said she and Jim would come out that night but she thought it was safest to tell me by telephone what the doctor had said, so William couldn't possibly hear it. "Though I think — I'm quite sure — he knows, Lisa. They almost always do." Then she told me we should be glad William had gone to this doctor because some doctors would have sent him to a specialist and a specialist might have put him in some distant hospital where they could insert a machine into his chest to regulate his heart action and keep it beating long after he wished it would stop. "You know Bill would have hated that," said Sue. "They're terribly heavy things, and it wouldn't have been Bill. He knows he's in the Lord's hands and that's where he wants to stay."

I didn't say anything all the time she was talking. I couldn't. But I listened to every word she said and it did help me. As days went by it helped more.

Sue came out at least once a day for the next three weeks. If it was daylight she gave William a bath, got him into a clean nightshirt between clean sheets, worked magic with his pillows and blankets. Sometimes Larry went for her, some-times Bri or Ron or Elaine brought her, and went in to see William for a minute after Sue had him all fixed up. If she came in the evening, Jim brought her, and after Sue had made William's bed and rubbed his back we all went in and Jim prayed. William was always glad to see them, all of them, and his eyes shone when they talked though he said less and less, lying there with Cat in the circle of his arm.

Sue really took almost all the care of William. It is a marvelous thing to have nursing skill. It is even more marvelous in a girl like Sue.

Larry could only keep his fires, turn him in the night, carry Betsy in for him to see, put his hand on his shoulder and ask, "How you feeling, man?", and read him the letters we wrote to Hod and that Hod wrote back. We told Hod only that William was being kept abed for a few weeks but would write him as soon as he got around again, and to keep the letters coming; which he certainly did. Larry heard from him once or twice every week and so did I, and there was always a letter enclosed for William. He wrote William mostly about what he remembered of all they used to do together and all the people they knew then. He said it seemed as if a door had opened that had been closed a long time, and his memories were rushing in on him. He wrote he was considering flying East next summer to see us all and of how he and William would go together to all the familiar places.

All I could do for William was cook things as nearly as I could the way he liked them (and Flo was a great help with that; I'd *never* have known what he meant by "porridge" if she hadn't told me), wash every day, keep his Christmas robe over the footboard of his bed where he could see it (he said he knew even in the dark if it wasn't there), and sing hymns, while I worked, loud enough so he could hear them. Yes, there was one other thing I could do; I could kiss him on his forehead. Nobody else could do that, though sometimes we held Betsy so her soft mouth touched him and that always made him smile. He usually didn't smile when I kissed him, but groped for my hand and squeezed it.

The last day I couldn't sing while I spread the Christmas robe, and then when I kissed him a tear fell on his nose.

He had seemed to be asleep, but that roused him and he snapped at me.

"What are you crying for, girl?" he demanded, almost in

his normal voice. "Ain't you all right? Don't you have a husband and a baby? Ain't you got a tight roof over your head and a tight chimney and plenty of wood to heat it up? Didn't your husband get into the cellar everything we raised last summer? Ain't Flo showed you how to put together a civilized meal? Didn't I get your six generations of Sturtevants? Even get you a grandfather? Ain't you a Sturtevant?"

Startled dry-eyed, I whispered, "Yes. Oh, yes, Sweet William."

"Well, then," he rumbled. "Act like one. Stop sniveling."

That night everybody came but Ron's little boys. Even Kathy and Une. They all sat in the kitchen and sang hymns, except Flo and Sue and Jim and Larry and me. We left the doors ajar and sat with William who seemed to be in a deep sleep and probably did not hear them singing, though he may have.

When I put Betsy to bed I had slipped the Red Stone out of the pocket in her sheet and when I went in to William I tucked it into the palm of his hand, under his closed fingers.

As much as an hour later, he asked suddenly, without opening his eyes, "What's this in my hand?"

I was the only one who knew so I had to answer.

I bent over him and said, "It is the Red Stone, dear. The one —"

He interrupted me.

"I know the one. It's for Sturtevant children. Give it back to the child."

"But — she isn't sick, William. You are."

"I'm not NEITHER," he said loudly. His own sound seemed to wake him. He opened his eyes. I don't know whether he knew who I was, but all the grimness went out of his face. He said very gently, "You didn't mean to do no wrong but *'tis* wrong. I ain't sick. I'm just old. I don't need the Red Stone. Any more. Put it back — where it belongs."

He uncurled his fingers. I took the stone. He closed his eyes. I tiptoed into Betsy's room and felt for the little pocket.

Around eleven o'clock they were still singing hymns in the kitchen, more and more softly, when William spoke again without opening his eyes.

He said, "Are you there?"

We didn't know who he meant but we all moved close to his bed and Jim said, "Yes, Bill. We're here. Is there something you want?"

"I've got wonderful news for her. I just had a telephone call . . . No, not — a telephone call . . . I talked with all the old ones out there in — California, I guess they was, and they want me to come out. They say the sun — something — is shining bright and warm and — and the apples is ripe. It's — it's Spring Week and they're all gathered together, waiting for me . . . The Alexanders and James and Holdfast and Orestes and Dobbin and Bart and all the rest of them and all their women, Elizabeth and Melura and Sarah and Roxy and Sophie and Kate and Grace and Jessica —"

He was sitting up, talking very fast, a smile spreading light across his face, when suddenly he coughed, fell back against Larry's arm, and lay breathing hoarsely.

Jim began to pray and kept on praying. When he said, "Lord, Lord, thy will be done. In Jesus' Name, Amen," William was still, and the little Crowley parlor was filled with his friends for whom it was not yet Spring Week.

Cat jumped off the bed and began pacing up and down, meowing loudly in the silence. Une picked him up and held him against her chin, stroking him, quieting him. I reached for Flo and hid my face against her shoulder.

"There, there, youngone," she whispered. "His time had come."

I carry as many of William's words as I can, at any one time, in my heart, and so far his last ones are always at the top, swelling my throat. Why did he speak differently in his last days than we had ever heard him before? Was he speaking as Bart and Kate had spoken and as he had spoken to them? Did he think, at least sometimes, he was speaking to them, not us? Or did he maybe think he was Bart, speaking to Kate? . . . And all "the old ones" who "called" him at the end. I don't think they said it was the sun that was "shining bright and warm" out there where they were. William didn't think so either. He was feeling for the right word. The word he wanted was "God," wasn't it? And it wasn't really that apples were ripe. *Something* was coming to fruition there for William that they had no words for in our language, that they could convey to him only through his memory of the ecstasy of a small country boy when he sets his strong young teeth into the first apple that drops from the Red Astrachan tree in September. And "Spring Week" was the nearest they could come to telling him what his new life would be.

I wonder who he meant when he said, "I've got wonderful news *for her*." Larry thinks he meant me. When he said it I supposed he meant Kate; that maybe he felt he was Bart, that the identification he had always felt with Bart, and increasingly in the last weeks, was then complete. But he named both Bart and Kate among "the old ones" who had talked to him . . .

And why did Jessica come to him with the others at that moment? He had scarcely ever mentioned Jessica to us. He

— and so we — knew of her only what Kate had heard the women saying in the Sturtevant front room while Grace and Bart, William and Hoddy were pushing Alex in the chariot his father had built for him up the hill to Adams's studio. . . . When did Kate tell William, or in William's hearing, what the women had said? That very night after she came home from Sturtevants'? Or not until many years later, when he might be expected to understand it? Perhaps soon after Grace died, or after Grace was taken away and the Sturtevant house was closed and deserted, and Kate recalled the conversation as she struggled to pay a last tribute to Grace? . . . Was Bart there when Kate told it? Was it Bart she was telling it to, not William, and William only overheard it? . . . And the night William died, was Jessica one of those who spoke to him? How could he recognize her voice, if he had never heard it? Or did she tell him who she was? Did she say, "William, this is Jessica. Jessica Sturtevant. I'm here, too. I'm waiting for you, too"? . . . And what had William meant when he told me he didn't need the Red Stone "any more"? Had he ever needed it?

I asked Larry one night in the dark of the Crowley parlor where we had gone back to sleep after William went:

"Do you suppose — is it possible — William was Jessica's son?"

". . . Possible, sure."

"Had you ever thought of it?"

"Yes. Once or twice."

"If he was — how did he get here?"

"No idea . . . Could she have sent him?"

"By train, maybe . . . In the care of a porter . . . But why would she? She thought Bart and Kate would do better by him than she could?"

"Could be."

"Then it had to be after Bart and Kate were married, and William must have been over a year old."

"That's what the dates show?"

"Yes. William was born in 1903. Bart and Kate were married in 1904 . . . Lar, do you think William may have been Bart's son, too?"

"Could be, I guess," Larry said again. Then, "But if it was the way those women seemed to think, how would Bart know whether he was or not?"

"He couldn't, could he? He would only know if the truth was that he couldn't be . . . Or if it wasn't the way those women thought and he knew *that*. Maybe Bart and Jessica really loved each other, but knew that a time had come when a Sturtevant would no longer be allowed to marry a Crowley. Maybe they had a last desperate hope that if they were going to have a child she could marry him. But instead she was sent away to have the baby alone. And then she got into some trouble, maybe was sick or in dreadful poverty, and all she could think of to do was find a home for the baby and maybe go to stay with her mother. I suppose in those days she couldn't come back here with the baby, even if she wanted to. Maybe she knew Bart had now married Kate. She must have if —"

Larry was getting sleepy.

He said, "Maybe, maybe. William would have said, 'May bees don't fly in February.' We'll never know how it was, kitten. Go to sleep."

But I couldn't, for a long time.

I lay imagining that a few months after Bart and Kate were married, the mailman left a letter in their box with the weekly newspaper. Kate brought it in and wondered about it, but it was addressed to Bart, so she put in at his place at the kitchen table. When he came in he saw it there, picked it up, turned it over, scowling at front and back. Did he know Jessica's handwriting? Or was this the first time he had ever seen it?

Kate said roguishly, for she was young then and they had lived together only a few months, "Now who's writing to you from 'way out in Illinois, Bartholomew?" Or Ohio, Nebraska, one of the Dakotas, or whatever the postmark said.

He shook his head slowly, answering, "Danged if I know." But did he suspect? He didn't look at Kate.

"Guess you'll have to open it to find out then, won't you?"

"Guess so."

He took off his jacket and cap, washed his hands at the sink, and sat down heavily at the table. Kate had brought the scissors to snip off the edge of the envelope. She was careful to take only a very narrow slip, for fear of damaging the contents. When he unfolded and spread out the paper, she read over his shoulder what was written there, the signature first.

Jessica Sturtevant . . . Jessica was asking Bart if he and his wife would take her little boy to bring up. She was ill and alone and couldn't do it. She could send him by Pullman train and had enough money to pay for it. When she was better, she would send more money. He was a year old now, a strong, healthy child. His name was William. If Bart would take him, no one was to know he was hers, now or ever. No one. He must come as a Little Stranger and grow up a Crowley. She would never claim him. Bart would never hear from her again, except that, if he took the boy, she would send money as often as she could.

Long after they had finished Jessica's letter they were
silent. Kate put dinner — or supper — on the table and they
ate in silence, made speechless by what had happened and all
it might portend. But once they began to talk they talked of
nothing else until they had agreed that Bart would answer
the letter and say they would take this child.

Otherwise . . .

Otherwise, Kate never saw Jessica's letter. After Bart
took off his jacket and cap and washed his hands he took it
into the bedroom or parlor to read it by himself. Or it had
not been brought by a mailman and Kate never saw the
envelope. This may have been before rural deliveries began,
and Bart had been called to the post office window in the
back corner of some dark little grocery store.

"Letter here for you, Bart."

Somewhere along his slow way home he stopped the horse
and sat beside the rutted road to stare at what had been
handed to him until he could bring himself to tear open the
flap with a square, brown forefinger and extract the paper
folded inside.

Bart, dear,

I am asking you for the only thing in this whole world I still want.
I have heard that you are married now. I have a little boy, a few
months more than a year old. Will you and your wife take him and
bring him up? I expect you will have a big family of your own. I
hope so, for all your sakes. But may William be one of the Crowley
children?

You will know why you are the only one I can think of turning to
in my extremity. (Or, you may wonder why you are the one I turn
to in my extremity. It is mainly because you are the only person I
know that I would turn to. You are the right age to father a child
and the home you have has to be a good home for children, for you are

a good man. The best man I have ever met, except perhaps my father who is far too old to become the father of a year-old boy and who, in such a case, would be burdened by the feeling that he shares my disgrace as you do not.) I am ill and cannot do for this child as a parent should, but without him, if I live, I can send you money so that he will not be a financial burden. Bart, please take him. Please, please let me send him to you. If you will, no one must ever know who he is. No one. I wouldn't want that: I couldn't bear that. Nothing I have done must reflect on him or on you. If wrong has been done — and I suppose it has — it was all my doing. Surely you and your wife could account for my William as just a little waif you were moved to shelter? And truly I believe you would be rewarded. He is your kind of little boy, Bart. Sturdy, grave, attentive, with bright, watchful eyes.

Please, please, Bart? For the sake of the past and the future? I am alone and so sick . . . so frightened . . .

She signed herself Jessica, but gave him another name to which to write. A name strange to him.

If Bart never let Kate see this letter, he told her all about it. As they began to talk about it, he asked her a question of great importance to both of them.

"Do you have any notion, Kate, that I am or may be the father of Jessica's child?"

Kate said, "No. No, Bart. No such notion at all."

Or she said, ". . . I don't know, Bart. Could he be?"

If she answered the question of great importance with this other question, Bart said:

"Yes, Kate. He could be, and I believe he is. Jess and I thought we was in love, and maybe we was — then. We wanted to get married, was desperate to get married. She said her folks would never let us. We wanted to have a child — to force 'em. For all that's been said, I don't believe she ever was with any other man. But they sent her away and I never heard from her, didn't know where she was, didn't think likely I ever would know . . . After a while I see you, Kate, sitting straight and pretty in a church pew, and I begun to have a feeling I'd never had before; a feeling that you belonged to me and always would and so I was the luckiest feller ever walked the earth. I am, too — if only you can figure out now how it was that when I was younger I wanted somebody as different from me as Jessica was . . ."

Or he said:

"No, Kate. He couldn't. I never done more than walk alongside Jessica Sturtevant in my life. I was where she was a good many times, and she kept getting herself into tight corners and I kind of watched out for her and got her out of 'em when I could. I got so I'd go to dances just to see if she was there, and if she was I'd hang around as long as she did, because some nights she'd tell somebody, sooner or later, 'No. And I *mean* no. I'm going straight home with Bart Crowley.' We'd gone paddling together, see, when we was youngones, Kate, and sliding on the ice, and picking berries. If you'd known her and watched her as long as I did, Kate, and seen the chances she was taking, you'd have worried about her just the same. You'd have worried about her, and about Orestes and Grace, too. I couldn't have done no different. But I never done her no harm."

And Kate said, "If you say so, it's so, Bart, and that's the end of it. Now what do you think you want to do about her little boy?"

But if any of this had happened, would Kate have told Bart several years afterward what the women said about Jessica at Sturtevants' Spring Week? Told him in such detail, in the hearing of William, that sturdy, grave, watching, listening boy who never forgot anything he heard but carried it all with him as if it were on tape? If she did, it was not in character, but no one is always in the character he commonly projects. A cruel person can have gentle moments, a kind person can have a vicious one. As she fixed supper or washed dishes at home, after a long day of cleaning on the hill, and Bart and William talked on and on about Sturtevants, did a flame shoot up in Kate and burst out into a torrent of words she could not suppress or did not try to, for once? Perhaps.

But I decided it was more likely Kate had never seen Jessica's letter or been told much of what was in it. I think it came, somehow, direct to Bart, and that he never felt he had the right to reveal a personal word of it to anyone. Jessica had said, "No one must ever know who he is. No one." And he was satisfied that, whatever else she may have been wrong about, she was right about this.

So I think he told Kate only that he had heard of a little boy out West who had no parents to take care of him and for whom a good home was being sought, that they could have him if they wanted him and bring him up as their own. I think he said, "It's up to you, Kate. You take your time and think it over. It's up to you. Whether we take him or whether we don't." I don't think she asked him how he knew of this little boy and his need. Men were always picking up odd bits of news when they went to market. She quietly thought it over, as Bart had told her to do; and her thinking was of where he could sleep, what he would eat, what clothes he would need. She may have talked with Bart about such matters, and he may have replied with some embarrassment, "You know better than I do, Kate. I was the youngest one in the family. You've got younger ones in yours. Can they walk when they're a year old?" Kate said, "Some can, some can't. Cora and Lizzie did, Budger didn't. Maybe girls are quicker at it than boys. Or maybe it all depends on how big you are, how much you've got to balance when you get on your feet. Budger was real heavy-set."

But one day soon — maybe the very next day — Kate said, "There, Bart, I can't stand thinking on it any longer, with that youngone getting along nobody knows how. I'm ready to take him, if you are. We may not have much but it's prob'ly more'n he's used to."

So Bart went somewhere — perhaps to the post office — and sent word to whatever address Jessica had given him that if she could get the child to the local railroad station and they knew what train he would be on, Crowleys would meet it and take him home and do the best they could by him. To write this probably took him some time because his fingers were used to grasping bigger tools than pen or pencil. If when he had said this much he thought he could manage a little more he probably added, "I hope this finds you well as it leaves me." And he signed his name with relief. His full name because he must have sensed this was an important document. Bartholomew Crowley.

Right after stamping and mailing his letter, he scratched a kitchen match on the sole of his boot and burned Jessica's letter, envelope, address, and all.

That must have been how it was, and now I was growing sleepy.

But the Red Stone William found in the bureau drawer after Bart died . . . He had given us some possible explanations for its being there, but said none of them seemed likely. Had a more likely one ever occurred to him? Grace had told Kate that once when she asked Orestes where it was he said he didn't know what had become of it, that he hadn't seen it for years. This would have been true if he had given it to Jessica when she went away, or if in his great anxiety and feeling of helplessness he had secretly dropped it into her purse or pocket, on the chance it would keep her safe and bring her back to him. He would not have wished to admit this to Grace, years later, when he knew nothing of Jessica, even whether she still lived, and so the worthlessness of the stone, he thought, had been proven. But if Jessica sent the stone East with William, as the only birthright she wanted him to have, didn't this prove otherwise? And didn't William, alone here in the Crowley house, thinking of so many things during those years after Bart died and before we came, think of that likelihood? . . . Was that why he told me when he found the stone in his hand that last night he lived, "I don't need it. *Not any more.* It is for Sturtevant *children*"?

Now I was satisfied. I believed William was a Sturtevant and perhaps a Crowley, too, and that he had figured this out. A wave of complete peace washed over me. I fell asleep. And the next day I wrote to my mother, enclosing it with one to Armand as William had suggested, and telling her that she could send a reply to him, or contact him if she should need me, as he knew where I was.

It was a long time before I heard from her. Her letter came just last week, and I hadn't known until it came what I hoped to hear.

She wrote as a pleasant stranger might write, saying she was glad I was well and with the Gallicos (which of course I had not said I was); she remembered I had always found them congenial. She hoped that when my daughter was a little older I could arrange to finish my college education.

However, it was possible for a woman to do very well without an academic degree. She, for instance, had risen from a secretarial position to become a buyer for a sportswear shop and was soon to leave for the Paris openings. The friend with whom she shared a penthouse apartment was the fashion editor of a leading newspaper, and they would travel together. She said she found her present way of life stimulating and delightful.

Now I knew that this was exactly what I had wanted her to say.

She put her new address on the envelope, but did not ask me to write again, and I don't expect to. I am as glad that she has freed herself as that I am free, and I trust she knows that. My letter probably seemed to her as much like one from a casual acquaintance as hers did to me.

My real life began when I met Larry Sturtevant. It began very small and tight, but it began. It unfolded a little in hiding and more as we rode and rode in the wind, and that was all wonderful but bewildering because I didn't know where it had come from or where it was going or how long it would last. It was from Larry. I had nothing but Larry. Without Larry I would be dead and that would be worse than being dead had been before I had ever lived.

Then we came here.

It is May again now, so we have been here a year.

In this one year all the basic experiences of life have come to me. Marriage, birth, and death. Through these and along with these Larry and I have found out where our life came from — his from the family he never knew he had and mine, too, from them through him. In this way, all because of William, we have a family of our own to pass on and our

Betsy need never wonder where she came from or, we hope, where she is going, or how long her heritage will last. It will last as long as she keeps it and passes it on. Even if she never has children, she can find other ways to pass it on. William did.

A few weeks after William died Jim and Sue came to stay with us, and we are no longer lonely. It saves their paying rent which they could not afford. They buy half the groceries, and Larry and Jim ride together to the University. Larry is taking six courses this semester. Through the late winter, on their days off, Larry and Jim worked in the woods, getting out next winter's fuel. Sue still goes to the hospital but they expect a baby in September. If it is a boy they will name him William. Jim will still have another year at the theological school, so Sue will go back to the hospital as soon as she can and I'll take care of Betsy and William. (We all so hope it will be William that sometimes it scares me and I tell them *Betsy* wants it to be another little girl.)

Meantime, we have continued our Monday night meetings, and more and more people come, some of them people who have never lived in town, or not since they were children, but whose parents or grandparents did and who have heard about us in letters from relatives and are curious. Most of them contribute either money or work to the restoration of the meetinghouse and Hod continues to stand ready to help more if it is needed, so now hired carpenters are there five days a week and all of us on Saturdays. We fully expect that by July we can have services in it. The walls may not be plastered and the pews may not be painted, but we'll get to that in time. There will be no carpet on the floor but we don't need carpet. Miraculously, most of the wide, pumpkin pine boards were still sound and the few that weren't we have been able to replace from floors in parts of the Sturtevant house we are not trying to restore. We'll feed those old boards with oil and wax until they are softer under our feet than any carpet would be; the same boards Sturtevants and Crowleys, Martins and Haseys, Watsons and the others tiptoed across for generations.

Larry, Betsy and I go up there with Jim and Sue every Sunday afternoon, as soon as they have come home from Mr. Standish's church and we've had dinner. We go in the pickup, and when Larry turns off the engine we are instantly surrounded by a vast, beautiful silence. If Betsy makes a sound it is like the song of a snowbird. We get out and stand looking at the little meetinghouse which has never had a steeple or a bell or a stained glass window, but which seems surrounded by a pale gold circle like the rim of a full moon riding the winter sky. We go up the path the workers have made, one of us carrying Betsy, and push open the door. From the dim inside a fragrance I can't describe comes to enfold us. It is faintly spicy, like incense, faintly waxy like old candles, faintly musty like a big book once much loved and much read but untouched for a long time. We tiptoe in and sit down together in the front pew, feeling all the pews behind us filled with Larry's people who now belong to all of us. We don't say anything aloud.

The first Sunday we went I whispered to Jim.

"Will you say a prayer before we go?"

He shook his head, smiling at me, and whispered back.

"Sh-h. All our hearts are praying."

So after a little while we tiptoed out again, reverently closing the door behind us. It has no lock. We never intend to have a lock for it.

But when we have a pulpit Jim will stand in it, and then

words will be spoken. When we have an organ someone will play it — I will play it if there is no one there who plays better — and all the voices in all the pews will sing. If we cannot see all the people who are singing, we shall hear their voices.

Also, at the same time, work goes forward apace at the Sturtevant house because Hod has definitely decided to come and spend the summer there. We can hardly believe it, but he seemed to make up his mind as soon as he heard William had gone. He wrote that too much time had already passed and, if he was to come, he must come soon. We are so glad. Without William, we suddenly feel a great longing to have Hod, and wrote him yes, come; come, come, come, and of course he would stay with us. By summer we would be sleeping upstairs with Betsy across the hall from where Sue and Jim were already sleeping; and Hod could have William's parlor.

He replied that indeed he would appreciate our hospitality if it proved impossible until later in the summer for him to stay "up home." But he begged us to make every effort to get the oldest section of the Sturtevant house safe and habitable as soon as possible. It would be a great pleasure to him to "stay on the old stamping ground," and perhaps he could be of some use to us in recalling just how the rest used to be, what we should try to bring back and what let go. For instance, he had a very clear picture in his mind of how Adams's studio had been when Alex used to rest there . . . And he asked if we knew of anyone who might be engaged to stay with him and look after his needs. "I am no cook, my dear," Hod wrote me. "And I'm not sure I should be at all handy with a broom. I know you would try to tend to me, but I also know your hands must already be busy

Next of Kin

enough, and should prefer to engage a woman or a couple to live in for, say, three months, if this is possible."

At first we could not see that it was, but the more we thought and talked of it, the less impossible it became.

The kitchen, front room, and three small back bedrooms were the old part of the Sturtevant house we had resolved to save. Surely we can have them ready for warm weather use by mid-summer if not sooner. Flo says when they are she and Eli will go up and see to Hod. "I don't know why not," says Eli. "T'aint fur for me to drive back home to my planted pieces and my haying."

I wrote Hod this, adding that the only problem we didn't see a solution to was that of furnishings, but Flo said that if things she had would do, Jim and Larry could help Eli haul over from Martins' what would be needed to get through the summer.

Hod replied that it was very kind of the Martins to offer, but when the old part of the house could be occupied it should have its own furnishings. Would we buy them and have the bills sent to him?

"Dreamy!" cried Sue. "We'll get old ones. We'll *haunt* the antique shops all up and down the coast. We'll try to find pieces we can imagine are the very pieces that were sold at that auction Bart went to at the Sturtevant place."

So that is where we are now, at the end of this ledger William began writing in just a year ago. It can hardly seem as incredible to anyone else as it does to me, but I know it is true. Every word of it.

Look at all we have behind us. Look at all we have ahead.

And it is William's legacy to us. He wrote his will that day he went to the lawyer's office and left everything he had to us. What he had was far more than this house and land

--❦ *247* ❧--

and a few hundred dollars in the bank. He had life; his life, and ours, and Betsy's, and that of this whole corner of the earth.

Thank you, William. Thank you, Lord. Thank you, Jesus. Lisa now signing off.

The living Lisa.

ABIGAIL E. WEEKS MEMORIAL LIBRARY
UNION COLLEGE
BARBOURVILLE, KENTUCKY